Awakening

Guardian from Trandor Series #1

By Phoenix Halloway

I0684826

Thank-you God.

Thanks to my family, for their love, support and patience through this process.

Table of Contents

Prologue

Inside the small spacecraft, the mood was tense, the occupants silent. Tajana looked back at the little girl strapped into the seat near the back of the cabin, and tried to keep the fear she was feeling from showing on her face.

"Have they detected us?" Tajana finally whispered to her husband, Kriden, in the seat next to her.

Kriden gave a slight negative shake of his head. His focus was on the instrument panel in front of him as he piloted the spacecraft through a small meteor field near the moon, trying to remain undetected.

"Kri Tajana?" the little girl in the back whispered, her normally blue complexion was pale, her purple eyes seemed to take up most of her face.

Tajana briefly closed her eyes and tried to school her features into a neutral expression. Since the little girl had used the formal title for 'aunt', she knew she was not successful at keeping her fear hidden. She knew her complexion must match that of the little girl, a sure sign of stress or fear. Tajana had promised her sister that she would get the little girl to safety, and she meant to keep that promise.

"We will be fine," she lied.

"Are you sure we have reliable information?" The captain of the Galdorian ship looked hard at his second-in-command.

"Sir, the information has come from a family friend. They are certain that the little girl will be smuggled away from the planet by her aunt and uncle." The second-in-command struggled to keep his voice steady under the intense gaze from his superior. "They did not know the exact time, but all indications are that it will be today."

"Perhaps the family friend is also trying to protect the little *shetanzie*?" The captain spat out the last, using the vulgar name given to the gifted young girls of the planet Trandor that they were at war with.

"No, sir. He, too, is tired of the special treatment these children receive; his child was refused acceptance into the preferred academy because of this *shetanzie*."

The captain looked hard at the view screen, as if his will alone, could make the spacecraft they were waiting for appear.

The navigator gave a sudden shout of triumph. "Sir! Small spacecraft approaching from the dark side of Trandor's second moon! Three life-forms detected!" The navigator grinned evilly at his commander.

"Excellent! Plot a course to intercept them once they clear the planet's detection fields." The captain turned to his gunner. "Prime the weapons, and lock onto them as soon as we are in range."

The bridge of the spacecraft was silent except for the sounds of the engines as they sped toward their unsuspecting prey. Too late, the small spacecraft detected the threat, but the weapons were already firing. The small craft took the first hit near the engines, disabling it. The next volley hit it hard, causing small explosions to light up the darkness of space.

"Sir! They got off a distress call!"

The captain shouted at his gunner, "Finish them! We cannot be caught here!"

The ship looped around to come at their prey for a final pass, all weapons firing. The explosions sent the small craft spiraling out into space, debris flying everywhere.

"Sir! Rescue ships approaching!"

The captain, torn between chasing down his prey and defending his ship, checked the scans himself to see how close the rescue ships were. As he brought up the scans, weapons fire hit them. Realizing that his prey was now gone, and hoping they had caused enough damage to complete their mission, he instructed his crew to attack the approaching rescue ships.

The battle was intense, as the Galdorians defended themselves against the Trandorian rescue ships. The Galdorian ship and its crew fought hard, but still lost the battle as they were outnumbered and outgunned. The Trandorian ships that survived limped back to the planet to tend to their wounded, the small spacecraft forgotten.

Chapter One

Kiara, sitting at her station aboard the spaceship Acadia, checked her navunit to make sure they were on course. Frankie, the pilot, was behind her at his station, whistling softly. They were headed toward a nearby space station to pick up some cargo, and so far, all was quiet. Captain Blackburne, when briefing them about this cargo run, had put the crew on heightened alert. Attacks on cargo and passenger ships in this area were on the rise, and Blackburne wanted everyone on the crew to be looking for anything suspicious.

Kiara checked scans of the area again, not expecting to find anything, but checking anyway. She was grateful to be on the Acadia and working as a navigator, as jobs for her race were difficult to get. At least good jobs. She was from Trandor, and her pale-blue skin, dark-blue hair and purple eyes told everyone what her race was. Trandorians were classified by the Galactic Transgate Alliance—the GTA—as a 'Protected Race'. They were protected because there were so few of her kind left, after her planet was destroyed by war. Being protected sounded great, but in reality, it made getting employment a little rough. No one wanted the responsibility of keeping a 'Protected Race' person safe.

Kiara was good at her job, but she was also good with computers and electronics. She supposed that's why Blackburne had hired her. On a small ship like the Acadia, the crew was minimal, and everyone had to have a working knowledge of nearly everything on the ship. Besides herself, the crew on the Acadia consisted of Frankie, Blackburne, and three Bendanite workers. She smiled as she thought of the Bendanites. They were large, bearlike creatures from the planet of Bendan, and their size and willingness to work made them great for cargo ships like the

Acadia. Kiara thought they looked like giant teddy bears. The three Bendanites on the Acadia had unpronounceable names, so Blackburne had given them shorter Earth nicknames. He called them Larry, Curly and Moe. Kiara had thought they would be offended by Earth names, but the Bendanites loved their nicknames. When they discovered where the names had come from, they had insisted that Blackburne find them video of the old movies so they could watch them. That's when Kiara learned that Bendanites also had a great sense of humor.

They were on final approach when Kiara received a warning from the space station. Unidentified ships were approaching quickly from the starboard side. Repeated attempts by the space station to get the ships to identify themselves were being ignored. The space station went on full alert, halting all approaching ships. Kiara quickly checked the scans, and could see several small spaceships approaching.

Blackburne ordered Frankie to hold their position until he could assess the situation. Kiara, watching those ships heading toward the space station, could feel her tension rising. The Acadia was a simple cargo ship; their maneuverability was limited, and their weapons were minimal. Blackburne took every precaution to keep them out of trouble since they would be no match for pirates or other enemy ships. Kiara counted at least four ships heading for the space station, and was grateful that they had received the warning while they were still a good distance away. Blackburne brought the space station up on the front screen of the bridge, and, as they watched, the approaching ships opened fire.

Kiara inhaled sharply as enemy fire began hitting the space station. They heard the mayday from the space station come over the coms, and Blackburne yelled for Frankie to back them off more.

"Shouldn't we try to help?" Kiara asked, turning to Blackburne.

"Their shields should hold, and since they got off a mayday, help should be quick to arrive," Blackburne told her, his tension coming through in his voice. "We'll hold here."

Kiara knew it was the right thing to do, but her compassion and worry for those in the line of fire was overwhelming. She was glad he was the one in charge and not her, because she'd probably get everyone killed trying to help. Blackburne was from Earth, and carried himself with such authority that Kiara had always been intimidated by him. Kiara was tall at six feet in height, but Blackburne was a few inches taller, fair-haired, broad in the shoulders, muscular, and frowned most of the time. She imagined he could intimidate just about anybody. Turning back to the screen, she watched as the space station took heavy fire, and the four enemy ships were soon joined by a few more. The space station was firing back, but couldn't seem to hit any of the enemy ships. Kiara knew that the space station was designed to defend against larger, less maneuverable ships than the small, agile ships that were attacking it now. She could hear Blackburne in the background, talking on the com, trying to assess how close help was. She guessed from the part of the conversation she could hear that help wasn't arriving fast enough.

Several ships docked at the space station were also taking heavy fire, and Kiara watched in horror as one of the ships exploded. Fortunately, the shielding and safety measures that the space station employed kept the damage from spreading, but the ship was a total loss, and Kiara knew that everyone on that ship was now dead. She watched the enemy ships swing back around, and her fear for the other ships and those on the space station caused her pulse rate and breathing to accelerate. Her skin flushed a deeper blue as she wished she could somehow help them.

"C'mon, c'mon," Kiara muttered as she watched the space station firing. "Get them!" If she hadn't been so focused on the battle, she was sure she would have missed it. She was concentrating on some of the enemy ships, willing the space station to hit them. As she watched in amazement, weapons fire seemed to curve and follow the enemy ships, and two of them exploded. In the chaos that followed, the space station got in another lucky shot and hit a third ship, disabling it.

"Yes!" Kiara jumped up from her station, her fist in the air.

Blackburne turned to look at her before looking back at the screen, questioning how those two enemy ships had gotten hit. The space station's weapons didn't seem to have the right angle to hit them. It seemed as if something had changed the trajectory of those shots. He could hear over the com that help was on its way, but was worried that the help would be too late. A few more ships had joined the enemy, replacing the ones that had been destroyed, and the battle was beginning to look hopeless.

"Back us off a little more, Frankie," Blackburne instructed the pilot.

Frankie nodded and slowly started to move them away, but it was too late. Several enemy ships had broken away and were chasing ships that were trying to escape, and one was coming straight for the Acadia.

"Check our shields, and get on the weapons, Kiara," Blackburne told her in a calm voice. "Larry, Curly, Moe, brace for battle," he said into his com to the three Bendanites in the cargo area.

7

Blackburne strapped into his seat, and worked another set of weapons to help defend the ship. He looked at Frankie, and received a nod from the pilot. Frankie would do his best, maneuvering the clunky cargo ship, and Kiara and Blackburne would do everything they could with the limited weapons.

Kiara could feel her pulse accelerating again, and told herself to be calm like her captain. The enemy ship would be in the Acadia's weapons range in a few minutes, and Kiara wanted to be ready and calm to help keep the ship and its crew safe. She got the Acadia's weapons locked onto the ship approaching them, and waited for it to get into range.

"Thank God," Blackburne muttered, and switched the front screen to show a contingent of ships fast approaching from behind them.

Kiara instantly recognized them as Ranger ships. She let out the breath she didn't realize she'd been holding, as the Ranger ships fired on the enemy ship. The enemy ship immediately turned from the Acadia, heading toward the moon it had just come from. It never made it. The Ranger ships were outfitted with the latest weaponry, and they made quick work of the enemy ships in the area.

Kiara briefly wondered why the Rangers had shown up. They were an elite group of space patrolling law-enforcement that reported directly to the GTA, and didn't usually respond to pirate raids. Whatever the reason, she was glad they were here.

The Acadia continued to hang back and stay out of the way until the Rangers gave the all-clear. A medical ship had already shown up to help with the wounded, so Kiara knew they wouldn't be needed for anything. Blackburne had her offer assistance anyway. The space station acknowledged the offer, but asked them to hold their position until they were cleared to dock. Once they were cleared, Frankie brought them into the space dock, and Kiara breathed a sigh of relief once they had safely landed. The space station's shielding had held through the attack, and damage was minimal. Blackburne checked on their cargo run, but with the attack causing so much disruption, it would be a while before they would be able to load it. Knowing the crew was probably on edge from the attack, he gave them an hour of personal time.

Kiara planned to take advantage of the time he had given them to head to the store on deck five. Before heading out, she helped her crew get their hoverlifts operating in preparation for the cargo they were picking up. Once the hoverlifts were working, she headed for the space lift, dodging crates, other crew members, and hoverlifts. She squeezed between a couple of hoverlifts, earning a hard glare from one pilot, and what she thought were curses from the other. It was an impressive dance of machines and cargo to get the stuff loaded without accidents or delays, and on any other day, she would have loved to watch from the safety of the ship deck. Blackburne had only given them an hour, and she didn't want to be late getting back to the ship. She'd only been crewing with this ship for a short time, and she wasn't sure she wanted his wrath at this point. She was pretty sure his frown could melt steel.

She finally made it to the space lift, and shot through the opening just as the doors were closing. She checked that they were stopping on deck five, and took a quick look around the compartment. She caught a glance of herself in the reflective surface of the lift walls, and tried not to wince. She wore the skinsuits that other crew members wore, hers, a blue-black color covering long lean muscles on her tall frame. She had some dirt and dust smudges on it from helping her crew get their hoverlifts up and running. She never felt comfortable walking around in just a skinsuit, so she always wore a long, flowing shirt in a bright color over it. Today, she had opted for a bright red one with an asymmetrical hem, and she could see wrinkles in it from sitting at her station on the ship. Her hair, a deep dark blue, was long and flowing down her back, almost to her waist, and a few tendrils were sticking out at odd angles from her hurried run through the cargo area. Her light-blue skin was flushed a darker blue from her run to the lift.

In the lift with her, she noticed a couple of tired looking Earthlings, a few Bendanites, and even a Volterran. Volterrans, similar to Bendanites, were great for transport and cargo work. Volterrans were reptilian-like creatures that were not only strong, but intelligent, agile, and multitasking as well. Kiara felt sorry for the Earthlings, their strength and size was no match for the others in the lift, and their faces showed it. They must have been desperate for work.

As soon as the lift doors had closed, she could feel the tension in the lift rise. She knew it was because she was from Trandor. The penalty for harming someone from a protected race was severe, and rumors abounded about people being sent to a penal colony for stepping on the toes of someone from a protected race. Kiara knew the rumors to be false, but it was useless to explain that to a bunch of strangers in a space lift. She knew her skin and hair color made her easily recognizable. Some protected races couldn't be distinguished from an Earthling, and she guessed that might be good or bad. She kept her head down and waited for the lift to reach her deck so she could exit. She was never good at interacting with strangers, and let out a little sigh when she was again on the move toward the store.

Okay, so she wasn't any good at interacting with strangers, but she loved her job. Space travel was her life, and she couldn't imagine doing anything different. Since her dad had found her all those years ago, she'd either been traveling through space on a ship, or stopping for a brief time on a space station. She knew her dad had hoped she would settle in one spot, but she loved traveling through space. Her rambling thoughts reminded her that she had better update her dad before he got worried.

Kiara reached the store and tapped her com unit on her hip. The com unit displayed a menu in front of her eyes, much like a hologram, and with her eye movement, she scrolled to her list of supplies. Many of the supplies could be ordered at the kiosk in front of her, the rest she would pick up on her way through the store. With a shift of her eyes, she linked her list to the kiosk, and set off to pick up the rest of the items. She was relieved to see that this store stocked her supplements. Trandorians needed special supplements to replace the minerals that used to be found on their planet. Not all stores stocked them, and when she found them, she made sure she grabbed as much as possible. She made quick work with the rest of the list, ignoring the looks that she received. Her race and her planet had been nearly wiped out decades ago due to war with the neighboring planet, so Trandorians were scarce. In all her travels, she had never seen another. She knew they were out there, and her dad had seen a few in his travels. Multiple species were on every space station, and usually on every spaceship, but she still felt a little out of place since there were so few of her kind around.

Kiara realized her thoughts were depressing her, so she concentrated on finding the rest of her supplies. She was nearly finished, when she walked by a display of Earth chocolate. She let out a gasp of excited surprise. Earth chocolate was her one weakness, well at least that she would admit to, and she was surprised to find it all the way out here. She grabbed as much as she could carry, thought maybe that was too much, and started to put some back. With a resigned sigh, she grabbed it all again, and justified it by telling herself she didn't know when she would find it again. Finished now, she completed payment with her com unit, and headed back to the space dock. Kiara entered the Acadia, loaded with supplies, and immediately saw Blackburne over by the ship's com unit. He acknowledged her with a nod, and went back to frowning over the message coming across the com unit. Frankie saw her and crossed over to her to grab a couple of the packages.

"We're delayed," he said as they headed back toward the small cabins midship. His eyebrows went up when he saw how much chocolate she had. "They shorted us on the Rubidium cargo, and Blackburne is trying to figure out where it is."

"Thanks, Frankie." Frankie was a mixed race of Earth and something else. He never really talked about it, but he was damned good at his job of piloting, and that's what mattered. "I'm going to give my dad a quick call while we're waiting. Let me know when we're ready to leave so I can head back to the bridge."

Frankie nodded at her and headed to the other cabins to distribute the supplies, and Kiara went to the cabin she shared with the only other female on the ship; Curly, one of the Bendanite cargo movers. The cabin was empty, which was a good thing. The space was small, like all transport ships. The room was needed for cargo, not crew. The cabin held two small beds, one on each side of the room, conveniently tucked into the wall. Kiara always wondered how Curly slept in that little bed, but since she never complained, Kiara supposed it must not bother her.

Above each bed was a storage space, and directly across from the entry door was a cubby hole with a small desk and a window. Kiara felt fortunate to have that window. Many of the transport ships she had worked on didn't have that little bit of luxury for the crew. They shared a common bathroom, except the captain of course, but, because Kiara didn't spend a lot of time on personal grooming, she didn't mind.

Kiara quickly put her supplies away, grabbed a quick bite of chocolate, and closed her eyes to savor it for a second. Moving to the small desk, she connected her com unit to the main booster of the ship, and with a couple of eye movements, called up her dad's profile and placed the call. She tapped her com unit to bring up the hologram-type display in front of her, and waited for him to answer.

"Kiara! How's my girl?" The connection to her dad was bad, even with the booster, and his face swam in and out of focus in front of her. Fortunately, the audio was coming through clearly.

She smiled, a genuine smile that lit up her face. That smile was a side of her that rarely came through in her short time on this ship.

"Hey, Dad! How's retirement?" She could see his smiling face, beaming back at her from his house on Earth.

Her dad, retired space pilot Kyle McCallister, was a legend. Whenever the crew she was working with discovered who her dad was, she was always questioned extensively about him. They weren't related by blood; he was from Earth, she was from Trandor. He had become her dad, though, since the day he had found her in the wreckage of a destroyed spaceship and had promised to take care of her. She'd been young, only a few Earth years old when he'd found her. He'd been on a routine cargo trip when he and his crew had come across the wreckage. They

13

presumed the wreckage had been floating for days, because when they found it, it hadn't been near any planets or inhabited moons. They'd discovered later that she was from Trandor, but by then, the planet had been nearly destroyed, the government nonexistent. The GTA was just forming, and Kyle had been reluctant to dump her at a space station and let some government child services group take care of her. Space travel near Trandor was considered extremely dangerous, and besides, they had become attached to each other.

They hadn't known her name, and she'd been too traumatized when they found her to remember anything. In those first few days, she'd stuck to Kyle like his shadow, and the crew began to call her little Kylie. Kyle had never married, had never actually wanted to. He'd never planned on having children either, but he seemed to have a connection with the little girl he'd found and rescued. With no other place for her, and his attachment to her growing, he decided that she should probably stay with him. Kyle thought he should find a better name for her than 'Little Kylie'. He valued his Irish roots, so Kyle searched for an Irish name that would fit. He had no idea what Trandorians named their children, so using his ancestry seemed the next logical choice. He finally settled on 'Kiara', which meant small and dark in Irish. It seemed to fit. She'd been in a small dark space when he'd found her, and still had the dark hair of her race. When he asked her what she thought of the name, she'd launched herself into his arms and cried. He later realized that giving her a name from his ancestry had solidified her belonging to him. Up until that point, she'd been worried that he would leave her somewhere. When she was twelve Earth years old, he filed paperwork with the GTA for custody and adoption. Trandor still hadn't recovered from the devastation of the wars, and the GTA had no record of anyone looking for her, so the petition had been granted. She was, as far as anyone was concerned, Kiara McCallister.

Her dad frowned at her with the mention of his retirement, and Kiara laughed.

"Awww, it can't be that bad, can it? Are you doing that fisher thing that everyone says you have to do when you retire?"

"Fishing, it's called fishing, and no, I haven't been fishing," her dad answered, his frown still firmly in place. "Were you close to that attack on the space station?"

The video part of the connection blurred again, and Kiara knew they only had a few more seconds before it failed altogether. This part of the sector always seemed to have the worst connections.

"I'd better make this quick! We were close, but we weren't in any danger." Kiara started speaking faster and faster, trying to say everything she needed before they were cut off. "The Rangers showed up, and everything is good. We're getting ready to leave Space Station Delta, heading out for a cargo drop. Blackburne hasn't told us where we are going yet. I'm doing okay—don't worry about me. I love you, Dad!" Kiara got that last bit in right before the connection dropped.

Smiling one last time, Kiara turned her attention back to getting the ship ready to leave. She knew her dad wanted more information about the attack, but she didn't have time to try to get the connection working again. Pirates were always a risk, wherever they went, and she was sure that's what they had witnessed. She sent a quick message to her dad reiterating that everything was okay, hoping it would relieve his worry a little bit. She quickly changed her shirt, knowing that she would be needed on the bridge shortly.

She'd only been with this crew a short time, and felt as if she needed to prove her skills at navigating every time she went on deck. None of the crew had ever questioned her navigating skills, so it was a silly notion that she had to prove herself, but she accepted it was how she operated. In fact, she got along with the crew on this ship better than she had on any other ship, and she was grateful for that.

Kiara headed toward the bridge, even though Frankie hadn't come to get her. She walked in on Blackburne and Frankie in a heated conversation. Kiara caught the end of the last sentence.

"—activated the Rangers."

Kiara raised an eyebrow. The Rangers were activated? They were usually only activated in a sector when there was serious trouble between planets. The GTA usually left the governing of individual planets to themselves, and only got involved in the most serious circumstances.

"Are we heading into trouble?" Kiara asked. She looked from one to the other. "I mean, more trouble than we already witnessed?"

Blackburne finally answered her. "There's been some additional trouble at the transgate in this sector," he said, frowning when he answered her.

Kiara nodded at him. "If you tell me where we're headed, I can see if there is another way to get there without adding significant time to the trip." She walked to her navunit and logged in. When she didn't get an immediate answer, she turned back around to look at them.

"What is it, what aren't you telling me?" She was starting to feel a little alarmed.

"We have to go through the transgate," Blackburne told her, "we don't have time to go another way."

Transgates were portals that made intergalactic space travel possible. Some ships could travel at warp speeds, but getting from one galaxy to another was still impossible because of the amount of time that it took. The transgates had been built to make it possible to send ships from one galaxy to another, and ships going through them had to have a navigator on board. Coordination with the transgate operator was necessary to ensure a safe trip through the transgate and reach your final destination. The transgates created artificial wormholes from one area to another, and it was the navigator's responsibility to guide the ship through the wormhole, dodging other planets, stars, meteor belts and space junk. In the early years of the transgates, most ships tried to navigate through the wormholes with just a pilot, and many ships were lost because of the collisions with something that the pilot failed to detect in time. For a time, ships tried using computer navigation to go through the transgates, but the cost to put in the necessary equipment prevented many from using them. The computer still required someone to program the variables and work with the transgate operators, so most ships used a combination of a navigator and computer. Coordination was required among the transgate operators, the pilots, and the navigators to make it safely from one side to the other. Kiara had learned how to be a navigator on her dad's ship, and her reputation for getting ships safely through the wormholes was well-known. If she hadn't been so talented at it, she doubted she could have gotten a job on a spaceship scrubbing toilets, because of her 'Protected Race' status.

Looking at the captain, she put it together. "You're worried about going through with me if we run into trouble?"

The captain's frown turned even more intimidating. "I brought you on this ship, and you've proven yourself time and again. I'm not leaving you behind." He turned his frown at Frankie. "The contract we have for the Rubidium delivery doesn't leave us room to take the long way, not if we want to get paid. We're going to have to chance the transgate."

Frankie turned to leave, the captain's orders following him, "Make sure the rest of the crew is on board, and double-check that shipment again before we sign off on it."

Blackburne turned to Kiara, entering some commands into his com unit. "I've sent the destination to you, let's make best possible speed."

Kiara nodded, and felt her stomach lurch. As much as she liked traveling in space, the kind of trouble that brought the Rangers out was more than she ever wanted to run into. Perhaps it wasn't simply pirate activity? She plugged the destination into the navunit, and made initial contact with the transgate operator to check the status of the transgate and set up preliminary communications.

"Um, Captain Blackburne, what kind of trouble should we be looking for?" Kiara asked. She could feel her adrenaline starting to spike, and worked to control her emotions, which were a mixture of fear and excitement. She knew she failed, when Blackburne looked at her and raised an eyebrow. She could feel a blush come over her, and for her race, a blush was turning a deeper shade of blue. Since her emotions had probably already deepened her color, she was pretty sure she was now almost purple. Pretty hard to miss.

"Take a deep breath, Kiara, we'll be fine," Blackburne told her. "We've received notice detailing threats against the transgates, so they brought the Rangers out to patrol. From what I understand, nothing has happened yet, so for now they are merely taking precautions. Space Station Delta sees twice as much commerce and travel through this sector and transgate than anything within ten sectors, so it's naturally going to garner threats and attention."

It was Kiara's turn to raise an eyebrow. She thought that was probably the most words Blackburne had spoken to her since he hired her. But at least she knew what they were dealing with now. She took a couple of deep breaths and turned back to her navunit just as Frankie joined them on deck.

"We're set Captain." Frankie took his seat and fired up the engines, while Blackburne and Kiara buckled in. They received permission to leave the space dock, and Frankie piloted the ship out and headed for the transgate. Blackburne watched the radar, but space traffic was light because of the threats the transgate had received and the previous attack on the space station.

"We have permission to go through the transgate," Kiara announced. "They already have our destination set, and are awaiting our go-ahead." Kiara waited for Blackburne to give the command, and with one last check of the radar, he nodded at her. Kiara set the controls, and they entered the transgate.

Kiara never tired of going through a transgate. She loved the sensation of being pulled, the visual tricks the wormhole could play on you, and the wonder of it when you came out the other side to a new planet or space station. For some, going through the transgates was not pleasant; they experienced nausea, dizziness, and some blacked out. Sometimes it depended on how well the wormhole was created and how long the journey through it was. Most modern ships were designed to handle the gforces exerted by the transgate and resulting wormholes, but many older ships were not, amplifying the effects one could experience. Kiara knew her race handled the stresses better than most; even on the older ships she never had any trouble, much to the envy of many of her shipmates.

They exited the wormhole and at first, Kiara thought they had reached their destination without incident. It soon became apparent, though, that not everything was as it should be. Kiara could hear an abnormal amount of voice traffic on the com channel for this area, and the radar showed a large amount of ship traffic. Blackburne, looking a little pale from the ride through the wormhole, told Frankie to hold their position while they evaluated what was going on, and instructed Kiara to contact the space station and get a status. Frankie moved them away from the transgate and out of the way of all the ship traffic while Kiara tried for several minutes to get through to someone at the space station. Kiara could see some debris floating around the space station, and between her attempts at hailing the space station, she could hear chatter of 'rescues' and 'destruction' over the com.

When she finally got someone to answer, they were instructed to clear the area, due to the recent attack on this transgate and space station. Kiara relayed the information to Blackburne.

"Ask if they need any help with rescue efforts," Blackburne instructed Kiara.

Kiara questioned the space station, but received a negative answer. "They say they have it under control," Kiara told Blackburne.

Blackburne nodded to let Kiara know he'd heard her, but he continued to study the monitor and radar of the area, his expression showing his concern. "Let's continue to our destination," he told Frankie.

Frankie got them on their way, but Kiara felt nervous. Who had attacked the space station? Were they still in the area? Was this related to the other attack?

Blackburne walked to Kiara's station, "Keep trying to get some information about the attack, if you can. The more we know, the better prepared we'll be."

Kiara nodded and turned back to her station, already relaying Blackburne's request.

As they neared the space station that they were delivering the cargo to, Blackburne reminded Kiara to tell them that they had Rubidium on board. "I believe they have special docks setup for this type of cargo."

Kiara nodded and set about contacting the space station and sending the docking information to Frankie. Rubidium was a fairly stable substance, but under the right circumstances, it could be lethal. Some space stations took precautions, some didn't.

Kiara contacted the space station again and inquired if they'd had any trouble since the other space station had been attacked. She was relieved to hear that all was quiet in this part of space. She relayed that to Blackburne, who also looked relieved at the news.

Once they were docked, all hands helped to unload, and Blackburne let them know that they would be here for at least a day. A day of downtime was rare, and the crew planned to take advantage of it. Blackburne suggested that they should all meet at one of the bars on the space station. After getting cleaned up, the crew headed out together. They made a strange group of two Earthlings, three Bendanites, and a Trandorian. It wasn't strange so much that they were all different, but more that they were all together. Larger ships didn't usually foster a culture of the cargo handlers socializing with the bridge crew, and vice versa, but Blackburne encouraged it on his ship. The culture aboard the Acadia was one of the reasons she applied for this navigator position.

They reached the bar and found an area big enough to accommodate all of them, including the three Bendanites. Bendanites were usually around seven to eight feet tall, and somewhere around four hundred pounds of solid muscle. Their strength was legendary. The female Bendanite, Curly, sat next to Kiara. Curly was around seven feet tall, with light-brown hair covering her body. Most people thought they resembled bears, but Kiara supposed it was because of all the hair and muscles. Their hair-covered faces had a distinctive humanoid shape, and Kiara assumed that they never got cold. Many Bendanites wore special clothing that didn't cause them to itch because of all the hair, but a few of them shaved to avoid the itching. Curly wore a gold, short-sleeve special skinsuit, and the hair on her arm brushed Kiara's arm as they sat. Kiara looked up at the gold and black ribbon around Curly's head to make sure it was her. Distinguishing female Bendanites from males was usually pretty hard because they didn't have distinctive body parts that told them apart. Because of that, many female Bendanites took to wearing colorful accessories around the short hair on their heads to help tell them apart. Bendanites themselves had no problems telling each other apart, it was simply a matter of smell to them.

Kiara willed herself to relax and have some fun. These were her shipmates after all. They'd only been together a short time, and most of that time had been spent working or sleeping, so Kiara still felt shy and slightly uncomfortable around them. She knew that before she joined them, this crew had been together for several years, so she was the new person. What was it her dad used to say? Oh yeah, the 'odd man out'.

Kiara brought up the drink menu on her com unit, and noticed that the bar had a large selection from multiple galaxies, so everyone should be able to find something they liked. She smiled when she saw some Earth drinks, including beer and Coke. Kiara loved everything and anything that had to do with Earth. If anyone looked into the little cubby above her bed, they would find Earth memorabilia. She kept just a few things, but it was enough to satisfy her cravings for Earth stuff. She knew it came from her dad and a need for a past or history, but that didn't matter. Stored in her com unit were Earth books, from early notable writings to science fiction books about space travel and the future. She always enjoyed seeing what people a few hundred years ago thought the future would look like.

She ordered a Coke, and noticed that she was the only one who ordered something from Earth. The Bendanites predictably ordered from their home planet, and Frankie and Blackburne ordered some alcoholic concoction that was a blend from three different planets. She thought they would be out of commission in a few hours if they ordered more than one of those.

Because of the threats to the transgates, patronage at the bar was light, and they had the back area next to an artificial window to themselves. The artificial window simulated the view out into space, and was currently showing the docking approach area on the lower portion of the space station. Conversation at first was all about the attack they had just missed and the earlier attack they were almost pulled into, but it soon turned to other topics. Blackburne started a story about one of his journeys from a few years back, and she saw and felt Curly chuckle next to her. Kiara smiled too, and started to relax slightly. Curly turned to her.

"Do you go back to Trandor?" Curly and the other Bendanites had been practicing English since they were hired by Blackburne. Kiara spoke English because she was raised by her Earth father, so it made crewing on this ship easier. Other crews had to use translating applications in their com units, which could make conversations slow and awkward.

At Curly's question, the conversation around the rest of the table stopped, and all eyes turned to Kiara. She assumed that Curly was asking whether or not she'd ever been back to Trandor. Kiara shifted in her chair, uncomfortable with the attention.

"No, I've never been back there."

"Have they started rebuilding there since the wars?" Frankie questioned.

"I've heard it's still basically a dead planet, atmosphere is toxic, with no food or water supplies," Blackburne said.

Kiara nodded, "That's what I've heard as well."

Frankie straightened in his chair slightly. "You know, I looked up Trandor when you first came on board," he said. "I'd never heard of your race before, and I think I've seen a couple of Trandorians through the years, but didn't pay much attention at the time." He looked around the table. "I had a difficult time finding information about your race and your planet." Now he looked slightly embarrassed. "I found some stuff out there about ancient races, women who were 'Guardians' with enhanced abilities, that kind of thing."

Kiara flushed a deep blue. "I read some of that a long time ago, but it seemed more like a myth. Kind of like Earth stories I used to read, like 'X-Men', or 'Superman'."

Blackburne smiled, and Curly next to her chuckled again, making Kiara's chair bounce.

"So, you can't see through clothes with your X-ray vision, or leap tall buildings?" Frankie asked with a smile and a wink at Kiara.

Kiara relaxed and laughed with everyone else. Really, a race of women with superpowers? Definitely stuff that stories were made of.

"I did discover why my skin is this color, though," Kiara said after a moment. "Trandor had minerals that permeated everything from the food to the water. Those minerals gave our skin its color; it was our body's way of adapting to the high mineral content."

"So that's why you have to order in those supplements?" Frankie asked.

Kiara nodded, "My dad figured it out early on. My body still needs the extra minerals. I can have other food and drinks, but I have to make sure I supplement with those special foods and supplements that I order."

"What happens when you don't get them?"

"I start to feel a little weak, mostly."

"Does your skin lose its blue color?"

"Actually, no." Kiara smiled at all the questions Frankie was asking her. "It gets a little lighter, but I'll always be blue. It has something to do with all the centuries of our bodies adapting to the conditions on Trandor. The pigment in our skin will always naturally be this color."

More drinks were ordered, and the talk turned to other adventures, and Kiara was glad the attention had moved to someone else in the group. She wanted to ask about the attacks again, but didn't want to earn a glare from Blackburne. Besides, they were all having a good time with the drinks and the conversation, and she didn't want to drag the group down. She'd try to ask about it tomorrow.

Frankie was telling a racy story involving him and four Sulverian women, when Kiara felt as though someone was watching her. The hair on the back of her neck stood up, and her skin flushed a deeper shade of blue. She shifted in her seat, and tried to look around the room without being obvious. She could see a half dozen or so customers in the bar, but none of them appeared to be looking at her. She turned back around, just as Frankie was getting to what he referred to as 'the juicy parts'. Kiara frowned, as she didn't really want to hear about Frankie's exploits with the notoriously sexual race of Sulver. She was about to excuse herself from the table, when the hair on the back of her neck stood up again. This time she also felt a tingling between her shoulder blades. She looked around the bar again, but still didn't see anyone looking at her. When she was younger, she'd had times when she'd felt someone looking at her, but it was usually when she was with her dad, and she would look up to find him looking at her. This feeling was strong, but strange, not like the times she sensed her dad. She shrugged, stood, and headed for the bathroom. No one at her table said anything, as Frankie was apparently deep into the interesting part of his tale.

After finishing in the bathroom, Kiara was making her way down the narrow hallway that contained the bathrooms, when someone else entered the hallway coming toward her. The hallway was dimly lit, and all Kiara could make out was that the person coming toward her was tall and broad shouldered. She thought it was going to get tight in the narrow space if she had to get by him or her. The hair on the back of her neck stood up again, and Kiara slowed her pace, her pulse accelerating slightly. Her hand went to her com unit; her thought was to call Curly or Blackburne. Before she could tap her com unit, the stranger stopped, seeming to sense her unease. His words did nothing to calm her.

"You are from Trandor." It wasn't a question.

"Do I know you?" Kiara kept her hand next to her com unit, ready to hit it if needed. She hoped her fellow crew members weren't too intoxicated to come to her aid.

"You do not know me. I have been waiting many years for you."

Kiara had heard more than enough. Waiting for her? Definitely creepy. Her pulse accelerated, and she could feel her adrenaline building. She moved up to the balls of her feet, ready to defend herself if needed. She wondered briefly at the heat that was building in her midsection with the spike of adrenaline, but instead she focused on the stranger in front of her. She hit her com unit, and in a slightly shaky voice, asked Curly to join her in the bathroom, and perhaps bring Larry and Moe with her.

"Do not be afraid, I am not here to harm you. I merely want to help you achieve your destiny."

"My destiny? What the hell does that mean?"

Before he could answer, Curly's big frame filled the hallway behind him. "Kiara?" Curly's voice was deep with worry.

"My apologies," the stranger said, bowing slightly at the waist. He turned and headed back up the hallway toward Curly, who now had Larry and Moe behind her. Sheesh, Kiara thought, the hallway was getting crowded. Bendanites were willing workers, but were dangerous when angry, and with their strength, most people were careful not to rile them. Curly blocked the hallway and looked at Kiara, waiting to see if she should do something to the stranger walking toward them. Kiara shook her head, and the three Bendanites shuffled back out of the way and let him pass. Kiara walked up to Curly, and noticed that not only had Larry and Moe joined her, but Blackburne and Frankie were only a few steps behind them as well.

"You are okay?" Curly asked her.

Kiara touched her furry arm, more than grateful that she and the rest of her shipmates had come so quickly to her aid. "Yes, I'm good. He scared me, that's all."

Blackburne led the way back to their table, the stranger long gone from the bar. "What did he want?"

"I'm not sure," Kiara answered. "He knew I was from Trandor, but he also said he had been waiting years for me." She tried to shrug off the feeling of unease that his statement brought on. "Maybe I should head back to the ship."

"We'll all go," Blackburne said. He quickly tapped his com unit to pay the bar bill, and received an immediate agreement from the others at the table.

"I don't want to ruin your evening," Kiara started to protest, but it had no effect, they were already heading out. She followed Blackburne, and noticed immediately how Blackburne and Frankie walked in front of her, the three Bendanites following behind, their gazes scanning the bar and the area outside the bar for anyone suspicious. Kiara wanted to roll her eyes, but found enormous comfort in their actions.

"Could you see what he looked like, or where he was from?" Kiara directed her question to Curly behind her.

"No," Curly replied. "He had hood covering." Curly gestured around her face with her furry hands. "I could not see his face."

Kiara didn't get a good look at him either, but thought she'd seen hair on his face, like the Bendanites, but he definitely wasn't a Bendanite. She mentally shrugged. They'd be leaving in the morning, so she thought she wouldn't need to worry about it.

They reached the space dock where their ship was, and the crew boarded in silence. Blackburne hadn't given them information for their next run, so Kiara supposed they didn't have anything yet. Blackburne was good at rounding up work, so he'd probably have several jobs lined up by morning, especially if he were willing to use a transgate while the threat was out there.

Chapter Two

Kiara's com unit signaled her alarm to get up the next morning, and she reached over to shut it off. She had been lying awake, in her little cubby hole of a bed for several hours. Her dreams had interrupted her sleep several hours before, the vividness and nature of them had left her heart racing. She'd been dreaming of other Trandorians, and strangers with furry faces. She knew the dreams were from the encounter with the stranger at the bar, but that didn't stop her unease. When she was a little girl, if she'd had a disturbing or scary dream, she'd run to her dad, and he'd let her sleep in his room until she felt better. She sighed. Now that she was an adult on her own, there was no one to comfort her after a night of disturbing dreams.

She rolled over and noticed that Curly was still snoring quietly, squished into her bunk. Kiara was amazed yet again that she even fit in there. Getting ready for the day, Kiara chose a forest-green tunic to wear over her skinsuit this time, and braided her hair down her back. She was always quick to get ready, with her pale-blue skin, and natural dark lashes, she never had to apply any enhancers, and probably wouldn't anyway, no matter what her skin and eye color was. She liked to spend her time on other things and not on trying to change the way she looked. She remembered one freighter that she had worked on; there was a mixed race human that she never really got to know. He spent several hours every morning working on his hair, his eyes, and his clothes. She never understood it. Apparently, neither had the captain, as the guy had gotten himself fired after only a couple of days on the job.

She checked her com unit for messages, and noticed that Blackburne had sent out the details for the next job.

They were picking up some freight here, and hauling it to a planet a few light-years away. They wouldn't even have to use one of the transgates to get there. She went up to the bridge to program in the route, and saw Frankie performing some preflight checks.

"Hey, Frankie," Kiara acknowledged him as she sat at her station.

Frankie grunted at her and continued his task. He wasn't a morning person, and Kiara had learned to give him his space until he got his humor back.

Kiara was leaning over her station, double-checking her navigation when she felt Frankie's hand on her shoulder. She turned to him, surprise making her eyebrows arch.

"What's going on, Frankie? Everything okay?"

"Yeah, yeah, just wanted to make sure you were okay, after that creep from last night."

Kiara was surprised. Yes, they were all part of the same crew, but they hadn't been together that long, and she usually didn't see this much interest in her from her fellow crew members. She knew it was her own fault, because she usually kept herself slightly apart from everyone. She had to admit; it was nice to know that someone besides her dad cared what happened to her and how she felt.

"I'm good, thanks Frankie," Kiara let a small smile come across her face. "A few weird dreams, but that's all."

Frankie chuckled. "I once had a female Volterran chase me through a space dock, screaming her undying love for me." He shook his head. "I had nightmares for weeks about her catching me."

This time they both chuckled as Kiara pictured the always self-assured Frankie running through a space dock.

"What's our cargo this time, Frankie? Anything we have to take special precautions with?"

Sometimes, depending on the cargo type, they had to stay minimum distances from populated areas, asteroid belts, or gravitational fields.

"Actually, it's a collection of junk that they want to send to the fifth planet over, I guess that's their dumping ground." Frankie said as he walked back to his station, and checked the navigational information that Kiara had sent over. "That planet is devoid of life—no atmosphere to speak of, but it's a dense planet. It has a huge gravitational pull, keeping everything they dump there on the surface." He nodded as he continued, "We're supposed to do a high-orbit cargo jettison for this haul."

"Junk? Is that legal?"

Frankie nodded. "Supposedly we have a certificate of 'no hazard', so we're legal."

Kiara would have never dared to ask Blackburne if a haul was legal, but before she took this job, she had checked in to this ship's background with the GTA. It didn't have any strikes against it for illegal cargo hauling, so she felt fairly confident that she wouldn't get involved in anything illegal. She hadn't been as fortunate on one of her early jobs. The captain had been secretive about their jobs, and she discovered later that most of the cargo had been illegal, including some human trafficking. She'd been lucky that she was only with them for a short time, and hadn't been part of that crew when the GTA had busted them.

Blackburne joined them a short while later, and Kiara watched the master com unit of the ship as Larry, Curly, and Moe finished loading the containers. The containers were large square metal boxes, with all the junk inside, which was fine with Kiara. Space dock junk could be anything from broken chairs to rotten food. With ten containers in all, it didn't take long before they were loaded and Blackburne gave the order to takeoff. It would take about nine hours to get to their destination, so Kiara knew she had some personal time before she was needed again.

Once they were clear of the space dock, Kiara went to the kitchen, grabbed a snack, and headed to the flex-space that served as exercise room, meeting room, and extra cargo space. Today, the room was empty, and Kiara set the holographic exercise program for one of her more aggressive workouts. It would help burn off the lingering effects of the dreams she had last night. Her workout consisted of Earth martial arts and boxing, mixed with some moves she had learned on her travels. Her dad had shown her the martial arts and boxing, and she'd been hooked. He said he introduced it to her so she could learn how to take care of herself, and he wouldn't always have to worry about her being safe. She didn't know about keeping her safe, she'd never had to use her skills on anyone, but she did know it kept her in shape.

She worked out for a good hour, and kept her com unit on in case the bridge needed her. She was heading back to her room to clean up when she heard Curly's voice come over the com unit, asking Larry and Moe to come to the cargo area. She thought it strange that Curly's request had come across her com unit, and not just Larry and Moe's, so she diverted from heading to her room to head to the cargo area.

She walked in on chaos. Curly was standing on top of one of the containers, emitting an ear-piercing shriek that can only come from a terrified Bendanite. Kiara was surprised to see Curly on top of the container, wondering how she had even gotten up there, but figured Curly's terror must have given her the impetus to make the leap. Larry and Moe were alternately yelling at her to be quiet, and running around banging on the containers and the floor with large sticks. Before she could shout out a question, Blackburne and Frankie walked in as well.

"What the hell is going on?" Blackburne's bellow finally got through to Curly, who shut her mouth with an audible snap. She stayed on top of the container, a small whimper coming from her now. Larry and Moe lumbered out from behind one of the containers, carrying the sticks, looking a little sheepish.

Larry, a large Bendanite at more than eight feet tall and light-brown fur, spoke first. "Curly saw spratna."

At the mention of the fist-sized spider/rat-like creature, everyone, including Blackburne backed up a step.

"Damn it!" Blackburne looked around the cargo area a little warily. "I was assured that this cargo didn't have any vermin or illegal stuff in it." He looked up at the still whimpering Curly. "I'm sorry Curly." He knew that Curly was terrified of the small creatures, not because they would cause any harm, but just because she was scared.

Kiara thought it was similar to someone from Earth being scared of spiders or mice. Kiara herself wasn't necessarily scared of the creatures, but definitely didn't like them. They multiplied like crazy, and their origin had never really been determined. They usually hung around trash and junk that sat around for a while, and once you got them, it was hard to get rid of them. The containers currently occupying the cargo area of the ship were not sealed up tight, allowing the creatures to move in and out of the containers at will. Fortunately, the ship's design would keep them from moving beyond the cargo area, but they needed to do something with the vermin that were here. Especially if they ever wanted Curly to work in this area again.

Blackburne turned to Kiara and Frankie. "Get some sticks; let's see if we can't get rid of them."

Kiara found some gloves as well, and the four of them slowly started to go through the containers. Curly stood on top and watched to make sure that none escaped the hunt. Most of the containers had scrap metal, paper, and other types of industrial junk, and it was tough work trying to find spratna in the containers. They were going through the third container when Kiara thought she saw something bigger than the spider/rat-like creature moving in the back. She turned to Frankie and asked for more light near the back of the container. A pair of red eyes reflected the light back at them, and both Frankie and Kiara stopped where they were.

"That's not a spratna," Kiara whispered.

"It's too big," Frankie whispered back.

"Do you have a bigger light?" Kiara asked, still in a hushed tone. What if it were some sort of supersized spratna? She might just join Curly on top of the container.

In answer to her question, Frankie tried to slowly move closer to whatever was hiding in the back of the container. His movement caused the critter to start a low huffing sound. Frankie froze.

"I think it's a drayek," Frankie whispered to Kiara. "It's probably been living off the spratna in these containers."

Drayeks were animals from a star system several transgates away that Kiara thought resembled the mythical Earth dragons, but drayeks never got more than a couple of feet tall. Some had wings, some did not. She'd only seen them once before, on the drayek's home world when she was doing a cargo run there. She'd never known them to leave their planet, and she wasn't sure if Frankie was right.

"Are you sure?" she asked Frankie.

Before Frankie could answer, Blackburne stepped into the container and pointed another light into the back. "What the hell is taking so long—is that a drayek?"

With Blackburne's light, it was evident now that the creature huffing at them from the back of the container was indeed a drayek, and from what Kiara could tell, it was young. It looked to be less than a foot tall, with small tufts of hair on the top of his head between his ears. A full-grown drayek had horns where the tufts of hair were. Blackburne muttered a few swearwords at finding more vermin in this load. Raising the metal stick he was carrying as he went forward, his intention to get rid of the drayek the same way they were getting rid of the spratna.

Without thinking, Kiara sprang forward, jumped several piles of junk and put herself between Blackburne and the drayek.

"No!!!!" Kiara threw her hand up. "Don't hurt it!"

Blackburne stopped in midstride, and frowned at Kiara. The metal stick he was carrying flew backward out of his hand.

"It's just a baby, don't hurt it," Kiara said.

Before Blackburne could answer, Kiara turned around to look at the little guy. She had no idea whether drayeks were friendly or not; she just knew that she had to protect this little creature.

Blackburne was alternately looking at Kiara and his hand. He was trying to figure out how he'd lost his grip on the stick, who was going to get rid of the drayek, and who was going to get fired for giving him a load of vermin.

"Did you know she could move like that?" Frankie whispered.

Kiara ignored whatever Blackburne said in response, and concentrated on the little guy in front of her. His little red eyes were locked on hers, and his ears kept going up and down as he studied her. She wished she knew more about them. Did they bite? Did they like people at all? She remembered her dad talking about finding a dog when he was a little boy on Earth, and how he had talked in a quiet voice to it. Well, she was in it this far, she might as well try talking to it.

"Hello, little one." At her voice, his little ears popped up. Kiara thought it was a good start, since he wasn't running from her and he wasn't baring his teeth at her. It had teeth didn't it?

"I won't hurt you, little one." She took a hesitant step toward it, and still it stayed where it was, eyes still locked on hers, ears up. She took another step, crooning nonsense at it. When she was about three feet away from it, she slowly raised her right hand toward it, palm up. From behind her, Frankie yelled at her to quit being stupid before she got bit. The little drayek flinched at Frankie's shout, his ears going back down against his head. His eyes darted past Kiara, but seeing that Frankie wasn't coming closer, he looked back at Kiara, his ears going back up. Kiara's hand was a few inches away from it, when it suddenly popped out a small set of wings on his back, and jumped straight at her. Kiara closed her eyes, hoping it didn't bite or scratch her, but refusing to move away from it. His little wings beat the air, and he landed softly on her outstretched arm. At the feel of him on her arm, Kiara's eyes flew back open. He had a tail as long as he was tall, and he wrapped it around her arm to steady himself. His wings folded back down his back, and he quietly stared at Kiara. As she watched in amazement, his skin, which had been a dark-gray color, slowly took on a bluish hue to match Kiara's skin. He was lighter than she thought he would be, but even so, her arm was starting to cramp at his weight. She didn't want to startle him, but she had to try to move him or risk dropping him. Before she could put a plan into action, he unwrapped his tail, dropped to all four legs on her arm, and crawled to her shoulder. He wrapped his tail around the top part of her arm, and rested his front legs on her head. She could feel a slight rumbling coming from his little body, and for some reason, felt a sense of contentment come over her, almost as if it were coming from him. Had he somehow sensed that she needed him to move? Maybe they had some sort of telekinetic ability.

Kiara slowly brought her hand up to him, and when it was close to him, the little drayek reached out and grabbed one her fingers. The rumbling increased in intensity, and Kiara felt the feeling of contentment increase. With the little drayek gently holding her finger, Kiara turned back around to Frankie and Blackburne.

Blackburne took one look at Kiara's face and muttered, "Aw, hell." He turned to Frankie. "Please tell me that Curly isn't afraid of drayeks. Looks like we're going to have one for a while."

All three made their way out of the container where Larry and Moe were waiting. At the site of the drayek, Larry smiled and nodded his head.

"Why are you smiling?" Blackburne asked. "You realize she's going to try to keep it, don't you?"

"Drayeks eat spratna," Larry responded, "and are good luck."

Blackburne shook his head. "You made that last part up, just to help sway me."

Larry just shrugged and went into the container to see if there were any more spratna inside.

Blackburne turned back to Kiara. "Are those things potty-trained?" he asked, referring to the earth custom of training young children to use a toilet.

"Um…"

"Just see to it that it doesn't make a mess, okay?" Blackburne headed for another container to look for vermin.

Kiara felt the drayek tense up on her shoulder, and turned around to find Curly's smiling face. The little drayek must have sensed that Kiara was fond of Curly because she could immediately feel the little guy relax again.

"You found drayek!" Curly made a low huffing sound, and the drayek mimicked it back to her. Kiara's eyebrows went up.

"It has bonded with you," Curly said. She made a clicking sound and the drayek mimicked that back to her.

"Why do you think it's bonded with me?" Kiara asked. The little drayek had one paw on her head, the other still holding one of her fingers. "Have you been around drayeks before?"

Curly nodded. "I had one when little." She reached up and scratched behind his ears. His rumbling increased again. "He has your blue. This is bonding." Curly coaxed it to her arm, and the little drayek stayed Kiara's shade of blue, and, even though it looked comfortable on Curly's arm, it kept looking back at Kiara. "Maybe that is not the right word—bonding?" Curly let the drayek hop back over to Kiara's shoulder.

"I think that's the right word, Curly." The little drayek was now holding her hair. "Why do you think it bonded with me? Is it because I was the first one to approach it?"

Curly shook her head, "They pick the person. If he bonded before, he would not bond with you now."

"They bond for life?"

"Yes."

"What happened to yours, Curly?"

Curly's eyes looked sad. "He died with war."

39

Kiara patted her friends arm at the sad look on her face. She watched as the drayek patted Curly's arm too. Parts of Bendan had been involved in a civil war years ago. Fortunately, the war hadn't spread to the whole planet, but many still died. The war was one of the reasons that Bendanites were out working on ships, space docks and other planets. They had fled their planet fearing that the wars would spread.

"Um, Curly, do you know what they eat, besides spratna, and what do I do about a toilet for him? I don't want Blackburne to get upset."

"He eats what you eat. You teach him to use toilet," Curly said as she started to turn away.

"Okay," Kiara said. She thought it sounded easy enough. She hoped it was anyway. "One more thing, Curly." Curly turned back around. "How do I know if it's a boy or girl? I've been calling it a 'him', but I'm not sure how you know."

"He is boy. He has two of these," Curly gestured to the top of her head, the same place that the little drayek's tufts of hair were. "Girls have one in middle; boys have two that become horns." Curly lumbered off, her panic about the spratna forgotten with the appearance of the drayek.

Kiara turned back to the nearest crate, her intent to see if she could help find more spratna. Her thoughts were elsewhere. Now that she knew that drayeks bonded for life, and this little one had bonded with her, she had to be committed to taking care of him. How long did they live for? She'd never had anything be this dependent on her before. Sure she had responsibilities as a navigator, but if she wanted to go to another ship, she just went. If she wanted to go to the bar with friends, she just went. Of course, that didn't happen that often, and come to think of it, she'd seen a couple of 'pet' type creatures in bars before, so maybe that wasn't an issue either. She reached out and moved some broken chairs out of the way, and a couple of spratna ran out from under them. Before she could move to intercept them, the drayek on her shoulder shot down to the floor and grabbed both of them. With his powerful hind feet, he quickly killed them, and just as quickly shoveled them into his mouth. His long snout and jaw held rows of sharp, wicked-looking teeth, and the two little vermin disappeared quickly. He turned back to Kiara, and with a hop and couple of beats of his wings, assumed his position on her shoulder.

"Well, okay then. Ah, good boy," Kiara hesitantly said to the little creature.

Kiara's com unit signaled and Blackburne's voice came over the unit ordering everyone out of the cargo bay. Apparently, they had reached their destination. Whatever spratna were left were going to end up going to the planet surface with the rest of the junk.

Frankie did a head count and security check before he jettisoned the load. Blackburne frowned hard at Kiara, and looked as if he were going to make a comment about the drayek, but Curly coming up to stroke the little creature stopped whatever he was going to say.

"It is good luck," Curly said, and headed off into the ship.

Blackburne sighed. "As long as it's good luck," he said sarcastically, and they all chuckled. "We have to monitor the dump for a couple of hours before we can head out." Blackburne turned to Kiara. "Be back on the bridge in an hour."

"Yes, sir," Kiara answered, as she headed to her cabin to see about getting to know the drayek better.

As she walked through the narrow corridor, she reached up with her free hand and slowly stroked the little guy's feet. He rumbled in her ear in response. She thought she'd better think up a name for him as well. A little panic went through her as she thought again about the responsibility that had just fallen in her lap. When her shoulders tensed up at the thought, a warm feeling of calm seemed to come from the drayek. Her shoulders eased back down, and she could feel the little guy stroke her hair. This could work, couldn't it? Besides, what other choices were there? Curly said he had already bonded with her, and wouldn't bond with anyone else. She knew she couldn't abandon him on some other planet, so she would just make this work. She was already starting to feel attached to him, anyway.

Kiara reached her cabin, but didn't see Curly when she entered. Curly usually stayed with Larry and Moe near the cargo area, so Kiara almost always had the cabin to herself. As she walked to her bunk, the drayek unwrapped his tail, unfolded his wings, and jumped to her bed. He hopped around her bed, making chirping sounds as he smelled the blankets and pillows. It made Kiara smile. She noticed that his skin still had the same blue color it had changed to when he had landed on her. Did he keep that color, or did it change, like an Earth chameleon? She sat down on the bunk and the drayek immediately came over to her side and curled up next to her. She tapped her com unit, and with a few eye movements and voice commands, brought up the information she could get access to for drayeks.

As she had thought, he was young, and judging by his size and the tufts of hair on top of his head, he was probably only a couple of years old. Her eyebrows rose when she saw that they could live more than one hundred years. She wasn't sure what her life span was supposed to be. She could assume it would be similar to other humans, but she couldn't be sure. There just wasn't that much information available about her race. Some documents said one hundred years, some said one hundred fifty. She was thought to be somewhere around thirty years old now. Nobody knew for sure, and her dad had just made up a day to be her birthday after she'd been with him for a while. They guessed that she had been about five years old when they had found her, and with nothing to contradict that, she went with it.

She read that drayeks usually bonded between the ages of one and seven, and as Curly had said, they bonded for life. If a drayek lost the person it had bonded with, they usually died as well. Kiara looked down at the sleeping drayek next to her and thought about how sad that seemed. She was definitely responsible for its life now.

They were fiercely loyal, protective, and she even found some information about decoding the sounds they made so she could understand him better. She flipped through some more information and saw that their wings didn't really enable them to fly; it just sort of helped them to jump higher and steady them.

At the end of one of the more obscure documents she found, was a reference to telekinetic abilities. Nothing definitive, just some information about knowing what the person they bonded with was thinking, and one reference that talked about enhancing telekinetic abilities. That was interesting. She looked down at him, and stroked her hand down his back. His skin was warm and smooth, and she couldn't feel any hair on him, except those two tufts between his ears. Did they get cold? She flipped back through the documents and finally found something that mentioned that they did get cold, so they usually stayed close to the person they bonded with for warmth.

Still petting him, she turned her mind to finding a name for him. She was terrible at coming up with names. Once, when she was younger, her dad had given her a small Earth goldfish in a fishbowl. It had taken her a week to come up with a name.

The drayek was now making a quiet snoring sound, and she giggled at the sound. He came awake with a start, and she felt bad for waking him. He probably hadn't been able to sleep comfortably for a while.

Kiara looked around her room, trying to find something to inspire a name. She looked at her small collection of Earth memorabilia, hoping something there might inspire her. She thought of famous Earth people that she had read about, or that her dad had told her about. Leonardo? She looked down at the little guy, but didn't think the name fit him. He was little, so maybe Napoleon? Kiara frowned, thinking he didn't look like a Napoleon to her, even if he was short. She sighed; worried that she was going to take a long time to come up with something. She didn't want to keep calling him 'little guy'. Thinking back through famous Earth people again, she thought about the famous singer, Elvis.

As the name 'Elvis' popped into her head, the little drayek bumped her hand with his head. The next name she was thinking of disappeared from her mind, and she glanced down at him.

"You like the name Elvis?" He bumped her hand again. "Okay, Elvis it is." Immensely relieved that she had found a name, she scratched the top of his head, earning another round of rumbling from him.

Glancing down at her com unit, Kiara figured she'd better head up to the bridge. What to do with Elvis? She stood up, and he immediately hopped up to her shoulder. Well, that answered that. She just hoped Blackburne or

Frankie wouldn't tell her to take him back to her room. She'd just tell them that she needed to keep an eye on him.

She reached the bridge and both Blackburne and Frankie eyed the little drayek suspiciously. Kiara ignored them and sat at her console. Blackburne had already keyed in the next destination. It would require two transgate jumps and several days flying to get there. She concentrated on plotting out their journey. Because both transgates had special rules associated with them due to their locations, it was imperative that she get the timing right. She turned back to Blackburne who was discussing something with Frankie.

"We'll have to do a layover near Transgate 29; they only staff it at certain times of the day, and we'll reach it at the off time," Kiara told Blackburne. "Also, it appears there's a queue of ships ahead of us, so I've got us in the queue, but it will delay us." She looked down to double-check her calculations. "It'll take us four days to get to our destination."

Blackburne sighed, but didn't seem too agitated, so Kiara assumed he had made this trip before and knew the constraints.

"I'll let the client know our time frame." Blackburne keyed in the message at his console and sent it off.

"Any more trouble at the transgates?" Kiara asked as she prepared her navigation report to send to Frankie's console.

"Some," Blackburne said, and left it at that.

Elvis was still on her shoulder, but he was so light that Kiara hardly noticed him, until he started snoring. The sound was soft, and she wondered how he didn't fall off her shoulder since he was apparently sound asleep.

Blackburne gave the order to leave, and Frankie piloted them away from the planet and toward the first transgate. It would take them the same nine hours to get back to the space station by the transgate as it took them to get to the planet they just left. Kiara knew she was once again going to have time on her hands. Once they were on their way, she headed to the kitchen to see if Elvis was hungry. She would get them some food, and maybe she would get some sleep before she would be needed at the transgate.

She entered the kitchen and found Curly rummaging through the cabinets. Curly turned toward them, and at the site of Elvis on her shoulder, her wide furry face broke into a grin. Kiara loved it when a Bendanite smiled—it was all sharp teeth and fur, and for those that didn't know them, it could be scary. An angry Bendanite didn't show their teeth–they simply tore apart whomever they were angry with.

"He has name?" Curly asked. She walked closer to them and made low huffing sounds to the drayek.

"Elvis," Kiara told her. At his name, the little drayek perked up his ears.

"Good, good," Curly said. "He knows already. Good." She handed Elvis a small piece of fruit, and he gently took it from her.

"You must practice the bonding," Curly told her.

"Practice the bonding?" Kiara could hear Elvis quietly eating the piece of fruit on her shoulder. She'd probably have fruit juice on her clothes after this. They would definitely have to work something out so she didn't look like something had spit up on her. Kiara turned a questioning glance at Curly, who was looking deep in thought, her brow furrowed, her eyes slightly narrowed. She was obviously trying to think of the right words.

"Here to here," Curly said, pointing first to Kiara's head, then to Elvis' head.

"Aaahhh," Kiara said, realizing she meant the telekinetic abilities the drayeks reportedly had. "How do you practice that?" Since Elvis seemed to be 'in tune' with her naming him, who was she to question it?

"Practice the bonding," Curly said, and lumbered out of the kitchen.

Kiara shrugged her shoulders causing Elvis to clench his feet and tighten his tail to keep his perch. All right, she would practice.

Concentrating, she silently asked Elvis to hop to the counter. She waited, but Elvis stayed perched on her shoulder. She turned her head to look at him, and at her gaze, he turned to look at her. He blinked slowly, but Kiara didn't think he looked as if he knew she'd just asked him to do something. Okay, that didn't work, so maybe it wasn't as easy as Curly made it seem. Never one to give up easily, she took a calming breath and pictured Elvis hopping from her shoulder to the counter. She sent him the request as she let her breath out.

With a slight swish of his wings, Elvis unwrapped his tail and hopped to the counter. When he landed he turned back to her, as if waiting for her to invite him back. She closed her eyes, not wanting to give away the signal with her eyes. She waited a few heartbeats, pictured him back on her shoulder, and asked him to come back. With no hesitation, he immediately jumped back onto her shoulder, his little body rumbling his pleasure at being back with her.

"Wow." She reached up and stroked his toes. "That was amazing, Elvis." He made a quiet chirping sound as if in agreement. "I wonder what else we can do."

Kiara grabbed a couple of snacks, intending to head back to her bunk for a quick nap. As she turned to head out of the kitchen, one of the snacks that she had grabbed fell out of her hand. She made a quick grab for it and missed, but watched in amazement as it seemed to float in midair before slowly descending to the floor. It landed like a feather on the floor. Kiara stared at it, realizing that she was bent over, focused on the snack. She straightened up and looked around the room, trying to figure out what was going on. She was almost afraid to touch the snack. She looked at Elvis, who was still staring at the snack on the floor. He didn't seem alarmed, so Kiara thought she must have imagined the whole thing. She must be more tired than she realized. Frankie's comments about 'Guardians from Trandor' replayed in her head, but she quickly shook that off. Taking a deep breath, she reached down and quickly grabbed the snack off the floor. Nothing happened, so she assured herself again that she had just imagined it. Elvis, still on her shoulder, chirped at her and reached for the snack. Kiara handed it to him and headed out of the kitchen.

They reached her cabin, and Kiara noticed that Curly wasn't there; she was most likely in the cargo area with Larry and Moe. Kiara closed her eyes, pictured Elvis hopping over to her bunk, silently asking him to go. He immediately hopped to the bunk and turned around to watch her. She dug through some of her cabinets, and produced an old blanket that she placed on the bed. She bunched it up near the foot of the bed to make a small, nest-like area. She was hoping that Elvis would sleep there. There really wasn't any room elsewhere in the small cabin, and if he didn't get much bigger, it shouldn't be a problem. As she straightened up from arranging the blanket, Elvis hopped over, jumped into the middle of the blanket and rearranged it a little. With one last look at Kiara, he curled into a ball and closed his eyes.

Kiara smiled as she changed into her sleeping tunic. For the first time in a long time, she didn't feel alone. She crawled into the bunk, and Elvis moved over to snuggle against the back of her legs. Kiara set her com unit to wake her in a few hours, and fell asleep with visions of flying drayeks and floating fruit racing through her mind.

Chapter Three

A few hours later, as Kiara dressed to head back to the bridge, a sudden thought of having to use the bathroom entered her head. She frowned. She really didn't have to go that bad. She turned around to see Elvis hopping around on the bed, and realized with a start that he had sent the thought to her.

"Oh, sorry Elvis! Let's go." She bent down and picked him up, her left hand under his back feet, her right hand holding him under his shorter front legs. She hoped taking him to the bathroom was the right thing to do; she had no idea what to do with him if he couldn't use the toilet. She was immensely relieved when she realized that he had used a toilet before, which became evident when they entered the bathroom. With their needs taken care of, she headed back to the cabin to finish getting ready before heading to the bridge.

When she reached the bridge and checked at her station, she realized the ship had made good time, and they were due to hit the first transgate within the hour. Frankie was at his position, but Blackburne was nowhere to be seen.

"Hey Frankie," Kiara called over to him. Frankie looked up from his console and smiled over at her. He looked at Elvis, now curled up at her feet, and smiled at him as well.

"For some reason, he looks as if he belongs there," Frankie said.

Kiara contacted the transgate, and frowned when she didn't receive a response. She checked the com frequencies, checked the message, and sent it again. Still nothing.

"Frankie, Transgate Control isn't responding."

Frankie briefly looked up from his console, sending a request for Blackburne to join them on the bridge. "I'm seeing a lot of activity around the transgate, so I'm going to slow us down until we figure out what's happening," Frankie told her.

Kiara felt the ship shift slightly as Frankie slowed them. She kept her contact message on a loop to Transgate Control, and brought up the scan that Frankie was monitoring. She too could see what appeared to be numerous ships around the transgate, some moving, some not. She magnified the scan and let out a gasp. She'd seen this before when she'd been traveling with her dad.

"Stop here, Frankie!"

Frankie brought the ship to a full stop, just as Blackburne joined them on the bridge. From his slightly sweaty appearance, Kiara guessed he'd been working out in the flex-space.

"What do we have?" Blackburne's presence on the bridge brought immediate relief to Kiara.

"Transgate Control isn't answering, but I think Kiara has seen something going on," Frankie nodded at her.

"I've seen this before—the transgate and the waiting ships are under attack." Kiara said quickly. "If you magnify the scan, you can see the debris from some of the ships that have been hit, plus the smaller ships, running in packs of three—those are the ones attacking."

Frankie brought up the scan on the main screen and magnified. Sure enough, they could make out the debris from several destroyed ships, and several packs of the smaller attacking ships.

"Scan the area, make sure we're not easy prey just sitting out here," Blackburne ordered, and Frankie jumped to do as he ordered.

Kiara brought up her radar and helped with the scan. The more eyes the better.

"There's a small group attacking the space station, and there appears to be several groups hiding behind the moon, but nothing near us." Kiara nodded her agreement of Frankie's assessment.

"Kiara, you've seen this before—who are they?" Blackburne questioned.

"They're hired assassins, different species, and different planets," Kiara answered. "I think they call themselves the Mercenaries. Not very original, but mercenary work is what they do. Assassinations, wars, whatever dirty work they can get." She looked back down at the scan. "I've never seen this many before."

"Too many for us to contend with," Blackburne said.

"The shielding on the space station and transgate is holding so far," Frankie told them while he continued to scan the area. "Looks like the space station got off a distress call to the Rangers."

At that moment, one of the ships under attack broke from the area and was trying to make a run for it. The ship was obviously crippled, but still had enough power to stay ahead of the Mercenary ships. Unfortunately, they were headed straight for the Acadia.

All three on the bridge realized it at the same moment, with Blackburne hitting the ship-wide alarm so the three Bendanites on board could get to a safe place. Frankie powered up the engines, and Kiara made sure their shielding was at full strength. They could hear the desperate cries for help coming from the approaching ship as it realized that another ship was out there. There was no question on the Acadia—they would help to the best of their ability.

Blackburne ordered Kiara to man the forward weapons. She knew how to fire them, everyone on board had gone through the training from Blackburne, but Kiara knew that their weapons were going to be no match against the Mercenary ships. She looked at Frankie, silently willing him to work with her on his evasive maneuvers. Elvis had gotten up from his position at her feet, and was now clenching her shoulder. Kiara reached up to touch him.

"I'm sorry, little man," she said, hoping that this wasn't going to be the death of all of them. "Hang on; we'll do the best we can."

Blackburne radioed the ship fast approaching them, trying to determine whether they had any weaponry left, or any defenses to help. It appeared to be some sort of passenger ship, and the captain was too panicked to answer Blackburne's questions. They were now within range, and the Mercenary ships had closed the gap enough to start firing. A couple of the shots hit the Acadia, but their shields held. Frankie powered their ship around, and Kiara got off a few shots that connected with a couple of the Mercenary ships, but she could tell it wasn't having any effect. The Acadia wasn't a battleship, so maneuvering was slow and cumbersome at best, but Frankie was performing miracles as most of the shots from the Mercenary ships missed them. The passenger ship had nearly reached them when they heard another voice coming over the coms. He identified himself as one of the Rangers, and told them that several other Ranger ships were coming through the transgate to help.

"Okay, let's try to hang on till they get here," Blackburne yelled as a volley of shots hit them. Kiara glanced at the shielding monitor, and saw that some of their shielding was nearly gone. She concentrated her shots on just one of the Mercenary ships, hoping to get through some of its shielding.

"C'mon!" Kiara muttered, her gaze focused on the ship she was firing on. She could feel Elvis clench his feet and tighten his tail on her arm, and as she watched in amazement, she could actually see part of the shielding on the Mercenary ship peel back. She didn't hesitate; she fired several shots at that area, and watched the ship explode. The explosion was so violent that it sent the ship next to it into an uncontrolled spin. The third ship however, had circled them, and was firing repeatedly. Frankie tried to maneuver the Acadia around, but it was no match for the smaller Mercenary ship. The Acadia was shuddering with every volley that hit them, nearly knocking Kiara from her seat.

The next few seconds seemed to happen in slow motion. Frankie yelled that their shields were gone at the same time that Kiara yelled that their weapons were damaged and they had lost their firepower. Blackburne was yelling at Frankie for evasive maneuvering, but Kiara knew there wasn't anything else he could do with the shields gone. All eyes turned to look at the front monitor as the Mercenary ship turned and headed back toward them, and Kiara knew they were going to die. She saw Frankie and Blackburne in front of her, she felt Elvis on her shoulder, and she pictured the three Bendanites in the cargo bay. The bridge was eerily quiet as they waited for the Mercenary ship to fire on them. No! Kiara silently yelled as she shook her head and stood up, still facing the front monitor. This couldn't be the end! Elvis chirped at her from his perch on her shoulder, as if agreeing with her. Breathing hard, adrenaline pumping, Kiara felt as if a volcano were building inside her.

The Mercenary ship began firing, and Kiara shot out her arms, palms facing outward, as if to ward off the attack.

"No!" Kiara screamed, her eyes squeezed tightly shut, arms still out in front of her. She felt as if the volcano had erupted, or a dam had burst within her. As each shot from the Mercenary ship hit the back of the Acadia near the cargo bay, Kiara felt as if each shot were hitting her in her midsection. She stumbled back a step, hitting the seat of her chair. Her eyes flew open in time to see the Mercenary ship streak past them, a Ranger ship right behind it. The Ranger ship fired on the Mercenary ship until it exploded.

Frankie, Blackburne, and Kiara all stared at the monitor, everyone breathing hard and trying to figure out what had just happened. Kiara held a hand to her stomach, still feeling those painful blows.

Blackburne got on the ship-wide com. "Larry, Curly, Moe—everyone okay?"

Curly's voice came over the com, assuring Blackburne that they were okay and that they had only minor damage to one of the cargo bays. Blackburne looked from Kiara to Frankie, and back to Kiara.

"What the hell happened?" Blackburne looked at the monitor, which now showed a half-dozen Ranger ships patrolling the area. No Mercenary ships were detected. They were either destroyed or had fled the area. A couple of the larger passenger ships that weren't too damaged were beginning rescue operations for the ships and crews that needed help.

"Frankie—status? Did you get the shields back up?" Blackburne asked the pilot.

"No, sir, the shields and weapons are fried," Frankie responded. "There's minor damage to cargo bay three, but the engines are good to go. We can help with the rescue effort as long as the Rangers help with protection."

Blackburne nodded. He looked again at Kiara, then at the front monitor, still trying to figure out how they had survived. Realizing the people out there needed his help; he mentally shook himself and turned to Frankie. "Let's go, it looks like they could use all the help they can get." He turned to Kiara. "Contact the space station and the Rangers—let them know we are ready to help."

The next few hours were spent coordinating rescue efforts to help get the injured transported to the space station, and to help tow in any ships worth salvaging. Through it all, the Rangers patrolled, but there were no more signs of the Mercenary ships.

They were finally able to take a break. More help had arrived through the transgate in the form of medical, transport, and salvage ships. The space station let them know that they were no longer needed, and, grateful for the help from the Acadia, reserved a spot in the space dock for them to land. Blackburne instructed Frankie to take them in so they could start on repairs. They landed with a thump, and Kiara blew out a breath of relief. No one could fault Frankie for the bumpy landing, she was just grateful to be in one piece.

After landing, the crew all gathered outside the ship near cargo bay three. Blackburne wanted to survey the damage to his ship so he could estimate the repair time.

Everyone stood looking at the damage when Larry spoke up. "We should be dead." Curly and Moe were nodding their heads in agreement.

"The shields were gone, we had lost the weapons," Frankie said as he shook his head.

"We saw the shields go down," Larry waved his furry hands at the Acadia. "The ship was coming right here!" He waved his hand in front of his face. Curly covered her face. "Then—." Clearly at a loss for the right words, Larry was gesturing with both furry hands.

"The shots just bounced off?" Frankie said, trying to interpret Larry's hand gestures. At Larry's nod, Frankie turned and looked at Blackburne. "That's what it looked like to me, too. How can that be? The shielding had failed. Those shots should have just ripped through us." Frankie looked back up at the ship. "We should all probably be dead."

Blackburne looked from Frankie to the ship, and then at Kiara. Kiara had been alternating between horror and disbelief while Larry and Frankie had been talking. She saw Blackburne look at her, and shifted her feet uncomfortably. Elvis, still in his position on her shoulder, clenched his feet and huffed at Blackburne. Kiara turned and went to Curly and gave her a big hug, thinking to divert Blackburne's attention from her. Besides, she was so relieved to see everyone, including the three Bendanites alive and well, that she just wanted to hug someone. Kiara laughed a little when her arms barely made it halfway around Curly's bulk, and Elvis was trying to hug Curly's head. Apparently, her laugh broke the somber mood, and the others joined in, laughing at the silliness of the three of them—Kiara, Curly, and Elvis, trying to hug.

"Let's take the night off," Blackburne said when the laughter died down. "And get something to eat—I'm buying." He turned to Kiara, "You okay if we go to the same place as before?"

Kiara nodded, extremely grateful that he had even thought to ask her after the day they'd had. The last time they were here (was it really just a day?) she had run into the creepy guy near the bathrooms. Besides, she didn't want to examine the thought that had implanted itself in her head. Did she have something to do with what happened, or rather, didn't happen to cargo bay three? She pushed the thought away, it was just too overwhelming.

The space station itself had come through the attack relatively unscathed. The shielding on the space station was top of the line, and had held through the attack. The damage they could see was mostly superficial. As the crew of the Acadia made their way through the space station, they noticed an increased security presence, with space station security officers patrolling with weapons clearly visible. Alarm and warning lights were still flashing throughout the station, and Kiara knew that the medical deck was overflowing with wounded.

When they entered the eating establishment, they noticed how packed it was. Kiara supposed they were either in for a long wait, or Blackburne would get impatient about having to wait and head everyone back to the ship. On her shoulder, Elvis seemed to shrink, and Kiara could feel his unease. She reached up to stroke his toes, and sent thoughts of protection to him. She could feel his grip on her shoulder relax slightly, but he was still hunched down, as if trying to hide. Before they could reach the harried-looking hostess, they heard a shout from the right. Kiara and Blackburne turned to look toward the shout, and Kiara noticed out of the corner of her eye that the hostess had stopped in mid-sentence, and was also looking toward the shout. A very tall, very large, mixed race humanoid came out of the crowd of people. His hair and complexion were dark, making the scowl on his face rival that of Blackburne. He was looking at Kiara and the drayek on her shoulder, and Kiara worried that he would kick them out because she had the little drayek with her. He started gesturing at the hostess and Kiara's group, speaking in a language she didn't recognize. Blackburne, also tall, but still a couple of inches shorter than the man approaching them, stood in front of Kiara to intercept him.

"I am Varnov," he announced to Blackburne. With one hand gesturing to the hostess, and the other hand gesturing to Kiara, he moved around Blackburne to Kiara. "Please, please, you must come to eat. "Seeta will take you." The hostess had finally reached them, and Varnov turned to her and spoke rapidly in that language that Kiara didn't recognize. Blackburne caught a couple words here and there and turned to smile at Kiara.

"It appears that they like your drayek," He told her.

"He is good luck!" Varnov exclaimed. "He has helped you, yes? He is yours—he is blue!"

Varnov was babbling at them as the hostess led them through the mass of people to a quiet corner in the back that also had a large window out into space. The area was roped off, and obviously was saved for special groups.

Once they sat down, Kiara could feel Elvis relax. He jumped off her shoulder and curled into her side next to her on the bench seat. She pulled out her com unit, sent a quick message to her dad that she was okay and would call him later. She figured that any minute now, word of the attack would have reached the other planets and transgates, and he would be worried.

Frankie looked at Blackburne. "Aren't you glad she saved him? Look what having the little guy gets us."

The waitress came over and took their drink order, and when she left, the talk at the table turned to the repairs of the ship.

"I think we can get it done in a couple of days if we can get all the parts," Blackburne said. "With all the destruction, parts are going to be hard to come by."

The waitress came back over and set their drinks down, and handed Kiara some special fruit that she told her was for Elvis. Elvis smelled the fruit from his position on the seat, and immediately jumped up on the table to eat.

Frankie turned to the waitress and asked her if she and the others on the space station were okay. Clearly Frankie was fishing for information, but the waitress seemed eager to share what she knew. After detailing the panic aboard the space station, she told them that she overheard one of the Rangers say that the Mercenary ships were piloted by CyRAINs. CyRAIN was the acronym for Cybernetic Artificial Intelligence, and were the latest robotic creations. They were used for everything from domestic duties to piloting spaceships. Unmanned spaceships were nothing new, nearly every species had some sort of drone spaceships, but this was the first time that Kiara knew of that an artificial intelligence had participated in an attack like this. Most CyRAINs were programmed to protect life, so it was a very scary thought that someone had reprogrammed them to kill.

Kiara excused herself from the table and went over by the window. She figured she had better call her dad, by now he would have heard of the attack, and she wanted to make sure he wasn't too worried about her. Elvis chirped at her as she stood up, and she patted him and silently asked him to stay at the table. She made sure she didn't leave his sight, but she wanted some privacy when she talked to her dad.

She made the connection to her dad's com unit, and enabled audio only while she waited for him to pick up.

"Kiara? You okay?" Her dad's worried voice crackled over the com unit.

"Yes, I'm good."

"I heard about the attack—was it near you? Were you involved? Why don't you have video enabled? Are you hurt?" His voice had become increasingly louder as he yelled his questions at her.

"Dad, I'm fine! Really! I'm in a public area, and just wanted a little privacy when I called you." She smiled as she heard his relieved sigh on the other end.

"We did get caught up in the attack, but we only received minor damage to the ship, and no one on the Acadia was hurt." She realized that her words had gotten faster and faster in order to ward off her dad getting panicked again.

"We've heard that CyRAINs were involved in the attack—is that what you are hearing?" Kiara asked him. Her dad may be retired, but Kiara knew he still had his connections. If anyone had heard anything, it would be him.

"That's what we've heard too," her dad replied. "We've also heard that they were piloting Mercenary ships. Is that what you saw?"

"Yeah." Kiara looked back at the table. Elvis was keeping an eye on her while he ate his fruit, and it looked like the waitress had brought him something to drink as well. He was holding the cup like a child, and Kiara thought he was pretty dexterous for something that wasn't humanoid.

She wanted to talk to her dad about what had happened on the ship, but knew this wasn't the place. The events of the day were making everyone more worried about each other, and she knew that those at the table weren't going to let her out of their sight.

Kiara and her dad exchanged a few thoughts on who might be behind the attack, but nothing seemed to fit. Neither could think of a motive for attacking the transgates in the first place. She told him about finding Elvis, and promised to send a picture. Before disconnecting, she told him that she needed to talk to him more when things had settled down and she could call from her room.

"You okay?" Her dad's worry came through the connection.

"Yeah, it's just that something happened on the ship today, during the attack, but I can't talk about it here." She glanced back at the group at the table. Blackburne was looking at her. "I promise I'll call when we get back on the ship. We're going to be here for a few days making repairs, so I'll have time." She spent a few more minutes trying to reassure him that she was okay. In the end, she had to enable video so he could see for himself that she wasn't hurt. She smiled, really smiled, for the first time that day, as his love and concern for her comforted her.

She disconnected and went back to the table. As soon as she sat down, Elvis climbed into her lap, reaching up to smell her hair and one of her ears, and made little huffing sounds at her. She stroked his ears, and told him she was okay.

"How's your dad?" Blackburne asked her. "Worried about you, wasn't he?"

Kiara laughed. "Just a little."

Frankie looked at her. "Did he know any more than we do?"

"No," Kiara muttered back, in between bites of the food left on the table for her. She felt as if she hadn't eaten in days. She'd always had a good appetite, but this was way beyond that. She crammed more food into her mouth, and found herself eyeballing the other's food. Even her hands were a little shaky until the food got into her system. She thought it must be from the adrenaline she experienced during the attack.

She finally paused in her eating, and looked at Frankie and Blackburne. "We keep circling back to the same question—why? Why attack the transgates? Who stands to gain from the transgates being shut down, or commerce and travel being disrupted?"

"That's what we keep coming up with, too," Frankie said. "Somebody hired those Mercenary ships, and stocked them with reprogrammed CyRAINs."

The three of them, Frankie, Blackburne and Kiara, exchanged puzzled looks before they went back to eating. Kiara could feel Blackburne looking at her throughout the meal, and supposed that when they got back to the ship, he would want to talk to her. She was hoping to talk to her dad first. Maybe he could help her make sense out of what happened.

They headed back to the ship, the security in the space station still at a heightened level. Larry, Curly, and Moe headed to the cargo bay to see if they could get started on repairs, so Kiara went to her cabin to call her dad back. Time to face what had happened earlier.

She connected her com unit to the booster and enabled both audio and video. Elvis was curled up on her bed, a soft snoring sound coming from him.

"Dad?"

Her dad's face floated into view in front of her face. His brow was furrowed, and she recognized that look of concern and impatience.

"Kiara! How's my girl?" Kyle McCallister forced his voice to lighten up. He'd been sitting in his house, waiting for her to call back. Knowing she had been in danger, and he couldn't get to her quickly, was nearly killing him. He'd even debated with himself about calling in a favor from one of his buddies to get a personal spacecraft and fly out to be with her. He knew she would be really upset if he showed up like that, so he restrained himself—barely.

"I'm good, Dad." She paused while she studied that worried look on his face. "Soooo, how many times have you talked yourself out of coming to get me?"

They both laughed, and Kiara was relieved to see his face relax a little bit.

"Dad, something happened today during the attack, and I don't know what it was exactly, or what it means. It was a little bit scary, too." Kiara took a deep breath, and tried to organize her thoughts. She didn't want her dad to think she was crazy, or that she had made it up.

"Just spit it out, Kiara. Whatever it is, I'm here for you. From that first minute I saw you, all those years ago, you've been my daughter, and there isn't anything that will change that."

"Okay." Kiara took a deep breath, and just plunged in. "When we approached the transgate, we saw that it was under attack. We weren't going to approach—we're just a cargo vessel, and shields and weapons are minimal as you know." She paused, and saw her dad watching her face, patiently waiting. "One of the passenger ships started heading for us with three of those Mercenaries right on its tail, so we got pulled into it." She paused again, swallowed hard, and just dove into the rest of it. "I was firing our weapons at one of the Mercenary ships—they have really good shielding—and I remember thinking, really hard, that if I could just peel back the shielding, I could hit the ship. Elvis was on my shoulder, and I could feel him tighten his feet on my shoulder. Then, suddenly, I could see the shielding peel back, and I was able to hit it and destroy it." Kiara watched her dad's face for a sign that he had heard her, but he still had that same worried look on his face.

"Well, that's good isn't it? You destroyed one of the enemy ships. It was either them or you." Her dad thought he had it figured out. She was upset that she had destroyed the ship. "It probably had a CyRAIN in it, so you shouldn't be upset about that."

Kiara sighed. He didn't get what she was trying to tell him. "I'm not upset about hitting the ship, Dad. I think I peeled the shielding back on it. I mean, how did I even see the shielding? But I swear I saw it peel back."

"What?" Kiara's dad looked confused.

"Wait—that's not all that happened." Kiara interrupted her dad's next words. He closed his mouth and simply nodded at her to continue.

"When I hit that ship, it took out the one next to it. The third one, though, it circled around us, and Frankie couldn't get the ship around, and we lost the shields." Kiara started breathing faster, the terror she felt hitting her almost as hard now as when it had happened. "The three Bendanites were back in the cargo area, and that ship was coming around and was going to destroy the back part of the ship. Maybe even the whole ship."

Kyle watched her pause again and attempt to regain control of her emotions, and wished for the millionth time that he could be there to comfort her. He watched in amazement as a little drayek suddenly appeared on her shoulder, wrapping his tail around her upper arm, and stroking the side of her head. He figured it was the drayek she had told him she'd found. He watched the terror on her face recede, her breathing start to even out. He wasn't sure how the little guy was bringing on this amazing transformation, but he was extremely grateful that the drayek was helping Kiara.

"Keep going, Kiara," he said gently.

Kiara nodded, and with the Elvis on her shoulder, helping to keep her grounded, she finished the story. "There didn't seem to be anything I could do. The weapons were in the wrong position to defend that part of the ship, and I panicked that we were all going to be killed. I thought, this can't be it, we can't all die today. I felt as though a volcano was building inside of me. When that ship came around, I closed my eyes and screamed. It felt like that volcano erupted." She watched her dad's face, it told her nothing. "When the shots from the Mercenary ship hit our ship, it felt as if they were hitting me." Her dad's eyebrows rose, but he still didn't say anything. "Larry said later that the shots from the Mercenary ship just bounced off the Acadia, and that we should all be dead."

She took a relieved breath, and looked expectantly at her dad. If anyone could figure this out, it would be him. When he didn't answer right away, Kiara looked closer at his face.

"What is that look, Dad? What are you thinking? Is there something wrong with me?" Her voice had risen again, and Elvis was desperately trying to comfort her.

"It's okay, Kiara, there's nothing wrong with you." He paused for a second before continuing. "I was just thinking about when we found you."

"When you found me?" Her brow furrowed. "What does that have to do with this?"

"You should have been dead."

"That's what I said about this attack." Kiara was staring intently at her dad's face, which still showed her nothing. Did all captains go to school to learn how to hide everything from their face?

"I meant when we found you, as well."

Kiara thought back to the stories her dad had told her. Her ship had been nearly destroyed, and they weren't close to any planet. She couldn't remember any of it, she had been too young, and it was probably too traumatic to remember anyway.

"The ship you were on was nearly destroyed. We thought for sure we wouldn't find any survivors." He shook his head. "Even the emergency beacons had been damaged so badly that they weren't working."

"You never told me that part." She sat down on the bed, jarring Elvis who was still on her shoulder. Since she was calm now, he jumped down on the bed and curled into a little ball next to her. She absently patted him, while her mind naturally jumped to what he was thinking. "You think I had something to do with that?"

"Maybe, I'm not sure. When we found you, you didn't have a scratch on you. The other two in the ship had massive traumas to their bodies, they most assuredly died quickly." He paused and looked down; the emotions from that day were still raw. "Then I saw you, still strapped into your seat. At first I thought you were dead, but I could see you breathing. You had your eyes squeezed so tightly shut, that it was making your whole face scrunch up. And I couldn't figure out how you were still breathing, since the hull of the ship was compromised, and I was in a space suit myself. We'd brought a couple of emergency breathers with us, and I went up to you and put it over your head, and you opened your eyes and looked at me." He took a deep breath and continued. "I knew it was a miracle that you had survived whatever had attacked your ship, and I knew in that moment that I had to keep you safe."

"Wait, wait," Kiara interrupted her dad. "You never told me that my ship was attacked. I assumed we got hit by a meteor or something. Why did you think it was an attack?"

"You could see the burn marks from the weapons that had hit your ship. Plus, it was overkill. Whoever had attacked your ship, hit it multiple times, even after the first shot had disabled it." Her dad let out a big sigh. "I didn't think, I just grabbed you and got back to our ship. When you were older and we talked about how I had found you, I just wanted to protect you, and I didn't want to worry you."

Kiara smiled at her dad. "I know."

They smiled at each other, their bond as strong as if they were blood-related.

"So you think I did something similar today, without realizing it?"

"That's where my thoughts are going," he told her. "There's no other way to explain how you weren't hurt. Your seat was even intact." He noticed the look that crossed her face. "What is it?"

"Frankie said something the other day that's got me thinking. He read that some from Trandor had special powers. I laughed it off, but what if he were right?" Her face went from fear to hope, and back to fear. "What if I can't control it? What if it's like a brain tumor or something, and I'm going to die from it?"

"I don't think there's anything wrong with you, but if you're worried about it, get a scan in your med-bay." He looked closely at her, trying to see through the connection, with a dad's eyes, whether or not his little girl was sick. Other than worried, she looked the same to him.

"What about the drayek?" He asked her. "I seem to remember reading something that said drayeks had telekinetic abilities. Have you read that or seen anything like that? Maybe it's all connected?"

"Maybe," Kiara said. She thought back to those incidents, and realized that during both, Elvis had been firmly planted on her shoulder. "Elvis was with me both times, dad, so maybe that's why it happened that way." Kiara suddenly remembered the incident in the kitchen with the snack that had floated above the floor. That had to be part of it, too.

"Maybe. Listen, Kiara, I'll see if I can find more information about Trandor beyond what we've found before. You're going to be there for a couple of days making repairs, right?"

"At least. I don't know whether Blackburne has found all the supplies to repair the ship yet. Why?"

"I'm going to come out there, see for myself that you are all right." He interrupted her, when he saw she was going to say something. "I'm your dad, and I'm coming out to be with you, and that's that!"

Kiara smiled. "I was just going to say that I was happy you were coming out." Her dad looked a little chagrined at his outburst. "I know I'm supposed to be all independent and everything, but I miss you, and with all that's going on, I could really use my dad."

"Okay." He looked down at his com unit as he plugged in some information. "One of my Ranger buddies is heading to that transgate due to the problems there, so I'll catch a ride with him. I'll be there in less than a day."

"That quick?"

"I'm riding with a Ranger—we get special priority."

"That's good," Kiara smiled her relief that her dad would soon be joining her. "Oh, one more thing, Dad. I think the captain suspects that I had something to do with keeping the ship intact." She frowned at her dad, her expression becoming worried again. "I don't know what to tell him."

"Honey, just be honest. You know that's the way to go. He's been a good captain from what you've told me, I think he'll handle this okay." Her dad wiggled his eyebrows at her, "Unless you want me to talk to him for you, but that will surely blow your independent image."

"No!" She giggled, and her dad reveled in the sound. "I'll talk to him. Have a safe trip Dad."

"Love you, Baby."
"Love you too, Dad."

Kiara disconnected her com unit, and looked down at Elvis, snoring quietly beside her. Sleep sounded really good, but she supposed she had better check-in with Blackburne and Frankie. If Blackburne wanted to talk to her about the attack, she might as well get that out of the way. She felt she could handle it now—her dad had allayed her fears, and she was beginning to feel more like herself.

She contacted Blackburne with her com unit, and he immediately asked her to come to the small kitchen area.

When she got there, Frankie and Blackburne were sitting at the small table in the room, drinking what looked like coffee. Kiara was a little apprehensive, but as she entered the room, Frankie smiled at her and asked her if she wanted something to drink, and motioned to some snacks on the counter. Kiara relaxed slightly and realized that she was still hungry, even after eating all that food not that long ago. Elvis was on the floor behind her, he had wanted to walk on his own when they had left her little cabin. Kiara looked down at Elvis and saw that his long snout was high in the air as he sniffed for the food up on the counter. She moved some fruit to the table for him and waited to see what he would do. With a quick flap of his little wings, he jumped to the table to eat the fruit. Kiara grabbed something to drink as she started the conversation.

"Were you able to find supplies to fix the ship?" Kiara asked into the silence.

Blackburne answered her between sips of his coffee. "Most of it, there are still a couple of things we're waiting for a response on." He took another sip and set his coffee down on the table. "Your dad contacted me to let me know he's on his way out here." At Kiara's raised eyebrows, he hastily added, "Professional courtesy, you know—captain to captain." He smiled. "Besides, I'm going to put him to work when he gets here."

Kiara sat at the small table across from Blackburne and next to Frankie. Elvis scooted over on the table to sit closer to her while he ate. The little guy was making little chirping noises between bites, and Kiara, Blackburne and Frankie all smiled.

"My dad will love it if you put him to work, I'm sure. He hates this retirement thing. I can get started on the wiring issues, and any computer problems." Kiara glanced at Elvis again. "I don't remember stocking that kind of fruit." She looked back over at Blackburne and Frankie. "He really seems to like it."

Kiara could have sworn that a look of embarrassment crossed Blackburne's face when he answered her. "Curly said that drayeks really like it, and I ordered some when I was getting the materials for the ship ordered."

"Thanks. You can take it out of my pay." At his questioning look, Kiara told him, "Any of the special food for him. I don't want him to be a nuisance."

"That's okay, Kiara. Apparently, he's good luck, and everybody likes him." He cleared his throat and looked uncomfortable again for a second, before he stuck his chin out in a defensive move. "Even me."

"Okay, thanks." She looked over at Elvis and smiled at him. "I'm getting kinda attached to him myself."

Blackburne cleared his throat again, and tapped a couple of fingers of his right hand on the table. "Kiara, let's talk about what happened on the bridge during the attack."

Kiara nodded. "Sure."

"Are you okay with Frankie being in here?"

71

"Absolutely." Kiara looked at their faces, trying to judge their mood. Blackburne, of course, was impossible to read—that captain thing again. But Frankie looked—Kiara blinked—he looked excited. She wasn't expecting that.

"Frankie thinks that what happened had something to do with that stuff he read about Trandor." Blackburne looked at Frankie. "Curly thinks it has something to do with Elvis." He looked back at Kiara. "Care to tell me your theory?"

Kiara shrugged. "I talked with my dad. We think it has something to do with both of us. I can't explain it yet, I just don't know enough about my race or drayeks to tell you exactly what happened, or what I did or didn't do."

Frankie was nodding enthusiastically. "Can you do something now?"

Kiara looked at him in surprise. "Um, no."

Frankie looked disappointed, Blackburne looked annoyed.

"Frankie, stand-down," Blackburne ordered him. He looked over at Kiara. "We see some strange things in our travels, and telekinetic abilities are pretty rare, but not unheard of. But something of this magnitude is—." Blackburne paused, at a loss for words.

"Exactly!" Kiara exclaimed.

All three exchanged looks and nodded.

"Kiara, get some rest. You look wiped out." Blackburne stood up from the table and headed toward the door. "Let me know if anything else happens. We'll sit down and discuss it more, perhaps after you dad gets here."

Chapter Four

The dream started like any other dream. Kiara found herself walking in what looked like a space station. The ships in the docking bay seemed foreign to her though, and she frowned at them, trying to place them. She thought to stop and take a closer look at one, but her body in this dream wasn't responding to her. She continued her walk through the space dock, and watched as several people approached her. She was surprised and delighted to see that they were also from Trandor, judging by their blue skin. She thought to greet them, but again, her body didn't respond the way she wanted. Instead, she kept walking toward a small group. When she reached them, her right hand reached out to a male in the group, and they grasped forearms together, and slightly bowed forward at the waist. A thought that wasn't hers entered her head.

Watch, do not fight this.

Kiara thought she must be dreaming of her ancestors. Her outstretched arm was decorated with drawn symbols and silver and blue bands. Her ancestor wanted her to watch this dream and not participate, so who was she to argue? She relaxed in her mind, and tried to absorb everything she could. The thought came again—definitely female.

Very good.

Kiara watched as her host exchanged greetings with others in the group, three males and two females. The group was making a diplomatic run to a neighboring planet, and her host was to be their Guardian. Kiara wondered at her host's name, and she was immediately responded to.

I am Mirona.

Mirona escorted the group to a waiting ship, where the ship's pilot greeted them before boarding. As they climbed aboard, Kiara caught a reflection of Mirona in the metal paneling in the hallway of the ship. Light-blue skin, dark-blue almost black hair, she wore a black skinsuit with blue piping along the sleeves. Kiara thought if she had a sister, the sister would look like Mirona.

We are related. You are from me.

Once they were settled, the ship left the space dock, slowly moving away from the planet below. Mirona sat next to the pilot, and as soon as they cleared space dock, she began doing some controlled breathing, her eyes closed, and Kiara could feel her focusing and gathering her power. Kiara recognized the same feeling of power she had felt herself, but in Mirona, it was stronger, sharper. They cleared the planet's detection field and headed to their destination, the pilot reporting that the radar was clear.

The dream seemed to skip ahead, and Kiara was suddenly aware of the pilot yelling a warning, and Mirona releasing some of her harnessed energy as a protection field around the spacecraft. An enemy ship fired on them, but it had no effect on the spacecraft. Mirona's protection field was bouncing everything back at the enemy ship. The enemy circled around, this time coming straight for them. Mirona's pilot had obviously worked with her before; he kept the ship on its course, even when it became evident that the enemy would try to ram them. Mirona gathered a different type of energy within her, and released it toward the enemy ship. Kiara watched in amazement as the enemy ship exploded.

Kiara woke with a start in her own bunk. She stayed there for moment, thinking back on the dream. The force of the explosion must have snapped the connection she had with Mirona. Back in the present, she realized that Elvis

Phoenix Halloway

was draped across the top of her head, his tail under her chin. The end of his tail had a small tuft of hair on it that was tickling her nose. She pushed his tail away and sat up.

"Elvis, you can't sleep on top of my head like a hat," she admonished the quietly snoring drayek. He didn't move or even acknowledge that she had gotten up. Sitting on the edge of her bunk, Kiara thought back on the dream. Had it been a dream, or something else? The dream was so vivid, and even now, she could remember every second of it. She couldn't remember ever having a dream like that before. She scrubbed her hands over her face, trying to wake up and make sense of things. Mirona. They were related, or at least they were in the dream. Maybe she could look for information specific to that name. She knew it was a long shot since records of actual inhabitants of Trandor were very limited. Most documents were about government officials. She made a mental note to bring it up to her dad as well.

She looked over at Elvis as she was braiding her hair, and thoughts of her dad reminded her of the time she had wanted a puppy. She remembered watching an Earth movie about a little girl that wanted a puppy. When the little girl finally got the puppy, the joy that the movie conveyed had stayed with Kiara for a long time. Kiara had pestered her dad, nonstop for about six months, begging for a puppy. It didn't matter that they were living in a spaceship with no room, or no way to take care of a dog, Kiara had emphatically insisted that she needed one. Her dad had tried giving her a virtual pet, but it wasn't the same. He also tried a robotic pet, but Kiara ended up frying the circuit board in it when she tried to reprogram it to be more realistic.

Elvis wasn't really a pet, but more like a cross between a pet and a child. Either way, she was glad to have found him. She definitely wasn't as lonely with the little guy around. She thought back over the last few days, and realized that she was also feeling a connection to her other shipmates that she hadn't had on any of her previous jobs. She hoped it continued because she liked feeling connected.

Dressed now in a black skinsuit and purple tunic, she walked back to the bunk to wake up Elvis. He was probably hungry again, and she needed to make sure he made a trip to the bathroom before heading out. She had some time before her shift working on repairs, so she figured she'd get some food for herself and Elvis, and go for a walk around the space station to pass the time. She knew that she should also take some time to find out if she truly had 'powers' or not, but she didn't think she was up for it yet. The thought of having powers was a little scary at this point. She took a deep breath. If she had powers, shouldn't she feel different? She closed her eyes and tried to see if she felt any different, but, no, she felt exactly the same. With a shrug, she grabbed Elvis and left her cabin.

She didn't see anyone else as she and Elvis left the ship, but she could hear drills and hoverlifts behind the ship and around the space dock. The reassuring sound meant repairs were under way. Blackburne had sent a schedule to all the crew members telling them when they would be needed to work on the ship. She was grateful he scheduled them in shifts—it kept everyone from getting burned out from too much work, or causing irritation if there were too many crew members in the same area.

She didn't need anything from the store, so at first she just wandered through the common areas of the space station. She walked by the restaurant they had all eaten at, and patronage was light at this time of the day. It was still early for anyone looking for dinner, and most of the patrons appeared to be crew members from other ships taking a break from repairs. She thought back on the old movies from Earth that she had watched. They couldn't have known back then what people from other galaxies would look like, but it always amused her to see the guesses. She watched a couple of cephalopods move slowly through the restaurant, their many legs moving them slowly across the room, their grayish skin making them almost blend into the background. On Earth, cephalopods lived exclusively in water, but out here, they had adapted to land. Speaking to one was a challenge, and most didn't travel much. She walked a little further along, and found herself in a section of the space dock that she hadn't been to before.

She could see a few office-looking spaces and a small museum a few doors down from there. The museum boasted that it had pieces on display from planets in this area, so Kiara tentatively opened the door. She wasn't sure if Elvis would be welcome, so she cautiously proceeded into the museum, looking for someone to ask. A small woman with orange frizzy hair was behind the desk as they walked in, and Kiara wasn't sure of the woman's race. The woman smiled at Kiara and Elvis, waving them into the museum. Kiara smiled her thanks and walked into a maze of corridors and small rooms with display pieces of all different sizes. She walked around, noticing that the small woman appeared to be from one of the nearby planets. Kiara smiled when she saw that holographic images of people from that planet showed them all to be short in stature, and frizzy hair was also very prominent.

There hadn't been anyone else in the museum when she entered, but as she walked around, she felt a tingling between her shoulders, as if someone was watching her. She looked around the small room she was in, and even looked out into the corridor, but she still didn't see anyone. Elvis, sensing her unease, tightened his grip on her shoulder, and stuck his nose in the air, as if trying to smell whatever was making Kiara uneasy. She thought she should head to the front of the museum, and as she made her way through the narrow passages, the hair on the back of her neck stood up. She immediately thought of the night when the stranger had talked to her in the hallway by the bathrooms. Just before that stranger had appeared, the hair on the back of her neck had stood up.

Kiara kept going until she reached the lobby area of the museum, and let out a sigh of relief when she saw the receptionist still behind her desk by the front door. Her relief was short-lived, however, when Elvis tightened his grip, and let out a high-pitched whistle. Kiara looked on the opposite side of the room, and immediately recognized the stranger from before. Even though it had been dark that night, she knew who it was. His words confirmed it.

"Please do not be afraid. I am not here to harm you."

Kiara judged her distance to the door, and put her hand on her com unit. Elvis began making hissing sounds at the stranger.

Sensing that the situation was quickly deteriorating, the stranger moved to sit in one of the chairs in the lobby, trying to look as harmless as possible. He was wearing a dark cloak that had a hood covering his head and part of his face. He slid the hood off his head, revealing brown skin, and dark-brown hair. The hair covered his entire head, but was short and fine around his face. His eyes resembled those from Earth, but his forehead, chin and hair on his face told of some ancestry to a Wolf-like race that she had come across a few times. Most races were traced, in some form or another to something on Earth. The Wolf-like race, the name escaped her at the moment, could also be traced to

Earth. And like wolves on Earth, this race was powerful, smart, and cunning. They were often hired to track or hunt people, both legally and illegally.

"What do you want?" Kiara took another step toward the door, wanting to make sure she could get there before the stranger could get to her.

"I have been waiting for you." He purposefully relaxed into the back of the chair, hoping to keep her from bolting out the door. He'd had to be patient, waiting for her to come back to the space station, and he didn't want to lose her again without getting a chance to speak to her. He knew his appearance didn't help, and because he was trying to keep his contact to her a secret, it made the situation that much harder.

"You said that before." Kiara frowned at him. "I don't even know you, why would you be waiting for me? And who are you?"

"My apologies for the way I have been approaching you, I do not want to attract the attention of anyone that would harm you."

"Harm me? Why would anybody want to harm me? I'm just a navigator on a spaceship, I'm a nobody."

"You are from Trandor."

"That makes me protected."

"Not from some."

At that last statement, Kiara's eyebrows rose. "You think someone is trying to harm me?" She glanced at the door again, considered leaving, but thought she had probably better hear the rest of what he had to say.

"My name is Stryker," he told her before she could try to leave again. "I work with others from Trandor to find those who need help, guidance, or protection."

"You're Stryker?" She started to take a step toward him, and Elvis hissed in her ear in reaction. She stopped, but studied his face intently. Yes, there it was, in his eyes, and the shape of his nose and mouth—she had seen him before. She struggled to bring the memory out.

Stryker frowned at her. There could be no way she remembered him, she had been too little. And yet, the way she had reacted to his name, and the way she was studying his face, made him reconsider.

"We met before," Kiara gestured with her left hand, "way before this, right?"

"Yes, I did not think you would remember." He shifted slightly in the chair. "You were very young. I was informed that you had survived the attack on the ship you were in. I tracked you to your adoptive father a few years after he had found you."

Kiara was nodding. "You talked to my dad."

"Yes."

He seemed reluctant to continue.

"So why are you here now? And who wants to harm me? Right now, you appear to be the only threat, except maybe those Mercenary ships."

"We should talk elsewhere," he said as he glanced toward the door. "I have already been in here too long, and I do not want to attract the wrong attention."

"If you think I'm going anywhere with you—."

"No, no. We must set a time and place." He stood and checked his com unit. "I will contact you. Bring your father if you wish." He moved toward the maze of corridors that led deeper into the museum.

"My father? How did you know—?"

He merely smiled at her, pulled his hood up over his face, and disappeared into the museum.

Back on the Acadia, Kiara immediately went to find Blackburne. She supposed that what happened in the museum qualified as 'something else happening', and wanted to let her captain know what was going on in case Stryker wanted to cause any problems. She'd also have to see if she could contact her dad before he arrived at the space dock. Communications through the transgates was impossible, but if she caught him in-between, she might be able to reach him. The conversation with Stryker kept replaying in her head, especially the part about someone wanting to harm her.

She opened the door to the flex-space and found Blackburne and Frankie working through a sparring program. She smiled as she recognized the holographic background as early Earth, with both men dressed in something from that time. She couldn't remember the name of the clothes—blockers or bakers or something like that.

"What are you guys wearing?"

Blackburne took a wide swing at Frankie, his timing off due to Kiara's question.

Frankie, light on his feet, ducked and answered her. "Boxers."

Ah, that's right, Kiara thought, they were boxers. She winced in sympathy as Blackburne finally connected to Frankie's jaw with a well-placed uppercut. She herself preferred to use her feet as well as her hands, her elbows, her knees, and whatever else was handy. She practiced some boxing techniques in her training, but she combined it with other martial arts training. She watched Frankie shake off the hit as Blackburne went to the main console in the room to turn off the program.

"Everything okay?" Frankie was studying her face as he crossed to her. Blackburne turned at Frankie's question, raising one eyebrow as he too, studied her face.

"I thought I was hiding it, but I guess I wasn't," Kiara said, as she sat on the bench near the entrance to the room. "I ran into that guy again—that one from the other night in the bar."

"You okay?"

"What did he want?"

Frankie and Blackburne simultaneously yelled their questions at her.

Kiara smiled, Elvis chirped. Frankie, of course, would be concerned first and question the 'why' later. Blackburne would want to know the 'why' first.

"I'm good," Kiara said and recapped her strange conversation with Stryker.

"He said his name was Stryker?" Blackburne's gaze was practically drilling a hole into her head. Before she could answer, he continued, "I've heard of him. Well, more like the 'legend' of him."

When he didn't continue, Kiara prodded him. "Good or bad?"

Blackburne shrugged. "Depends on which side you were on. If he was hunting you to kill you, it was bad, if he was tracking down someone for you and found them, it was good. He's known to be ruthless, tenacious, and very discreet. Most of everything we know is rumor and conjecture." He paused before continuing. "No pictures, no videos, no surveillance of him, so nobody knows what he looks like for sure."

"I got a good look at him, but then, it seems I had met him before," Kiara said.

"Don't go off by yourself to meet him if he contacts you."

Kiara rolled her eyes at Blackburne's order. "If my dad's not here, I'll bring you and Frankie, okay?"

"He didn't say who he thought would want to harm you?"

"No, he didn't." She sent an apologetic look to Blackburne. "I'm sorry if this is causing you trouble. I was grateful when you took me on, knowing I was from Trandor—most ships steer clear of Protected Races."

"Right now, the way I see it, we owe you. So stop apologizing."

Kiara smiled in relief, until Frankie opened his mouth.

"Have you tried to do anything else, like move objects or read minds?"

Blackburne frowned over at Frankie, while Kiara tried to think of the best way to answer him.

"No, I haven't tried to do anything," she said as she glanced at Blackburne. He was still trying to stare down Frankie. "I really haven't wanted to try. I'm feeling anxious, afraid, and excited, all at the same time. I wanted to wait for my dad to get here."

Blackburne nodded at her. "That's a good idea."

Kiara's com unit signaled that it was time for her shift working on repairs, and Blackburne nodded again at her to let her know she should head out. As she left, Frankie's disappointed look left her grinning.

According to the schedule on her com unit, Blackburne had her working below deck, replacing some damaged wiring, which had her sighing in relief. She had been worried about what to do with Elvis if she had to work on some of the heavier repairs. She'd been worried that Elvis would be in the way or might get hurt. Stopping by the cargo area, she grabbed the supplies needed for her repairs, and with Elvis in tow, headed below deck. Before reaching the first repair area, Kiara tried to reach her dad, but couldn't, so she thought he might be going through one of the transgates. She set her com unit to keep trying to reach him while she started on the first area of repairs.

As she worked, she made an interesting discovery about Elvis. With his connection to her, Elvis was handing her tools and supplies before she had fully formed the thought to grab them herself. She found herself smiling while she worked.

Kiara finished the repairs quickly, and after testing the connections, sent a message to Blackburne that it was complete. Heading back to her room, Kiara checked her com unit to make sure it was still trying to reach her dad, and checked for an update from the space station on repairs and overall security. She saw some updates on the Rangers still patrolling the area, and noticed a bulletin on trouble at other transgates that was affecting the delivery of supplies. She flagged the bulletin for Blackburne, thinking it might help him round up jobs for the Acadia. As she cleaned up from crawling around in the bowels of the ship, she wondered, yet again, where all the dirt came from. It never ceased to amaze her how dirty it got down there. After all, they spent most of their time traveling through space where there wasn't any dirt.

After getting cleaned up and something to eat for her and Elvis, her com unit signaled. Her dad had arrived, and wanted to meet with her and Blackburne in one of the office units of the space station. Kiara frowned. Why didn't he just meet them on the Acadia? She checked the authentication of the message, and found it legitimate. She still thought it was weird, and wondered why her com unit hadn't gotten through to his if he were on the space station. Checking her com unit, she saw that he had acknowledged her signal, but had declined the connection. Now she was getting worried. Her com unit showed Blackburne near the cargo area of the Acadia, so Kiara headed there first.

Blackburne was standing by Larry and Curly, reviewing the latest repairs of the cargo area, and what was left to do. Kiara saw that most of the major repairs were finished; there were just a few cosmetic things left. Blackburne acknowledged her presence with a nod, and finished his conversation with Larry and Curly. Turning to her, he tapped his com unit.

"It appears your dad wants to meet us on the space station," he said as he looked down at his com unit and back up at Kiara, "right about now."

Kiara nodded, "Yeah, I got that message, too. It seemed a little strange."

"I think he's got some people with him, but he wanted to keep things quiet."

"Oh." Kiara glanced down at Elvis sitting by her feet. "Let me see if Elvis will stay with Curly while we meet with my dad and whoever he has with him."

Blackburne nodded at her as she headed over to Curly. Curly was clearly excited to watch Elvis, and Elvis was clearly not excited. It took some convincing, with Elvis hopping from Curly's shoulder back to Kiara's shoulder several times before Kiara could convince him to stay with Curly.

With Elvis finally settled, they headed into the space station to meet with her dad. Following the directions from their com units, they arrived at an innocuous-looking door, which had the number three written on it in several languages. Kiara noted that they were on the same level as other security offices, which made her feel a little better. Since the attacks on the transgate and space station, the extra security and presence of the Rangers helped to reduce the level of anxiety she was feeling.

Blackburne didn't bother knocking; he tapped the door mechanism and entered the room when the door opened. They entered a small waiting room that held an empty receptionist desk, and several uncomfortable-looking chairs. A door on the other side of the room was opened slightly, and Kiara could see what appeared to be a larger room with windows that looked out into space. Kiara saw her dad as soon as she entered the small waiting room. He was standing in the far corner of the room, deep in conversation with two Rangers. The Ranger's distinctive black uniforms were recognizable anywhere.

Kyle McCallister, though he was supposed to be retired, took pride in staying fit and up to date on current events, and was getting an update from a couple of Rangers. He saw his daughter enter the room, and immediately held up a hand to the Ranger that was speaking.

"Hold on a sec, John. My daughter's here."

The Ranger nodded, and Kyle headed over to embrace his daughter. He hugged her tightly and thanked God once again that she was okay. She'd been telling him she was okay, but he didn't realize until this moment, when he could hold her and see for himself, how much worry he'd been carrying around.

"Dad," Kiara whispered, "you can let go now."

He gave her one last squeeze before letting her go. He knew he'd embarrassed her; the color of her face had deepened to a dark blue. He smiled an apology at her, but kept his arm around her shoulders, feeling the need to have her close to him for a while. He extended his right hand to Blackburne for a handshake, and introductions were made. The two Rangers—John and Hannah—were part of the security at the space station brought in since the attack. After the introductions, Kiara turned to her dad.

"Why are we meeting here, Dad?"

"Sorry for the secrecy and ignoring your calls, Kiara." He pulled her off to the side while Blackburne talked with the Rangers. "There's more going on here, and I didn't want to alarm you, or let anyone else know what's going on yet."

"What is going on?" Kiara realized they were both whispering.

"I don't have time to explain everything right now, but I will as soon as I can."

Kiara studied his face. She could see worry there, but something else. He was definitely keeping something from her, but she knew from experience that he wouldn't tell her until he was ready.

"Are we waiting for something?" she whispered.

"We're waiting for the District General Ranger."

Kiara's eyebrows shot up. The District General Ranger was meeting them here? Whatever was going on was big if they were having a meeting with a high-ranking Ranger official.

The door to the hallway slid open, and the District General Ranger entered, along with three other Rangers. The tiny waiting room was starting to get crowded. The two Rangers already in the room came to attention, but a wave from the DG Ranger had them relaxing slightly.

Kiara could feel the suspicious glare from the three new Rangers, but when the DG Ranger saw her dad, he let out a booming laugh.

"Kyle McCallister!" the DG yelled and moved forward to give him a hearty handshake. The DG was the same height as her dad's own 6'4", but was bigger in bulk. Both men had fair hair, but Kiara could see another race mixed in with Earth on the DG's face. Apparently, they knew each other well, and Kiara could see genuine affection on her dad's face. That was good enough for her.

The DG turned to Kiara. "You must be Kiara," he said, and extended his hand to her.

Kiara smiled and shook his hand. "I'm pleased to meet you, Sir."

"Please, call me Daniel. Your father and I are old friends. He's told me quite a bit about you over the years."

The DG turned to Blackburne. "Captain Blackburne?"

"Sir."

The DG waved everyone to proceed into the larger room, and once everyone was settled, he took his time getting started on whatever he wanted to say. Standing at the head of the large table in the room, the DG seemed content to stare out into space through the wide bank of windows in the room.

Finally, the DG turned back to the room, cleared his throat, and began speaking.

"As some of you are aware, we have had several attacks over the last few days on space stations and transgates. We are investigating the attacks, and who is responsible for them, as they were well coordinated and organized. Also, as some of you are aware, the attacks were carried out by Mercenary ships piloted by CyRAINs."

Several in the room nodded.

"I've invited Captain Blackburne to join us for this meeting, but not to talk about the attacks. We need his help to organize supply runs to space stations that are currently cut off and in desperate need of medical and food supplies."

Kiara and Blackburne exchanged a quick look.

"We've inventoried the ships in this sector, and Captain Blackburne's ship is the only one that can be repaired quickly enough to make the runs. Otherwise, this situation goes from desperate to tragic."

"Exactly what is it you need from me and my crew? Even if we get the repairs completed, my ship is no match for those Mercenary ships."

The DG nodded at Blackburne, silently letting him know that he understood those concerns. "Information from the space stations we are most concerned about is sporadic, but what we have gathered shows little or no Mercenary ships in the area. The Rangers are spread thin, and we haven't been able to send a contingency of Rangers to reinforce those areas yet. Our plan is to send you with a squad of Rangers for protection. We'll also upgrade the firepower and shielding on your ship."

Blackburne didn't immediately say anything, and the DG took the opportunity to drive the point home, sensing that Blackburne might be seriously considering the plan.

"You come highly recommended, Captain Blackburne. You and your crew."

Blackburne looked over at Kiara's dad, trying to gauge what he thought of the plan, but Kyle sat with an unreadable look on his face.

"I'll need to talk with my crew, make sure they want to take the risk." Blackburne glanced at Kiara. "When do you need my decision?"

"As soon as possible," the DG said quickly. "We have the upgrades ready for the Acadia, and I think your repairs are almost complete. The supplies will be ready in a few hours."

Blackburne nodded once and stood, as did everyone else in the room.

"For security, please only discuss the plans with your crew, and those in this room."

"Understood."

Back on the Acadia, Blackburne gathered his crew. Elvis flew to Kiara's shoulder as soon as Curly entered the room, his front paws combing Kiara's hair as he made little chirping noises at her. Kiara reached up and stroked his toes, which were now firmly anchored on her shoulder. She glanced over at her dad, who had followed them back to the ship when they left the meeting. Conversation had been sparse—Kiara wanted to get some private time with her dad before she opened up, and she supposed her dad was thinking the same thing.

They were gathered on the bridge of the ship, and once everyone was settled, Blackburne quickly briefed them on the DG's request. He looked at each crew member's face. He had a good crew, one of the best he'd ever worked with. He knew, even before he told them of the possible 'mission', that they would all agree to do it. Every one of them would follow him as the captain, but people needed their help, and that would also drive them to agree.

Frankie, of course, was the first to speak. "Let's get them to upgrade the engines while they're at it. We could use a little more maneuvering capability."

Blackburne took that to mean that Frankie was in. He looked at the three Bendanites. All three nodded their heads. He looked at Kiara last.

"You know we have to help," she said in response to his look.

Blackburne looked at Kiara's dad. He knew if he had children, he would be objecting vehemently right about now. Kyle didn't look happy, but more resigned.

"Do they have a job for you?" Blackburne asked him.

"Yes, they do." He looked from Kiara to Blackburne. "They're deputizing me and letting me pilot one of the Ranger ships that will be escorting you." He smiled fiercely. "I knew you would all agree to help, especially Kiara. This will be my way of helping to keep her safe."

Blackburne let out a bark of laughter that had Elvis flinching on Kiara's shoulder. "Perfect!" He turned to Frankie. "Supervise the weapons and shielding upgrade, and see what they can do with our engines in the small amount of time we have." He turned to the three Bendanites. "Supervise the loading of the supplies. Make sure they don't load anything but medical and food supplies. I don't want this to turn into a weapons run." He saw Kyle frown at that, but he always looked out for his crew. Finally, turning to Kiara, he said, "Get our course and other logistics. And for God's sake, go catch up with your dad. But make it quick!" The last was yelled at their retreating backs, as everyone headed out to get started.

Kiara led her dad to the kitchen, and got him a cup of coffee from the food processor unit before he could even ask. He smiled at her, his gaze going from Elvis to Kiara and back to Elvis.

"Will he let me touch him?" Kyle asked. He'd never seen a drayek in person before, and found the little creature fascinating.

Before Kyle could reach out toward him, Elvis, with a quick flap of his little wings, jumped from Kiara's shoulder to her dad's. He landed softly, and reached out his front paw to touch Kyle's face. He made a couple of chirping noises before looking back at Kiara.

"Do you know what he's saying?" Kyle asked his daughter.

91

"No, it doesn't work that way." She studied Elvis, absorbing the feelings he was pumping out. "I can tell that he likes you, but that's about it."

Kiara looked down at her com unit. "Looks like the Rangers sent the route for our supply run, so I'm going to need to head up to the bridge pretty quick." Elvis hopped back to her shoulder as Kiara studied her dad's face. "Are you okay with this mission?"

"I don't want you in harm's way, that's for sure." Kyle looked toward the door of the kitchen. "We need to do this; those people need our help, and I'll be there to help keep you safe."

"What is it that you aren't telling me?"

"This is bigger than just making a few supply runs. There's more to this, who's behind it, what they want to accomplish."

Kiara nodded, "I figured as much. Do you have any theories? Do the Rangers have any ideas?"

"Somebody wants control of the transgates, and to take all the power from the GTA."

"What?" Kiara shot a glance at the door, then back to her dad's face. Her voice dropped to a whisper. "Do they know who? Who would be crazy enough, or powerful enough to try something like that?"

Kyle slowly shook his head. "The GTA and the Rangers are working on it. Nobody's talking right now."

"Dad, you're supposed to be retired, how did you get pulled into this?"

"I guess I pulled myself into it. I keep in touch with my buddies in the Rangers, so I've been monitoring stuff for a while." He walked over and put his arms around her, thankful again, that she was okay. "When you got pulled into that last attack, I called in some favors so I could be closer to you. Even though I was never a Ranger myself, I completed enough runs for them that they feel like I'm one of them. I didn't think at the time that all of us would get asked to do something like this, I just wanted to be closer to you in case you needed me." He let out a big sigh. "It's hard being a dad, when your daughter is so far away."

Kiara returned his hug, and felt Elvis rumble in her ear. "I'm glad you're here," she whispered to her dad.

She pulled away from her dad and checked her com unit again.

"Things are moving fast, Dad. The shields and engine upgrades are almost complete. The weapons are taking slightly longer." Kiara entered a few commands into her com unit. "There, now you're connected with the Acadia, so you'll know what's going on when I know."

Her dad nodded his thanks, and with one last hug, headed for the door of the kitchen. Kiara suddenly remembered something else she was supposed to be talking with her dad about.

"Dad, wait!" He turned at the urgency in her voice. "With all this other stuff going on, I almost forgot to tell you. I know we don't have time to discuss it right now, but we need to sit down and talk about it as soon as we can."

"Discuss what?"

"That stranger that tried to talk to me outside the bar a few days ago—I ran into him again earlier today."

Her dad immediately came back into the kitchen, concern all over his face. "Did he try to hurt you?"

"No, it was okay, and I think you know him. He said his name was Stryker."

At the mention of the name, Kyle stiffened.

"What is it, Dad?"

"If he tracked you down, it's not good."

"What do you mean, it's not good? I don't think he wanted to hurt me, just the opposite."

"No, he wouldn't hurt you." Her dad checked his com unit. He looked back up at her as he came to a decision. "We can't do anything about it now, but when we get back to the space station, we'll try to meet with him. I assume he knows I was coming here?"

"Uh, yes?" Kiara felt as if she was coming into the middle of the story without reading the beginning.

"Okay, don't worry; we'll have more time to discuss it later. Let's keep our focus on one problem at a time, okay?"

Kiara opened her mouth to protest, to ask for more information, something, but the look on her dad's face had her nodding in acceptance instead. He had that look she'd seen a hundred times before. He wasn't going to say anything until he was ready.

Chapter Five

Back on the bridge, Kiara finished her preflight programming with the information she had received from the Rangers. She also opened a direct link on her com unit to her dad so they could keep in contact during the mission. Frankie soon joined her, wiping grease and grime off his arms and face, but he was grinning from ear to ear.

Kiara took that to mean that the engine upgrades were successful. Her com unit signaled, and she glanced down to see that Blackburne had sent out information on the weapons upgrade. She studied the information, and hoped she didn't have to use it. Elvis, firmly planted at her feet, pushed his nose into her calf muscle, and looked up at her. Kiara reached down and stroked the tufts of hair on his head.

"We'll be okay," she told him. "We've got my dad and the Rangers looking out for us."

Kiara wished she had more time to be with her dad before heading out. She wanted him around while she explored her possible 'powers', but with the aggressive timeline they had for this mission, it just wouldn't be possible. She hoped, if she did have 'powers', and needed to use them again to protect her shipmates, that she would be able to do it.

Blackburne joined them on the bridge and immediately opened the com links to the other ships. Introductions were made—Kiara recognized John and Hannah from the earlier meeting, and the fourth Ranger joining them was Torin, a thin, wiry, mixed-race man. All the Rangers, except her dad, had that same unsmiling look on their face. Kiara figured that mastering that look was part of the Ranger training.

Blackburne let the group know that they would be taking the ship on a couple of practice runs around the space station to get a feel for the engines and the ship's maneuvering abilities. He sent questioning looks at Kiara and Frankie, and received ready nods from each of them. Blackburne noticed that Kiara's color was a little darker blue, and hoped it was because she was nervous or anxious about the mission. He verified with Curly that their cargo was aboard, and gave the order to take off. Kiara coordinated their movements with the other Ranger ships as they headed out of the space dock.

Frankie, all business now, piloted the ship around the space station, simulating battle maneuvers as he tested out the engines. The ship made a few groaning noises as the stresses on the hull increased, and Kiara kept a good eye on the sensors to make sure they weren't exceeding the limits of the ship. An unexpected high-pitched whine came from the engines, and Frankie shut them down before any damage was done.

"Damn!" Frankie exclaimed.

"What happened?" Blackburne wanted to know.

Frankie didn't answer right away as he waited for the computer to spit out the diagnosis. He finally let out a sigh of relief. "Looks as if we have a phase mismatch between a couple of the new components, should have it righted shortly." His fingers flew over the console, as he worked to correct the problem. "Kiara, I could use your help correcting some of this programming." He never even looked up at Blackburne or Kiara as he spoke.

Kiara relayed their status to her dad and the other Ranger ships and connected her console to Frankie's to help. It didn't take her long to find the issue and once she corrected it, she turned and nodded at Frankie.

Everyone breathed a sigh of relief when the engines rumbled back to life. Frankie looked up at Blackburne, gave him a nod, and took the ship through a few more maneuvers. This time, the engines stayed a constant rumble, and Blackburne told Kiara to relay to the team that they were ready.

They headed for the transgate, their contingent of Rangers flanking them. They knew that going through the transgate and emerging out on the other side was going to be the most dangerous part of this mission. An ambush as they emerged from the transgate would be the most likely scenario if someone wanted to stop them. Kiara checked with both ends of the transgate one last time, and received an all-clear. Her dad and John headed into the transgate, separating their ships by a minute for safety. Then it was the Acadia's turn, and Frankie piloted them into the transgate, following Kiara's navigation. This trip would be a short one, just over an hour, but they had three other transgates to go through before they reached the first space station to drop off supplies.

They emerged through the transgate without incident, and Kiara could see her dad and John's ships patrolling the area. Frankie had the Acadia in an evasive pattern as a precaution while they waited for Hannah and Torin to come through the transgate. Kiara took the time to scan the area, her feeling of unease starting to increase. No other ships showed up on the scans. The space station in this sector was small, staffed by only a few people for the transgate. Several inhabited planets were close by, but Kiara thought it strange that she couldn't detect any ship traffic. She relayed her unease to Blackburne and her dad, and found that they, too, thought it strange. Her dad communicated with the other Rangers to be on high alert as they waited for the other two ships to join them. Still scanning, Kiara sent the route to the next transgate to Frankie, and tried not to hold her breath while they waited for the last Ranger ship to come through.

Finally, the group was together, and they set off for the second transgate that was still a few hours away. Communications with the transgates was still normal, but Kiara couldn't seem to get rid of her unease. They reached the next transgate with no mishaps, but Kiara felt like screaming. Her tension was flowing into Elvis, who had a death grip on her shoulder. She briefly acknowledged the mark it would leave, and turned her attention back to the mission. Conversation was nonexistent, which just seemed to heighten the tension. An alarm on Kiara's navunit suddenly went off, and everyone on the bridge jumped. Kiara looked down at the alarm message, and immediately yelled a warning.

"Hold!" She communicated her hold message to the Ranger ships as well. Her dad's ship was almost into the transgate when he got the message. He immediately backed his ship off.

"What is it?" Blackburne asked.

"There's an unknown object in the transgate," Kiara told him.

"I'm not picking up anything, and Transgate Control isn't picking up anything." John's voice came over the com.

Kiara muted communications with the other ships, except her dad, and turned to Blackburne. "A few months ago, we had some downtime between jobs. I made some modifications to my navunit and the sensors." She shrugged at the intense look that Blackburne was giving her. "I looked at the sensitivity settings that the transgates were using, and modified my navunit. I didn't think the settings they had were good enough, or were keeping us safe enough."

"That's my girl," Kyle's voice came over the com.

"Is it just space junk that our shields can deflect?" Blackburne questioned.

"No sir," Kiara quickly responded. "Part of the adjustments I made was to distinguish between harmless items and something that could cause serious damage. The alarm went off because it was detecting explosive residue." She looked back down at the screen. "If we hit whatever is in there and it caused an explosion, we'd destroy this end of the transgate, even if we didn't sustain serious damage."

Blackburne nodded. "Let's loop the others in and figure out a plan to get whatever that is out of the transgate safely."

In the end, they had to bring in a ship from the Transgate Controllers that was used for this type of situation. They went in with the special ship, encompassed the object, and brought it out. It took hours to accomplish. Once they had it out, they were able to use more sophisticated sensors to examine it. They found an impact-sensitive bomb, encased in material made to look like space junk. Someone had planted it along the most traveled path through the transgate, and its position near the entrance would have ensured the destruction of the transgate.

The space station in this sector was small, so the Acadia and two of the other Ranger ships couldn't dock with it. They had to orbit the station while they waited for the all-clear. The crew of the Acadia was in the kitchen getting something to eat and waiting for an update from Blackburne. The kitchen was small, and with three Bendanites, Frankie and Kiara, it was almost claustrophobic. Elvis, however, was in heaven. He jumped from Bendanite to Bendanite, grabbing treats from each, and making happy chattering sounds. Kiara smiled while she watched him, and was glad he was here to help lighten the mood. Even Frankie was smiling at him.

Blackburne finally joined them, but stood in the doorway instead of trying to squeeze into the already overcrowded room. He relayed the thanks from Transgate Control for catching the bomb. Frankie reached over and grabbed Kiara's hand and gave it a squeeze.

"Good job," he whispered.

"Yes, good job," Blackburne told her, but he was also frowning at her. "Next time, tell me when you get bored and make unauthorized modifications to my ship."

"Yes, sir." She couldn't tell if he was mad at her or not. Back on her shoulder, Elvis made a low huffing sound at Blackburne.

"Whoever planted it knew that it would pass the standard sensors of the transgate and most ships," Blackburne told them. "And now, thanks to you," he nodded at Kiara, "the Transgate Controllers are recalibrating their sensors to detect these types of objects."

Kyle's voice broke in on Kiara's com unit. "We're ready to proceed through the transgate when you are."

Blackburne looked at Kiara. "Are we good to go?"

"I'll run another sweep before we head through," Kiara said as she stood up to head back to the bridge. She let her dad know the plan, and heard him relay it to the others.

"Kiara?"

"Yeah, Dad?"

"I'm proud of you."

Kiara flushed a deep blue at the words from her dad, a smile of pure love on her face. "Thanks, Dad."

Kiara reached the bridge, and set her navunit to scan. While it did, she turned back to Blackburne and Frankie, and knowing that her dad could still hear her, she posed the thought that had bothered her since they had arrived in this sector.

"Where are all the ships? It's as if someone cleared out this sector so they could plant that bomb in the transgate."

Blackburne nodded. "My thoughts as well."

Kyle and Frankie echoed those words.

For a moment, no one spoke until Kiara's dad voiced what they were all probably thinking.

"Let's keep this between us. It doesn't look good for the Transgate Controllers and the GTA if they are somehow involved in this." Everyone murmured their agreement. "This situation throws suspicion everywhere, and until we know who we can trust, let's keep our eyes and ears open, and keep the information to this small group."

Kiara's navunit signaled that it had finished scanning with no objects found, so Kiara gave the all clear. Due to the elevated threat level, it was decided that the ships would enter the transgate spaced farther apart. Since communications through the transgates was impossible, this would be the best way to ensure safety.

Kiara watched John enter the transgate, followed by her dad a few minutes later. The Acadia entered the transgate, and Kiara relaxed slightly. This wormhole was the shortest on their route, and the most isolated, but also had some of the best color displays in it. She had purposely left the large front display screen on so the blues, yellows and greens currently splashed across the screen could be enjoyed. For Kiara, it was like visiting the most exclusive art gallery, but with ever-changing paintings.

As they neared the exit, the Acadia began to experience turbulence, so Kiara checked her scans and frowned. The turbulence was unexpected, and she couldn't immediately identify the source. Blackburne was studying the front view screen, when his eyebrows shot up.

"That looks like weapons fire!" Blackburne shouted. "Brace for impact, and be ready to return fire!" Their shields were already at maximum to go through the transgates, which was fortunate, as some of the weapons fire was already hitting them.

Frankie shifted up in his seat, ready for evasive maneuvers when they exited, and Kiara made sure the weapons were ready to fire. As they exited the transgate, Frankie immediately shot them up and to the right. A piece of ship debris was heading right for them, but Frankie's maneuver kept them from getting hit. In one corner of her brain, Kiara realized the ship debris was not her dad's or John's, even as she scanned for where the threat was coming from. Her scan showed four ships in the area, all of them engaged in combat. Her dad was holding his own, but John's ship had taken some serious hits, and looked to be losing some engine power. Kiara immediately trained the Acadia's weapons on the enemy ships, while Frankie maneuvered them closer to help protect John. Blackburne was calmly talking with both ships while giving Frankie directions on maneuvering.

Kiara got off a few shots at the enemy, and the Acadia took a couple of hits, but everyone involved sensed the swing of momentum since the Acadia had joined the battle. The two enemy ships suddenly broke off the attack, heading toward some far-off planets. Kyle gave chase for a few seconds to make sure they were leaving before heading back to join the others. Hannah and Torin's ships exited the transgate, and together the group moved a safe distance away.

After confirming that everyone was okay, Kyle told them that there were three ships waiting outside the transgate. They had immediately engaged John when he exited the transgate, so his ship had taken the majority of the hits. When Kyle had come through, he was able to help, and they managed to destroy one of the enemy ships. They also tried to lead the battle away from the transgate, knowing that the Acadia was going to be exiting the transgate at any moment.

"Knowing that the bomb was in the other end of the transgate, these ships were probably here to intercept whoever made it past the bomb," Kyle told the group.

Kiara contacted Transgate Control, and frowned at the response she received. She turned to Blackburne.

"They aren't even acknowledging that we were attacked."

"We need to keep moving," Blackburne told the team. "John, status on your ship."

"Badly damaged, leaking fluids." John's voice crackled over the connection. "I'm sure it can be repaired, but it will take more time than we have. I suggest we destroy it, and I ride on the Acadia."

"Agreed."

"Anybody catch the markings of those ships that attacked us?" Kyle asked.

"Markings were not visible, and they appeared to be single occupant fighters. Perhaps they are refurbished ones from this sector." Hannah's voice came over the com.

"I'll alert Ranger Command to investigate when they can spare the men," John responded. "Prepare for docking."

John docked his ship with the Acadia, and they transferred all the supplies they could. With one last look at his ship, he manually undocked it from inside the Acadia. Once they were a safe distance away, John detonated the self-destruct. Everyone was on high alert, but no other ships were detected in the area. Kiara supposed that Transgate Control was either threatened or bribed, and neither was good for their safety. She nodded at John as he joined them on the bridge, and watched him stare at Elvis on her shoulder with his eyebrows raised. Kiara just smiled and Elvis huffed at him.

Blackburne checked with the other ships to ensure their status was good, and once he received confirmation, checked with Curly to make sure the cargo was still in good shape. Receiving a positive reply from Curly, he nodded to Frankie to head for the third transgate. After they passed the planets clustered near the transgate, they had hours of travel time through nothing but space and a few meteor belts, so an attack would not be likely. Kiara sent the navigation information to Frankie, and as soon as they cleared the last planet, she excused herself from the bridge to try to relax a little bit. As she walked by John, she could hear him on his com unit talking with someone else in the Rangers, trying to get extra support for them. From the side of the conversation she could hear, it didn't sound promising.

Kiara decided to head for the flex-space, perhaps a good workout would help get rid of the tension from the mission. She shook her head as she walked down the narrow hallway of the ship. She was usually calm under pressure, and knew that when she agreed to this mission, there would be danger. Nothing she had imagined, or stories from her dad had prepared her for the reality of it. She knew that being a Ranger required a special type of person, and right now, she was sure she wasn't that type of person.

Kiara reached the flex-space, and was relieved to find that it was empty. Because the Bendanites on board weren't needed for this part of the mission, she thought they might be passing the time in here. She entered the room and considered what program to run. She decided to run one of her favorites, hoping it would help center her. The program was a run through an obstacle course, with jumps, climbs, and a lot of running. She slid a small bench out of the wall near the door and set Elvis there so she could work out without trying to hold him or worry about where he was. She was nearly finished with the program, cooling down with a slow jog when she sensed that Elvis had jumped off the bench. She closed her eyes and pictured him hopping into her arms, and with her eyes still closed, felt his weight settle on her. Still jogging with her eyes closed, she silently asked him to shift around to her back, and leaned forward to make it easier to balance him. He held her braid in his front paws, using his back legs and tail to keep his balance.

Completely focused on the holographic exercise program and Elvis, Kiara didn't hear the door open as John walked into the room. He stood watching her, enjoying the way her body moved, appreciating the athleticism it took to do what she was doing. Realizing that it might look like he was stalking her, John noisily cleared his throat as he walked toward her. Elvis let out an ear-piercing screech, just as Kiara turned to see who had entered the room. Elvis' screech sent her into overdrive, and without thinking, she threw out her arms to protect them, and John walked straight into the invisible force field she had thrown up.

Just as she recognized that it was John in the room, the solid 'thunk' of John's forehead hitting the force field reached her. Kiara dropped her arms and tried to regain her composure, while John stumbled back a few feet.

"I'm so sorry," Kiara said as she rushed forward to make sure he wasn't hurt. "Are you okay?"

John put his hands up to ward her off, not quite sure what had happened. "What the hell was that?"

Kiara stopped short, not sure what to say, a feeling of dread coming over her. She didn't want people to fear her.

"You startled me," she finally said. Elvis was huffing at him, feeling Kiara's unease about the situation.

"You did that?" John had regained his balance and some of his equilibrium. "Was that some sort of force field?" Before Kiara could answer, he answered his own question. "No, that would be ridiculous. Was it part of the holographic program?"

"Um, yes." Kiara smiled in relief. "I programmed it to do that when someone approaches me from behind." She fought to even out her breathing from the exertion in the program and the sudden adrenaline rush of John startling her. "Are you okay?"

"Sure, no problem." John smiled his best 'win-her-over' smile. "You were doing pretty well there."

"Oh, thanks." Kiara realized he was trying to flirt with her, and suddenly feeling self-conscious about how she looked, she reached up to smooth back the hair that had escaped the long braid down her back. She was feeling out of breath again and completely at a loss for words. It wasn't often that someone flirted with her. She looked down and realized that not only was her hair a mess, but she was also sweaty. Why would anyone find this attractive? Feeling the need to escape, she shuffled her feet toward the door at the same time that she gave the command to terminate the exercise program. John was still smiling at her, so she smiled back as she maneuvered around him and headed for the exit.

"I should go get cleaned up." Kiara pointed awkwardly at the doorway.

"Sure, no problem." John still had his best smile on his face, but he was beginning to wonder whether it was working. Usually by now, he had the female he was smiling at nearly swooning at his feet.

Kiara turned and fled the room, feeling like an idiot. She was sure her face was nearly purple from the exertion and the embarrassment. Men didn't usually flirt with her, due to her protected race, so she was definitely out of practice recognizing and responding to it. She realized she was nearly running again, so she slowed down to a walk and tried some slow deep breaths. Sheesh! You'd think the guy had tried to attack her or something the way she was acting. She gave herself a stern lecture on not overreacting, and promised herself that she would try to smile back at the guy and be friendly, but not too friendly. After all, they were on a mission.

She saw Curly coming down the hallway toward her, and Elvis immediately started to chirp on her shoulder. The closer they got, the more excited he got, until he was nearly vibrating with excitement. Curly murmured to him in her native language and held out her arm. Elvis didn't hesitate, and immediately jumped from Kiara to Curly. His little front paws were busy petting Curly's fury face, and Kiara smiled over the picture they presented. Kiara was amazed that Elvis had bonded with her the way he had, and hadn't tried to bond with Curly. After all, Bendanites understood drayeks a lot more than she did.

Kiara reached out and touched Curly's arm to get her attention.

"Are you guys doing okay?" Kiara asked her, referring to Curly and the other two Bendanites in the cargo area.

"Yes, we are good." Curly grasped Kiara's hand, her large, furry paw-like hand swallowing up Kiara's hand. "I know you will keep us safe."

At first, Kiara felt the weight of that statement bear down on her. What if she couldn't keep them safe? What if she failed? She looked into the kind eyes of Curly, and knew that she would do everything in her power, and her new power, to keep them safe. They had become her family, and the current mission they were on only served to emphasize that fact.

"I will do my best to keep you safe," Kiara finally replied.

Curly smiled, and Kiara smiled back. She loved to see a Bendanite smile, as they didn't do it often. Their smile was very toothy and wide, with large scary teeth showing. The first time a Bendanite smiled at her, she had nearly run off screaming.

Curly continued on to the cargo area, and Kiara, after coaxing Elvis back to her shoulder, headed to her room to clean up. After cleaning up and getting food for her and Elvis, she check the ship's position, and knew she still had a little extra time. Back in her room, she used her com unit to contact her dad.

"Hey, Dad."

"Hey Kiara, you doin' okay?" Kyle studied his daughter's face. Something was definitely wrong.

"I'm okay." She took a deep breath, wishing he was on the ship with her instead of trying to explain all of this over the com unit.

"Just spit it out, Kiara. You'll feel better, you know."

"I know." She took another deep breath. "I was in the flex-space with Elvis, working out, when John came in. I didn't hear him come in, and he startled us." She saw her dad frown. "He just came in to say hello, but he startled us." Kiara smiled embarrassingly. "I reacted without thinking, and threw up some sort of force field."

"You did what?"

"I threw up a force field, and John walked right into it!" Kiara realized she was whisper-shouting, and immediately cleared her throat, and attempted to speak normally. "He didn't see it, and at first, I think he was afraid of me, before he concluded that it was the holographic program that had put up the field."

"Why did you think he was afraid of you?"

"When I walked toward him, he threw up his hands to keep me from touching him." She blinked back tears, only now just realizing how much she didn't want people to fear being touched by her. Elvis tried his best to comfort her when he sensed her distress. He was in her lap, and tried to burrow his head into her stomach to be closer to her.

"I'm sure that wasn't it, Kiara," her dad responded to her distress as well. "I'll bet he was just reacting like most people, and didn't want to get clocked again." Her dad suddenly started chuckling. "Did you knock him down?"

"Noooo," Kiara drew the word out as she frowned at her dad. "Why are you laughing? This is serious!"

"Oh, honey, I know it's serious. It's just that I would love to see what you are describing. I've known John for a lot of years, and he thinks of himself as quite the ladies' man. To see him brought down a few pegs would have been great!" Her dad was now into a full belly laugh.

His laughter had the desired effect on Kiara; first she smiled, and then, she too, was full out laughing.

"Okay, it was kinda funny." Kiara's laughter died down as she had a sudden thought. "Hey Dad, we still have time before we get to the transgate and the planets around it, do you think you can stay on the com unit with me while I go back to the flex-space? I want to see if I can create a force field or do something without it being an emergency."

Her dad checked his com unit and their position, and agreed that they had time. "I wish I was on board with you, but let's try it this way for now. Just keep it simple for this first time."

"Okay." Kiara was already hustling down the hallway of the ship. She reached the flex-space and found it still empty. She sent a quick message to Blackburne and Frankie to let them know where she was, and this time, put the privacy lock on the door so no one could enter without her knowing.

"I brought some stuff from my cabin to throw at it, since; conceivably, anything from the holographic program would pass right through it."

"Good idea."

Kiara took a couple of deep breaths, planted her feet about shoulder-width apart, and threw out her hand in front of her, thinking of a force field. She didn't feel as if anything happened, but just to be sure, threw a small hair clip at it. It fell harmlessly to the floor.

"Blast it!"

"Hey, take it easy, little one." Her dad's calm voice came over the com unit. "Surely you didn't expect it to be that easy, did you?"

They both chuckled and Kiara relaxed a little bit. "You're right."

"That's why I'm the dad."

Kiara smiled. He'd always said that when she was little, and it was helping her frustration now.

"Okay, we know the other times that it happened, you had a major surge of adrenaline going. I think, until you discover how to tap into it, you're going to have to imagine something to get your adrenaline or emotions going."

They both thought about it for a moment, and anyone watching would have assumed they were related, if their skin had been the same color. They had the same look in their eyes, the same furrowed brow.

"I guess I can try thinking back on the first attack when the shields went down, see if I can get enough emotion going with that."

Kiara braced her feet, and took a quick look up at Elvis. "Ready, little man?"

At his answering chirp, she closed her eyes, took a deep breath, and thought back to that day when they had been attacked by the CyRAINs. Her breathing quickened as the thoughts of that day flooded in. With her heart hammering, Elvis tightened his grip on her shoulder, and Kiara flung her arms out, thinking of putting a force field around her and Elvis. This time, she felt the pull of something leaving her body, and in the silence of the room, heard a slight hum. She opened her eyes, but couldn't see anything. She dropped her arm to reach for something to throw, and felt the energy in the room plummet to zero, the humming disappear. Kiara threw the hair clip anyway, but it hit the floor just like the other one.

"Well?"

"I, uh, I think I did it." Kiara looked down into her com unit at her dad's questioning face.

"What happened?"

"I could feel the energy leave me, but when I dropped my arms to pick up my hair clip, it stopped. I wasn't able to hold it."

"Okay, but you did have something happen this time, right?" At her answering nod, he continued. "You can build on that. Why don't you try again, but this time without Elvis?"

Kiara nodded, and silently asked Elvis to move off her shoulder and go sit by the door. She could sense his reluctance, but he finally went. The little drayek planted himself by the door, his ears up and alert, his eyes following Kiara's every move. Kiara braced her feet, closed her eyes, and tried to bring up the emotion from the attack as she had before. She threw out her arms, but this time, nothing happened. She let out her breath in a loud sigh.

"Does that mean nothing happened?" Kyle's voice came over her com unit.

"Nothing happened. But I'm not sure if it's because I couldn't do it, or I couldn't do it without Elvis." She coaxed Elvis back up to her shoulder so she could try again.

This time, there was a definite hum in her body, and Kiara, keeping her arms up, slowly opened one eye to see if she could see anything. There didn't appear to be anything visible, and when she realized she was holding her breath, she opened both eyes as she let her breath out. The humming immediately stopped.

Kiara smiled down into her com unit. "I was able to do it again, but holding it takes quite a bit of concentration, I think. Any little thing breaks it immediately."

She could see her dad nodding, but he was also looking at one of the monitors on his ship.

"Time to go?" Kiara asked.

"Yeah, we're getting close."

"Okay, do you see anything?"

"Not yet."

They said their good-byes and Kiara headed out of the flex-space and arrived to a quiet bridge. Blackburne was studying his computer screen, and Frankie looked like he was napping in his pilot's seat. Kiara knew he wasn't napping; he was deep in a kind of meditation. He said it helped to keep him calm and focused when he was piloting. To Kiara, it was a contradiction; Frankie was high-energy, outspoken, and one of the best pilots she'd ever worked with. Yet, he meditated. Maybe she should try it sometime, but it seemed to her to be a waste of time. She shrugged slightly and walked toward her navunit, and noticed John sitting in her seat. Kiara frowned, feeling territorial. She was glad she had added a program to her navunit that kept track of changes. She would easily tell if he tampered with anything. She didn't question her suspicion of him, in her experience, you had to earn trust, and he hadn't earned hers yet. Elvis huffed at him, and John looked up as Kiara approached.

He tried out his winning smile on her again, but it only earned him a frown. It suddenly dawned on him that she was probably frowning at him because he was in her seat, and he quickly jumped up and gestured for her to sit.

"Seating is limited in here, so I borrowed your seat for a while." When her frown stayed firmly in place, he added, "I didn't touch anything, I swear." He placed his hand over his heart and smiled his most charming smile.

Kiara made an effort to relax her frown. "No problem, John." She pointed to a panel behind Frankie's seat. "There's a seat over there in that panel, you can use that one when we go through the transgate to make sure you're strapped in."

"Thanks." John headed to the panel, and thought he might be making progress with Kiara since she didn't kick him off the bridge. Out of the corner of his eye, he could see Frankie smirking, even though his eyes were still closed. John let out a sigh. Nothing like striking out in front of her shipmates.

Kiara logged in to her navunit, checked that nothing had been tampered with, and began her check of the transgate. They were still a good distance out, and the ship's sensors wouldn't reach all the way through the transgate at this distance, but it would give her a baseline to work from. She contacted Transgate Control, and received a normal response this time. She relayed that to Blackburne, who nodded his acknowledgment. As they approached the transgate, Kiara received a message from Transgate Control that they would be delayed going through the transgate. Apparently, since the attack at the other transgate with the Acadia, extra precautions were being taken, slowing down the whole process. Several ships were already in the queue ahead of them, and it appeared that Transgate Control would only let the next ship go through the transgate when the previous ship had cleared the other side. This was one of the longer transgate trips in this sector, and Kiara did a quick calculation that they would be waiting for about ten hours before they were up.

"Blackburne, it looks like it's going to be about ten hours before we can go through the transgate. Do you want to use a Ranger priority override to move us up in the queue?"

Blackburne turned to John, "What do you think? We don't come through this sector that much, so I'm not familiar enough to know whether we want to announce ourselves or keep it quiet."

John contacted the other Rangers, and after a brief discussion, it was decided to keep their mission and affiliation quiet for now. The Ranger ships were easily identifiable, but the consensus was that they shouldn't try to draw extra attention.

Frankie backed them off the transgate and the space station into the nearby holding area. He set the main engines to idle to conserve power.

Kiara checked the scans and didn't see anything unusual, but she still felt as if they were exposed. What was that phrase her dad always said? Oh yeah, like sitting ducks.

"We got a ship fast approaching from the starboard side," Frankie called out.

"Affiliation?" Blackburne questioned.

"Unknown," Frankie said, as he studied his screen and waited for the computer to spit out the ship type and planet it was from.

Kiara suddenly felt uneasy, and it wasn't because the computer hadn't found the ship type yet. She looked down to see Elvis staring intently at her, and with one thought had him jumping up to her shoulder.

"Something's not right, Blackburne." Kiara stood up from her seat, her gaze focused on the large view screen at the front of the bridge.

"I agree," Blackburne opened communication with the other ships. "I need everyone on high alert with the ship approaching from our starboard side!" Blackburne turned to look at Frankie, who shook his head to indicate he still didn't know the ship type.

"What's the deal?" Torin's voice came over the com units. "I'm not scanning any weapons trained on us."

Blackburne turned to look at Kiara. She stood perfectly still, her skin color deepening to a dark blue, her eyes slightly glazed over. Blackburne immediately took a step toward her, but Kiara put her hand up to stop him.

"I'm okay," she said, and was grateful that she didn't hit him with a force field. "It's an old Galdorian ship."

Frankie immediately tapped some instructions into the computer, and received an instant confirmation. "It's a small two-person fighter craft—it doesn't have the range to be all the way out here."

Two of the ranger ships, one of them Kiara's dad, moved into position to intercept the ship before it could reach the Acadia.

"Weapons capability?" Kyle's voice came over the com unit. "That ship isn't in my ship's database."

"Assuming it hasn't been modified, it shouldn't have the firepower to penetrate any of our shields," Frankie responded.

"Let's assume it's been modified," Kyle said, and Blackburne voiced his agreement.

Kyle switched his com unit and attempted to hail the approaching ship. The ship didn't respond or slow its approach. Frankie powered up the main engines in case they needed to maneuver, and let Blackburne know that the scanners still didn't show any weapons trained on them.

"He's somehow cloaking his weapons," Kiara said into the quiet.

"How do you know that?" Torin asked.

"Don't ask," Blackburne said, "just assume she's correct."

"He's here for me." Kiara's voice was almost a whisper. "I can feel such hate coming from him, it's almost overpowering in its intensity."

Blackburne looked over at Kiara, and observed that she was now a pale blue, and starting to shake.

"Identify yourself or you will be fired upon!" Kyle's authoritative voice came over the com.

Finally, the ship slowed and came to a halt. It appeared that the occupant finally realized that he was outnumbered and outgunned.

"Another time." The eerily quiet voice came over the com, sending shivers up Kiara's back. The ship turned around and headed back the way it came.

"Should we pursue?" Hannah asked in the ensuing silence.

"There's no time, and since we are already one ship down, we can't spare anyone," Blackburne said with an apologetic look toward Kiara.

"Agreed," Kyle answered. "I've got video and audio of the ship, we'll send it back to the DG Ranger and the GTA, and see if we can get some support to investigate this further. If someone is after Kiara, they should be the ones to investigate."

Blackburne turned to Kiara. He noticed that her color looked normal, and her eyes were clear. "I'm sorry, Kiara."

"No need to apologize, we have a mission, and that takes priority," Kiara responded.

Blackburne nodded. "Contact Transgate Control, use the Ranger priority override, and get us through that transgate. We can't sit here and wait to see if he comes and back and brings some friends."

Chapter Six

The rest of the trip passed without incident, and Kiara supposed it was because whoever planted the bomb and sent the fighters after them didn't think they would make it past those attacks. They had dropped off the rest of their load at the second space station, and were now taking a break at one of the larger space stations in the sector. Security was still high, but upon their return the group had learned that most trade routes had been reopened without incident, and the areas with the most pressing need for supplies had been taken care of.

Kiara was currently hanging out in the gardens aboard the space station with Elvis and her dad. She loved the garden areas. True, they used artificial sunlight and the 'sky' above them was a holographic image, but the plants were real, and visiting the garden areas aboard a space station was one of her favorite things to do. Most space stations weren't large enough, so she took advantage whenever they got to a station that had them.

Kiara laughed at Elvis, now on his back, feet straight up in the air, wiggling around and making snorting noises in the grass. Her dad reached over and hugged her again. Kiara sighed into his shoulder.

"I'm really okay, Dad," she told him for what seemed like the hundredth time.

"I know," he laughed back at her. "I missed you, you know. Seeing and talking to you over the com isn't the same as being here."

They'd been here for a day, resting and recovering from the mission. So far, they hadn't received a request to go on another mission, but the DG Ranger had asked them to hold here for a couple of days. Kiara had been avoiding talking or thinking about anything serious. Feeling safe with her dad nearby, she'd been sleeping a lot, and hanging out with her dad when she did emerge from her cabin.

"I made a decision, Dad," Kiara told him as they continued to walk along. She had to keep a good eye on Elvis; she discovered that he liked the taste of the plants in here, and she didn't think the gardeners would appreciate his type of 'trimming'. She sent a silent 'no!' to Elvis when she saw his mouth closing around a purplish-red flower. He immediately pulled back, his happiness at being in the garden not diminished at all, even with Kiara not letting him eat the flowers.

"What decision is that?"

"I'm going to embrace this new side of me, and explore it, and not be afraid of it."

They had both stopped walking, and Kyle looked down at his daughter. He knew she would eventually embrace it. She was his daughter after all. She might have been afraid in the beginning, but her natural curiosity and desire to overcome her fears would win out every time.

Kyle nodded at her and waited for her to continue, he sensed that she had more to say.

"I'm going to work on developing this new power and controlling it, but, I think we need to learn more about my past, and why someone is trying to harm me." She was remembering her conversation with Stryker, and the lone Galdorian ship that had tried to attack them on their recent mission. She still hadn't told her dad about the dream she'd had, but since she hadn't had another, she was beginning to think it was more a product of her imagination and just a dream, nothing more.

"Learning more is going to be tough," Kyle told her. "We've already combed through just about every document we could find on Trandor."

They had started walking again, and Kiara acknowledged her dad's statement with a nod.

"Maybe we should ask Stryker?" Kiara hunched her shoulders, anticipating her dad's disapproval. His next words caught her off guard.

"Maybe we should."

Kiara relaxed her shoulders and felt Elvis' nose poke her calf. She reached down to scratch him behind his ears.

"The problem is, I don't have a way to contact him." Kyle said as he watched Kiara and Elvis interact. "He was always the one who initiated contact."

Kiara swallowed her frustration. She was always impatient, and once she had made up her mind, she wanted to take immediate action, and get instant results. She remembered her conversation with Stryker in the museum. "He did say he would contact me, after he met me in the museum that one time."

"I know it's hard, but let's wait for him to contact us. I think we might draw unwanted attention to you if I start putting out feelers to try to find him."

"I knooowwww," Kiara said in her best teenage-girl whining voice.

They both laughed.

As they approached the Acadia, Kiara saw John coming toward them. He'd been helping with repairs after they had gotten back, and was waiting for the Rangers to send him a new ship since they'd had to destroy his. Kiara smiled at him, determined to work on this 'flirting' thing. It wasn't hard, John was handsome, tall, and fit, if the cut of his uniform was any indication. Besides, he seemed to be interested in her, as far as she could tell.

John saw her smile and smiled back at her, thinking perhaps they were making progress.

"Hi, John," Kiara said. Elvis, on her shoulder merely stared at him for a few seconds.

"Kiara, Kyle," he said, nodding at Kiara's dad. "Where you guys coming from?"

"We went down to the gardens," Kiara answered him, suddenly feeling awkward.

Kiara and John looked at Kyle for a second, who seemed oblivious of his surroundings, as he studied the display on his com unit. John cleared his throat, knowing he would just have to continue the conversation with Kiara's dad present.

"Are you hungry? They have a great little place to eat on deck ten, if you'd like to go."

"I could eat," Kyle answered absentmindedly, still looking at his com unit.

Kiara looked from John, who had a surprised look on his face, to her dad, who still hadn't looked up. She burst out laughing.

At her laughter, Kyle finally looked up, and to his credit, it only took him a fraction of a second to figure out what was going on.

"Actually, John, I need to take care of something, so you two go ahead and get something to eat." Kyle looked back down at his com unit and climbed the steps into the Acadia.

Kiara, still laughing, looked back at a now grinning John.

"Well, how about it? Feel like accompanying me to get something to eat?" He glanced at Elvis, who looked half asleep on her shoulder. "I asked earlier if your little drayek could eat with us, and they said no problem."

"Sure," Kiara said. "And thanks." She was incredibly touched that he had gone to the trouble to make sure Elvis could go.

She followed him to the space lift, feeling awkward again, and searched her brain for a conversation starter. The doors opened for the space lift, and Kiara entered first, noting that there was one other occupant in the lift, a small, web-footed, green-skinned man. She noticed his feet had clear coverings on them, showing his webbed feet, but Kiara would have known just by the shape anyway. Kiara and John both nodded at him, but he simply ignored them.

"Deck ten, forward." John instructed the lift before turning back to Kiara. She was wearing a green tunic today over her skinsuit, and his mind pictured her in the gardens she said they had been to. He figured she looked stunning in the gardens, but, he supposed she looked stunning no matter where she went. He smiled at her and moved a little closer, his intent to try for a more intimate conversation, since they had another occupant in the lift. However, as John got closer, Elvis started huffing at him, getting louder as he got closer.

"Is he okay?"

"Sure, sure," Kiara said nervously, and took a step back. Elvis immediately stopped huffing. She wasn't going to tell John, but Elvis had been voicing her nervousness for her. She'd felt as if he was invading her personal space, and was a little uncomfortable. Unsure of the proper protocol in this situation—space lift, another occupant, drayek on her shoulder—she simply didn't say anything. Her little drayek had picked up on her feelings and conveyed them in the only way he knew how.

"He's probably nervous about being in the space lift," she lied, and smiled to try to cover up the awkwardness.

The lift stopped to let out the little green man, and as he exited, he turned and frowned at the three of them.

When the doors closed again, Kiara and John both let out a laugh.

"What do you think bothered him more—the drayek, or that we even got on the lift?" John asked, still laughing.

Kiara shrugged her shoulders, not sure what a good response to that would be. Luckily, the lift stopped again for them, and they exited into a crowded lobby area. Shops, dining, and gambling; it was all available on this level. She hadn't been to this area of the space station before, and immediately disliked the number of people and noise here. Unsure of their destination, she worried she would lose John in the crowd.

John turned and headed to the left, motioning for Kiara to follow him. She thought he might have said something to her, but the crowd noise was so bad, she couldn't make out what he said. She tried to keep up, but someone jumped in front of her, and someone else bumped into her, and she soon lost sight of John. Elvis was holding her hair, and his back legs were clamped tightly onto her shoulder. She could feel her anxiety rising, and tried to move quickly around a group of very big Andonites, trying to see if she could spot John again.

Someone bumped into her, and she stumbled into the back of one of the Andonites—seven feet of solid muscle, and from the smell, very intoxicated. She started to mumble an apology, but apparently, the Andonite didn't like it that she had stumbled into him, and reached a massive arm out to push her from him. His push sent her flying like a rag doll toward another group, and Kiara, with a little squeak, threw up a protection field to keep them safe. The impact of her protection field to the group behind her had everyone in that group flying back, several bodies hitting the ground.

Kiara regained her balance, and looked around her. Everyone was staring at her, and there was a good twenty feet of space around her now. She looked at the faces surrounding her—some expressions held fear; some held surprise, and one or two looked angry. Her eyes locked onto John's, and his was probably the most surprised of all.

Kiara stuck her chin in the air and squared her shoulders. She'd told her dad she was going to own this didn't she? Well, now was as good a time as any to put that into practice. She looked around the group until she saw the Andonite that had pushed her.

"I don't like to be pushed."

She walked toward John and prayed that he wouldn't flinch from her, or tell her he didn't want anything to do with her. Elvis was huffing and chirping on her shoulder, and those around her were giving her a wide berth, but John didn't move. When she reached him, he held his hand out for her to grasp. She grabbed his hand, thankful that her protection field had dropped on her walk over to him. Conversation around them was starting to pick up again, so John leaned toward her so she could hear him.

"Are you okay?"

Kiara nodded, letting out a sigh of relief.

"I'm sorry we got separated back there, I didn't think it was going to be this crowded up here. The last time I was here, there were only a few people."

"It's okay."

"Do you still want to eat something? The place I was thinking of has tables away from the noise and crowds of the main area, so I could ask if we can sit at one of those."

Kiara nodded, grateful that he seemed to sense she needed that.

This time, as they headed out, John held onto her hand.

In the restaurant, John was true to his word, and got them a table away from the main crowds. He kept the conversation light, talking about his childhood, getting Kiara to talk about some of her adventures with her dad. Kiara soon relaxed, which in turn had Elvis relaxing enough to leave her shoulder and sit next to her. The food was good, and the restaurant even had the fruit that Elvis was fond of.

"Aren't you going to ask me about what happened back there?" Kiara finally voiced her concern after the dishes had been cleared from their table.

"I thought if you wanted to tell me, you would."

Kiara smiled. She was beginning to like John. She told him what she knew, which wasn't much. She left out the part about the attack on the Acadia and the first time she used her powers. She wasn't sure why she left that out, but it just seemed too private at the moment.

John nodded, "I remember reading something about the Guardians from Trandor when I was younger. More like far-fetched legends was our thought."

"I don't know about the 'Guardian' part, but my dad and I are exploring the rest." She looked down and saw that Elvis was starting to look sleepy after eating.

John noticed the sleepy drayek as well, and suggested they head back to the Acadia. The crowds had thinned considerably, and Kiara was grateful that the walk back was uneventful. John dropped her off at the Acadia, and Kiara immediately went looking for her dad. She wanted to get started on practicing, but she also wanted to tell him about the incident in the crowded area on deck ten.

Kiara found her dad in the kitchen with Blackburn and Frankie, and after exchanging greetings, managed to drag her dad away from the group. She knew he enjoyed talking with her shipmates. They headed to the flex-space, and Kiara was glad to see that Elvis looked more alert now. She wanted his participation in her practice session. Once they reached the flex-space, Kiara told her dad what happened up on deck ten, and John's reaction to it.

"So John knows now, and so do a bunch of people on deck ten," she told him.

"It was bound to come out sooner or later," her dad told her, "we'll deal with it."

With her dad by her side, and her decision made, she felt calm and determined to work on this. Her dad always seemed to know the right thing to say, and in no time, Kiara felt as if they were making progress. It was taking less and less effort and concentration each time to bring up a force field and hold it. At one point, while she held it up, her dad walked around, testing the field. He used the onboard computer to map it out, and together they looked at a perfect sphere around her and Elvis.

"Wow!" Kiara said as they looked at the computer representation of her force field.

"Pretty impressive, little one," her dad said as he put his arm around her and pulled her into his side. "How are you feeling?"

"Pretty tired, and hungry again."

"I imagine that this is like any muscle in your body, it'll get stronger with practice. We don't want to overdo in the beginning."

"I know, I know, it's just that I feel like I was just starting to get the hang of it."

"Why don't you go grab some food for you and Elvis, and maybe a quick nap, and recharge your engines, so to speak?"

"Okay, what are you going to do?"

"I'll go catch up on some correspondence, see if the Rangers have passed on any more information." They exited the flex-space. "Come get me when you're back up, if you're feeling up to it, we can practice some more."

After grabbing a quick bite, she and Elvis went back to her little cabin to lay down for a bit. Kiara felt tired and sluggish, and she could feel Elvis' fatigue as well. As soon as they entered the cabin, Elvis jumped up on the bunk, spun a couple of quick circles on his blanket, and flopped down with a big sigh.

"That's a good idea," Kiara said, and threw herself into the bunk as well, falling asleep almost as soon as her head hit the pillow.

When the dream started, Kiara immediately recognized the space dock and ships from her earlier dream. She caught a glimpse of her reflection, and recognized Mirona looking back at her. Today Mirona was dressed in a black skinsuit with a white, flowing, long tunic that came to her knees. The drawings and bands were still on her arms.

Mirona?
Yes, my child.
Is this before or after I was here last time?
It is after.
Is this a dream, or something different?
We are joined, through time and space, for you to learn.
Did you bring me here?
No, it is your power, from within, that has determined that you need me.
My power is not like yours. I have just discovered it. I have no one else to learn from.

127

Then it is true what the others have told me. Our annihilation is coming.

Kiara could feel the sadness coming from Mirona.

I have been told that there are others, but I don't know where they are.

I can teach you to find them.

My power seems to be linked to the drayek that I found. We have bonded. Does that happen often?

A drayek?

Kiara could feel the confusion in Mirona's thoughts, so she brought a picture of Elvis into her mind.

Aaahhh, yes. This happens sometimes. You are very lucky. He will help you become more powerful than if you were on your own, more powerful than I.

Than you? Kiara didn't think that would be possible, not from what she saw the last time.

The connection was snapped when Kiara's com unit signaled her, causing her to sit up in her bunk, confused for a moment about where she was and what she was doing. She scrubbed at her face with her hands in an effort to clear the fog. Elvis nudged her leg with his nose, and Kiara looked down at him, finally starting to feel like herself again. She checked her com unit and found a message from her dad, stating they needed to meet someone in an hour. Stryker? Probably. She checked the time, and realized that she'd been sleeping for a couple of hours, and the message from her dad had come about twenty minutes ago. She sent a quick message to her dad to meet outside the Acadia in a few minutes, and straightened out her hair and changed her tunic.

With Elvis trailing behind her chattering and jumping, Kiara headed out to meet her dad. She saw

Frankie heading to the kitchen, and he confirmed that Blackburne hadn't issued any orders yet. She let Frankie know that she and her dad were going to possibly have a meeting with Stryker. She wanted to make sure that someone else knew where they were going, just in case anything happened to them. Frankie wanted to go, but Kiara told him that Stryker wouldn't meet them if he did.

"Don't worry, we'll be fine," she assured him. "My dad knows how to handle himself, and I've been practicing." Kiara wiggled her eyebrows up and down with the last part of her statement.

Kiara laughed at the look of excitement on Frankie's face.

Kyle was waiting for her when she exited the Acadia, and they exchanged a quick hug.

"Is it Stryker?" Kiara whispered to her dad.

"Yes, but we'll approach it like it's a trap, just to be safe." They headed into the space station, Kyle taking her toward the back of the space dock instead of toward the space lift. "I'll go in first, and we'll keep our com units open so you'll know whether it's okay for you to come in."

"Maybe I should go in first—with my protection field, and—,"

"Absolutely not!" Her dad interrupted her at a near shout. "You can barely control your power, and I won't send you into an unknown situation where you could get hurt!"

"Okay, okay," Kiara put her hand on her dad's arm, "it was just an idea."

"I know," Kyle looked chagrined and pulled her in for a hug, "it's the 'dad' thing."

Following the directions that Kyle received, they entered an area of the space station used for storage and maintenance, so the chances of running into someone else were remote. Surveillance was sparse, and Kyle supposed that's why Stryker chose it, but it was also a good place for an ambush.

Leaving Kiara near the entrance with a good escape route, Kyle entered one of the bigger bays, his hand weapon drawn and ready. At first, he didn't see anything; the bay was poorly lit, and there were deep shadows everywhere. He entered a little farther, keeping close to cover, as his eyes adjusted to the dim light. He sensed someone else was in the bay, but didn't say anything, choosing to wait and see if Stryker announced himself.

"My apologies for the meeting place, Kyle." Stryker's voice came from somewhere to Kyle's right. "We must keep your daughter safe."

Stryker emerged from behind a pillar, slowly approaching Kyle. His stride was long and purposeful, giving the observer a sense of strength and determination. He was taller than Kyle, and broader in the shoulder, and Kyle knew from his experience, that this race of humanoids was powerful and ruthless when provoked.

"Stryker."

Stryker had reached Kyle, and bowed slightly at the waist, his sign of respect for the father of Kiara.

"Perhaps you could invite Kiara in?" Stryker looked down at Kyle's com unit as he said it, and Kyle knew that Stryker realized the connection was open.

"Hello, again," Kiara responded from behind Stryker.

Kyle could see slight surprise in Stryker's eyes at having Kiara approach him from behind, unawares. Stryker turned slowly, lowering the hood on his cloak. He bowed even lower to Kiara, uttering a greeting to her in a language she didn't know. Stryker gestured with one hand for Kiara to join her dad. As she walked toward her dad, she dropped her protection field, and guessed that her protection field was how she was able to sneak up on Stryker. That was good information to know.

As she passed Stryker, Elvis suddenly jumped from her shoulder, and with a couple flaps of his small wings, wobbled his way over to Stryker and landed on his still outstretched arm.

"Elvis!" Kiara cried out in alarm. Why would he fly over to Stryker?

"It is fine," Stryker said calmly, his free hand holding one of Elvis' tiny front feet. "He knows I am not here to harm you, it is his way of helping you understand."

Kiara opened herself to Elvis' thoughts, and felt confirmation of Stryker's words. She looked at her dad, and smiled. "He's right."

With a slight lift of the arm that Elvis was sitting on, Stryker sent him back to Kiara.

"Thank-you for meeting with me. We must stay in contact to keep Kiara safe, now that the Galdorians have decided to make a move to harm her." Stryker looked at Kiara. "When you began to use your power, they began to hunt you. If you had never come into power, they may have left you alone."

"We ran into a Galdorian ship on our last trip that tried to get close to us, he had his weapons cloaked." Kiara looked from Stryker to her dad as she spoke.

Stryker nodded, "Yes, we were aware of the aborted attack."

"We?" Kyle asked.

"Yes, there is a small group of Trandorian elders and others who work to keep their race safe, and hope to one day reunite them in a place that they can call home."

"Maybe I could meet them someday?" Kiara asked. "I've never met anyone from Trandor before; I'd like to be able to meet someone like me."

"Perhaps."

"What can we do to keep Kiara safe?" Kyle asked.

"This is a vulnerable time for you," Stryker said to Kiara. "You have power, but lack the knowledge and experience to use it well enough to protect yourself. The Galdorians hunting you know this; it is why they try to strike down potential Guardians before they fully realize their power."

"Then it's true, others before me were called 'Guardians'?" Kiara asked.

"Yes, those of your race with your powers were called 'Guardians'. They protected government officials, diplomats, and, of course, their families." Stryker paused, looking intently at Kiara. "We must get your power more fully developed, but protect you while you are training." This time he smiled at Kiara. "You have been practicing, this is good."

"Just a little."

"We have been hearing about the episode on deck ten earlier today." Stryker looked from Kyle to Kiara. "It is not bad yet, but the more you use your power in front of others, the more it will attract those that want to harm you. There may be others that will want to harm you just because they don't understand your power and are afraid."

"How do we keep her safe, for now?" Kyle voiced some of his frustrations. "She's practicing, yes, but we don't know what we're doing, so it will probably take much longer for her to reach her potential."

"I have a way for us to communicate so that others will not know—I will program your com units before we depart today. This way, you can let me know when you are in danger or have concerns. We have friends in many places that will help you in a moment's notice. In addition, I have a friend coming in that can stay near Kiara for protection, but will also help with her training. He has trained others, and knows almost as much as I do about Trandor."

"Like a bodyguard?"

Stryker could hear the dismay in Kiara's voice.

"No, not at all. Your father will not always be with you. The Rangers may ask him at any moment to help with another mission. And while your current shipmates will come to your defense, they are not experienced in dealing with this threat. Jax can help with your training. I hope you will become friends."

"His name is Jax?" Kiara and Kyle asked at the same time.

"Yes, he is from Soltus, like me, and has spent much of his life helping those from Trandor."

"But what about my job? I'm not willing to quit my job, or hide because I might be in danger." Kiara's chin went up a notch.

"Of course not, you must continue with your life. If you back down or hide, they win." Stryker was impressed with her courage. She would need it for what was to come. "We will talk to your captain about adding Jax to the crew. He has worked aboard spaceships before, so he will be a help, not a burden."

Kiara looked doubtful, but agreed to the plan.

"When will we meet Jax?" Kyle wanted to know. He hadn't wanted to say anything to Kiara, but Stryker was correct. The Rangers had already asked him to support another mission that didn't involve the Acadia, but he was torn between helping protect others with the Rangers, and staying near his daughter to help protect her. Perhaps

Stryker already knew, and that was the reason he had reached out to them.

"Jax should be here in a few hours. We can introduce him to your captain after you both meet him." Stryker looked at the emotions playing across Kiara's face—fear, hope, confusion. "Things are moving fast, yes, but it is necessary to keep you safe."

"I know," Kiara said, looking at her dad. "Change is always hard, and there doesn't seem to be any time to catch my breath before the next change comes." She kept her gaze on her dad's face. "They've already asked you to go, haven't they?"

Kyle sighed, and pulled her in for a hug. "Yes, they've been very insistent. I was going to tell you earlier, but I've been conflicted about whether or not I should leave."

"You can't follow me around forever, you know."

"I know, but I'm not going to accept the new mission if I don't think Jax can keep you safe."

"Daaad," Kiara drew the word out, letting him know that she didn't agree with his overprotectiveness.

Stryker watched in amusement. He'd kept tabs on this pair, ever since Kyle had found the little girl in the wreckage. Their bond was absolute, and he had vowed that if they needed him, he would be there, and do everything in his power to protect them. He'd been involved in helping others from Trandor, and there had been a few times when he'd found it very difficult. For a few of those Trandorians, their moral character was lacking, and it was only his sense of duty that kept him helping them. These two, however, were people of the highest standing in his eyes, and worthy of all his efforts. He was bringing in Jax, the only other person besides himself that he trusted to help Kiara. He would have preferred to stay and help her himself, but his secrecy was legendary, so it wouldn't help to have him on the Acadia. Jax, however, had been out of the shadows for years, so it wouldn't harm him or his reputation to work on the Acadia.

"Trust your little drayek, he will help you know when you are in danger, or if there is someone you can trust. His senses in this area are very well developed."

Before they departed, Stryker programmed their com units to work with his encrypted one, and let them know that he would contact them with the next meeting time and place once Jax was aboard.

As Kiara and her dad headed back to the Acadia, she asked him if they should talk to Blackburne before or after they met Jax.

"Definitely after. Let's make sure it's a good fit before we stir things up."

Kiara suddenly remembered the dream she had before meeting Stryker, and thought this might be a good time to bring it up.

"Speaking of my training," she began, and Kyle stopped walking and turned to look at her. "I've had this strange dream a couple of times, where I was back in time with one of my ancestors." Kiara struggled with the words, wanting to make sure she expressed the importance of the dream, and that it wasn't really like a dream at all. "I mean, it was like a dream, but it wasn't like a dream."

Kyle raised his eyebrows. "If it wasn't a dream, then what was it?" His voice expressed his confusion at her statement.

Kiara let out a sigh. "I don't know. I was in someone else's body, someone from Trandor. She said her name was Mirona."

"Do you think you were dreaming of someone that you made up in your mind?"

"I honestly don't know. She said I was there to learn, and my power had brought me to her because I needed her. I think it was before the wars."

Her dad's eyebrows drew together as he thought about what she said. "I guess anything is possible. Maybe Stryker or this new guy, Jax, will know whether this kind of thing is possible. There's so much we don't know about your ancestry, and we're just flying blind here. I'm glad we will have someone who knows more about you than just what we've read."

"I'm excited, but a little nervous about that part. I want to know more, but I don't want to hear anything that might be bad."

"Bad? Like what?"

"You know, like I come from a long line of serial killers, or everybody from my planet goes insane by the age of fifty or something like that."

Kyle studied her face for a moment, trying to decide whether she was serious or not. He'd always known where he came from, so he had no experience with the feelings that she was having. Deciding she was serious, he pulled her in for a hug.

"We'll deal with it together, no matter what it is, okay?"

Kiara sighed into his shirt. "Okay, Dad."

When they boarded the Acadia, they ran into Frankie in the hallway.

"Blackburne's been hustling up a job for us while we wait for the Rangers to decide whether they want to use us again. We'll be leaving in about four hours."

"Okay," Kiara answered as Frankie continued into the ship. She turned to her dad. "Timing will be tight."

"Let's go talk to Blackburne, and I'll send a quick message to Stryker. We'll work it out."

They found Blackburne on the bridge, working out the logistics for the latest cargo run. He looked up as Kiara and her dad entered the bridge. The two captains exchanged a quick nod, and Blackburne turned to Kiara.

"We've got a cargo run, you good to go?"

"That's what we came to talk to you about." Kiara took her usual seat at the navunit, her dad leaning against the wall next to her. Elvis jumped into her lap and curled into a ball for a quick nap.

"Everything okay?" Blackburne looked from Kiara to her dad, concern written all over his face. "Did someone try to attack you?"

"No, no, nothing like that," Kiara was quick to reassure him. "We're okay." She took a quick glance at her dad, who nodded back at her.

"We met with Stryker a bit ago, and got more background on who's trying to harm me, and what we can do about it." Kiara was relieved to see that Blackburne's expression had calmed down quite a bit. He was intimidating on a day-to-day basis, but when he was angry, his expression was downright scary. "I can explain more later, but the short version is, there are some Galdorians that hunt Trandorians that come into power, like me. He wants to bring someone on to help protect me and train me—someone that knows about Trandorians, and someone he trusts."

"Someone that Stryker trusts?" Blackburne looked at Kyle. "What do you think?"

"We haven't met him yet, but since you have a run coming up, it makes the timing a bit tight," Kyle answered him. "He's supposed to be here in a couple of hours. I'd like to make sure I trust him, before I trust Kiara to him."

"Agreed." Blackburne stood up, began pacing.

"Stryker wants him to be a crew member aboard the Acadia." Kyle said.

"Makes sense."

Kiara rolled her eyes at her dad and Blackburne. "I'm sitting right here, you know."

They chuckled at her, but kept right on with their conversation.

"See if Stryker will let the three of us meet and evaluate this person—what's his name?" Blackburne asked.

"Jax."

"See if Stryker will let us meet and evaluate Jax, and if need be, I can push back our run by a couple of hours." Blackburne deliberately stared at Kiara. "Kiara needs to be safe."

Kiara let out a sigh. She was happy that everybody cared, but really, did they have to act like she was a child or something? She hoped Jax wasn't overbearing, or they were going to be butting heads a lot.

"I'll let Stryker know what we're up against, so we can move quickly if needed." Kyle stood up and moved off slightly to send the message.

"I know you don't want me to apologize, but I'm going to anyway—I'm sorry," Kiara told Blackburne. As predicted, Blackburne frowned, and opened his mouth to say something, but Kiara interrupted him. "This is going to put a strain on everyone, I know that. If you want, maybe we should find a replacement navigator for you, at least until we can figure out if I'm going to put you guys in danger. I couldn't live with myself if one of you got hurt, or worse, because of me."

Her dad walked over at the end of Kiara's statement, and looked over at Blackburne. Blackburne was looking thoughtful.

"Okay, Kiara, here's what we'll do," Blackburne said as he crossed to her, his look still thoughtful, but slightly determined. "We'll ask everyone what they want to do. If they want you on board, and they know the risks, then we'll put the matter to rest, agreed?"

Kiara looked at her dad, doubt in her eyes. She didn't see the answer she was looking for there, so she turned back to Blackburne. He still looked determined, and she had no doubt that he would take the risk. She looked down at Elvis, still curled up in her lap, and knew that no matter what, she was going to need help. All of these people, at one time or another had agreed to help her and stand by her. If they wanted to continue, she would let them.

"As long as we make sure they know the risks, and we don't put any pressure on them." She nodded at her dad and Blackburne. "It has to be unanimous."

"Agreed."

Blackburne called the crew to meet in the flex-space because it was the only room big enough to hold all of them. The room was a good size, but with the three Bendanites, it was starting to feel a little cramped. Once they were all in the room, Blackburne explained the situation, making sure he emphasized that there was no pressure on anyone, from Kiara on down. If they were going to risk their lives, they needed to understand the situation.

"I know we haven't been together for all that long, but for me, this is the best crew I've ever had." Blackburne looked at each crew member. "Every one of you has exceeded my expectations for handling your position, and has stood by the other crew members without reservation, even when we took that last job for the Rangers. The situation with Kiara is slightly different, but if she stays on, we may all have to pitch in to keep her protected. So each of you let me know right now, if you want Kiara to stay on, or if we should find a temporary replacement." This time Blackburne looked at Kiara. "Kiara has volunteered to leave to keep us safe, so a vote for a temporary replacement is not going to hurt anyone's feelings. Kiara wants to keep everyone safe. And all of you know how much that means to her."

Blackburne looked over at Larry, Curly and Moe. They had been speaking to each other in their native language, and when Blackburne looked over at them, Larry moved slightly forward.

"She will stay." At his words, the other two Bendanites nodded.

Blackburne looked at Frankie.

"Of course she stays!" Frankie was fairly vibrating where he stood. "This is the most exciting thing that's happened to us, and I wouldn't miss it for anything!" Frankie danced his way over to Kiara, and enveloped her in a hug. "And if anyone tries to hurt you, they are going to have to deal with all of us!"

"Thank-you," Kiara's muffled voice came from the front of Frankie's shirt. When Frankie finally let go of her, Kiara wiped the tears from her eyes, and she could feel Elvis holding her leg down by her feet.

"Hey now," Frankie said. "What's with the tears? This is good news!"

"This is so overwhelming," Kiara said as she looked around the room. "I always thought it would just be me and my dad as family, but I'm realizing that you guys are like family to me, and it's an incredible feeling."

"Okay," Frankie joked, "group hug!"

Blackburne sent Frankie a disgusted look, but the Bendanites all laughed, their impressive teeth on full display.

"So, we're good, right?" Blackburne asked Kiara.

"Yes, thank-you."

Kiara's dad walked into the room, and told them that Jax was aboard the space station, and Stryker wanted to get the introductions started.

Blackburne answered first.

"Let's have the meeting aboard the Acadia. We're all in this together, so I think it's reasonable that everyone should be okay with a potential new shipmate."

"My thought as well," Kyle answered him. "Kiara, what do you think?"

"Only if Stryker brings him aboard."

Kyle walked back out into the hallway to communicate with Stryker, and Blackburne walked over to Kiara.

"Okay?" Blackburne asked her, and Kiara knew he meant about everyone agreeing to help her and keep her on the Acadia.

"Yes, I'm good with it. I still don't want anyone hurt because of me."

Kyle let the group know that Stryker was on his way over with Jax, while Frankie maneuvered himself closer to Kiara.

"So, Kiara," he leaned his head closer to hers, and wiggled his eyebrows up and down. "Can you show me some of your stuff?"

Kiara laughed and playfully punched his arm, but when he kept staring at her, she realized he was probably serious.

"Not now, Frankie," she whispered back.

"Okay," he whispered. In a more normal tone, he continued. "In all seriousness, Kiara, we'll keep you safe."

"Thanks, Frankie."

"So, who's this 'Jax' person?"

"Someone that Stryker said could help protect me and train me." Kiara looked over at the doorway as her dad motioned for Blackburne to accompany him. She figured that Stryker and Jax must be here, and Blackburne went to greet them and let them onto the ship. "Stryker said that between the time I discover I have powers and when I can use them well enough to protect myself is when I'm most at risk."

"You've never met Jax?"

"No, we'll all be meeting him today for the first time."

"Should we trust him?"

"Well, Stryker trusts him, and my dad trusts Stryker." Kiara shrugged her shoulders. "I know I need help with my training, so I guess we'll see."

Elvis suddenly climbed up her leg, and with Kiara's help, gained her shoulder. He chirped at Frankie, and touched Kiara's face with one of his front feet. Kiara felt anxious, but she couldn't tell if it was her anxiety, Elvis' anxiety, or a combination of both. She turned to the doorway as Blackburne came in, followed by two cloaked and hooded figures, then her dad.

Suddenly, Curly, who had been closest to the door, bared her teeth, and emitted a low growling noise that had the hair on everyone's neck standing on end. The tension in the room increased exponentially, as Curly stared at the hooded figures.

"You were there," Curly growled at them. Continuing to growl, she puffed herself up, making herself look even bigger. Larry and Moe puffed up as well, moved to surround the two hooded figures and keep them from entering further into the room.

"Wait, wait," Kiara shouted and sprinted to the doorway. Stryker and Jax, realizing their danger, had dropped their hoods and were in a defensive crouch, waiting to repel an attack if needed.

"Curly, what the hell?" Blackburne shouted. "These are our guests!"

Curly sniffed the air, and still puffed up and growling, pointed at Stryker. "You were there!"

Kiara saw that both Jax and Stryker had somehow produced baton-like weapons, and were keeping their backs to each other, ready to strike or defend. It suddenly dawned on Kiara that Curly was referring to the first time that she had met Stryker, in the hallway outside the restrooms. Kiara had called for help from her shipmates, and Curly had been the first to come to her aid. That knowledge wasn't helping now, as everyone was shouting, and Kiara knew at any moment the situation was going to escalate out of control, and someone was going to get hurt. Larry's big frame was blocking her way, and no matter how hard she shoved at him, he wasn't moving. Her dad was yelling, Blackburne was yelling, and Frankie was also trying to get one of the Bendanites to move. Kiara knew she had to do something. With one hand, she touched Elvis' feet, and closing her eyes, she prayed this would work. She could feel the power building, and putting her free hand out, pictured a force field enveloping Stryker and Jax. She had no idea if it would work that way, without the field being attached to her. She hoped that if Mirona, in her dream, was able to throw her force field, then something like this might work.

Holding her breath, she slightly opened one eye. All the noise in the room had ceased, and Kiara supposed that

143

was a good thing. Stryker and Jax were now standing up, their posture slightly less threatening. Curly had stopped growling, and slowly turned to look at Kiara.

"You protect him?"

"I protect all of you. This way seemed the easiest."

Larry finally moved his massive bulk out of her way, and as Kiara stepped forward, she watched Stryker put his hand out and have it stopped by her force field. It worked! She looked toward the other occupant in her force field, and met the dark, piercing gaze of Jax. Her force field fell, and she could hear Stryker's voice in the background.

"Kiara, meet Jax."

Chapter Seven

Kiara stared at her navunit a few hours later, trying to process everything that had happened. They had managed to calm down the Bendanites, and once the situation was explained to them, they not only accepted Jax, but welcomed him into the group. Kiara glanced behind her. Jax was strapped into the extra seat that John had occupied a few days ago. He was busy on his com unit, but looked up at her as if sensing her gaze on him. Kiara smiled a little and turned her gaze back to her navunit. He apparently passed the test to accompany the crew, as they were, even now, headed out to pick up some cargo. She'd had a quick and tearful good-bye with her dad, as he'd decided to go help the Rangers on the mission they'd asked him for. Stryker had left also, telling her and her dad that he would be keeping an eye on things. She sighed. She was all for adventure and everything, but this was getting ridiculous. So much had changed in the last couple of weeks that she felt as if she wasn't in control of her own life any longer.

"It will get easier," Jax spoke quietly from behind her.

Kiara turned and looked at him. She didn't question that he knew what she was feeling. "I'm not so sure."

He nodded and put his hand on her shoulder. Elvis, who had been sitting in her lap, stood up on his hind feet, and chirped at Jax.

"He likes you," Kiara told Jax.

"I like him as well. He is really good for you." He moved his hand from Kiara's shoulder to the little drayek's chin and scratched him lightly, sending Elvis into a blissful state. His chirping changed to a low rumbling. Jax moved back to strap into his seat, reminding Kiara that they were approaching a transgate, and that she needed to do her job, no matter how troubled she felt.

She contacted Transgate Control, received the expected response, and sent the navigation information to Frankie. She watched her console as she scanned the transgate for problems, and when it came back all clear, she nodded at Blackburne and Frankie. Transgate traffic was light, so they didn't have to wait, and immediately entered the transgate. This wormhole had a reputation for being one of the rougher rides, and Kiara watched Blackburne's face slowly turn an interesting shade of green. Kiara smiled. You'd think with all the advances they'd made with medicine, they could find a way to counteract the forces of the wormhole. Blackburne didn't like the side effects of the medicines he could take, so he usually just rode it out. Fortunately, this trip through the transgate was a short one, so Blackburne wouldn't have to suffer for long.

They reached the other side without incident, and Kiara was starting to feel more like herself. She sent a quick message to her dad that they had arrived safely, while waiting for Frankie to get them docked at the space station nearest the transgate. They would have a little time here while the cargo was loaded, so Kiara hoped she would have a moment to speak to Jax alone. She turned in her seat to look at Jax, but he was standing by Blackburne, deep in conversation. They moved to a ship console, and Jax brought up something that had Blackburne looking surprised. The captain motioned for Frankie to join them, so Kiara figured it had something to do with the ship's engines or performance. Her suspicion was confirmed when Frankie yelled 'alright!'. Thinking they might be at it for a while, and not exactly sure what to do with herself,

Kiara stood up, moved Elvis to her shoulder, and started to leave. She'd only made it a few steps when Jax joined her.

"I think we have a little time before you are needed, would you like to go talk somewhere?"

Kiara looked at him, somewhat befuddled. Since he'd joined them, he seemed to be the psychic one. "Sure." She looked back at Blackburne and Frankie, still huddled over the ship console. "I thought you were going to be there awhile."

"I wanted to make sure I was an asset to the group, not just a dead weight." He smiled down at Kiara, and she could feel her heart skip.

"What did you tell them?" Kiara asked, and felt some embarrassment when her voice came out a little breathlessly.

"I found some parameters that could be optimized for engine performance—increasing output, decreasing fuel consumption, that sort of thing."

"I'll bet that made them happy."

Jax laughed, "Yes, Frankie was like that Earth saying—you know—child in a candy shop, or something like that?"

"Oh, kid in a candy store?"

"Yes!" Jax laughed again, and had Kiara laughing too.

They seemed to be of the same mind, and headed to the docking tunnel to exit the ship. This space station was small, and to get off the ship, they had to go through the small docking tunnel, but it was worth it. Art, food, shops, and friendly people awaited them. Due to the cumbersome way to get off the ship, the number of travelers aboard the space station was reduced, so it wasn't overcrowded. Jax and Kiara walked around, exchanging stories, getting to know each other. She told him what she knew of herself, what she'd accomplished with her gift, what her dad had told her. He told her about working with Stryker, about some of his travels aboard other spaceships, where he'd gotten his experience from. Their pasts were not so different, and Kiara felt the beginning of a connection with him. She finally asked him the question that had been on her mind for a while.

"Are you psychic?" At his startled look, she hurriedly elaborated, "You always seemed to know what I'm thinking."

"Not psychic, no. Our species is very empathetic, and I work to cultivate that side of myself. Put that together with everything that Stryker has told me about you, and it makes it easier to anticipate what you need or what your questions are." He chuckled. "However, that particular question did catch me off guard."

They stopped at a small seating area near a bank of windows that had a view of the nearest planets. The area was empty, so Kiara thought this would be a good place to sit and perhaps get a few of the more in-depth questions answered.

"Can we sit here for a minute, and maybe talk about some of the more serious stuff?" Kiara sat first, picking the long bench that faced the windows. She checked her com unit to make sure they didn't need her back on the Acadia, before looking up at Jax. He was still wearing his hooded cloak, but with the hood pulled back and the light in the area, he looked a little less menacing than the first time she saw him. He still presented an aura of strength, and with his dark clothes and cloak, Kiara was sure that others saw him as menacing. It did make her feel protected, which slightly irritated her, because she liked thinking she could take care of herself.

Jax took one more look around them before sitting on the bench, but instead of facing the windows, he faced the room.

"What do you want to know?"

"Do you know anything about my Trandor family? How I ended up on that destroyed ship?"

"Stryker has not been able to discover anything about your beginnings. He became aware of you a few years after your dad found you. He tried to uncover information about your family, but so much has been destroyed that it has been impossible."

Kiara nodded, her look thoughtful. She looked down at Elvis, who was currently sniffing at something on the floor near the windows. He never strayed far from her, so she didn't worry about losing him.

"Do you know who is trying to harm me? Is it someone that we can be on the lookout for?"

"There is a small faction of Galdorians that want to wipe out all those from Trandor, specifically, Guardians and potential Guardians," Jax told her. "They keep hidden, and those we find are turned over to the GTA. We don't know how many there are. They are well-organized, and very determined."

"Galdorians don't have the blue skin of Trandor, so they look just like any other humanoid, right?" Kiara asked, thinking back to some of the information that she had looked up.

"That is correct, on the surface. Their faces, their hands, their feet, look like anyone from Earth. However, we have found that Galdorians do have a distinguishing feature. Their blood is purple. Also, those of the faction who are still hunting Trandorians have a tattoo over their heart that means 'death'."

"Their blood is purple because of the minerals they were taking from Trandor?"

Jax nodded, his eyes never leaving the room, constantly scanning. "We also have to be aware of those that are not from Galdor, but have chosen to join that cause. That could be anyone."

"It sounds like too much to defend against," Kiara sighed. She wished they could go back to the way it was before she discovered she had this gift.

"Do not despair," Jax said as he reached over and covered her hand with his on the bench.

Kiara noticed that like his face, his hand was also covered with short, fine hair, but she could see the strength in his hand, even with the hair. Her pulse jumped when his hand covered hers, and she quickly looked at the floor so he wouldn't notice. Elvis was under the bench sniffing at something, but when she looked at the floor, he came out from under the bench and poked her leg with his nose.

"I'm trying not to, but it's a lot. Why do you do it?"

"Help you and others from Trandor?" At her nod, he looked back into the room to continue his surveillance. "I was trained from an early age to take on this role. Not just for those from Trandor, but those from other planets who may be in similar situations. Some from our planet use their gifts and talents for nefarious gains, my family, Stryker's family, and a few others have chosen this path."

"That sounds as though your path was chosen for you, and you didn't answer my question."

Jax smiled. He knew he was going to like her.

"I have found great satisfaction in helping others."

When she raised her eyebrows in doubt, he chuckled.

"Okay, I see you have your doubts. I will tell you of another I have helped; it will help you in your journey, and help you to understand why I do it."

He told her of another young woman from Trandor, living on a planet with a foster family who didn't understand her ancestry, and had no tolerance for anything they didn't understand.

"When she began to exhibit signs of her power, they locked her in a room, and fed her through a small hole in the door. They were afraid of her, and thought that she had been taken over by an evil spirit. They brought a high-priest to the house and tried to excise the spirit, and when that didn't work, they tried to beat it out of her."

Kiara gasped at the horrible picture it painted in her mind. Elvis, sensing her distress, immediately jumped into her lap and chirped at her, poking her arm with his nose. She put her hand on his back and murmured to him that it was all right. He curled into her lap, reluctant to leave her.

"How did you learn about her?"

"A traveler through that sector heard about the 'demon girl', and when he asked about her, they showed him a picture. He immediately recognized that she was from Trandor. He contacted someone at the GTA, who contacted Stryker. Stryker sent an envoy to ask if we could take her to others that could help her, but the foster family was reluctant to give her up."

"Why? I would think they would be happy to be rid of her."

"Greed. They wanted the money that they were getting from the GTA to foster her."

"That's awful!"

Jax just nodded, his face grim. "That is the reality of it. For any race."

"I assume you were able to convince them?"

151

"No, we were not. The envoy that Stryker sent reported back that the girl was near death, so Stryker and I pulled off a midnight raid and took her."

Kiara let out a breath she didn't know she was holding. "Is she okay?"

"Yes, she is now. We took her to a colony of others from Trandor. I spent time with her, helping with her training, as did a few others in the colony." Jax looked back Kiara. "She doesn't have your abilities, but she is happy with what she can do. She is with others that will continue to look after her and help her now. She is accepted and revered for who she is."

"Did the GTA prosecute the foster family? We're supposed to be protected."

"They did not."

"Well, why the hell not?" Kiara was incensed.

Jax could practically feel the anger pumping off of her. "The foster family was given a religious exemption."

"That's ridiculous!"

"I agree. The best we could do after the fact was prevent them from fostering children with special abilities in the future. We had several representatives lobby the GTA for a change in law, which did eventually happen."

Suddenly, something that Jax said earlier penetrated Kiara's brain. "Wait—did you say there was a colony of Trandorians?"

"I was wondering when you were going to catch that."

"Where are they? Do you think I can meet them someday?"

"I can't tell you where they are—we're trying to keep them protected. But," he stalled her next statement, "I'm sure that we can arrange a visit someday." He thought it telling that she asked to 'meet' them, not go live there.

Jax knew it was one of the reasons that Stryker had brought him on in this capacity. Stryker had thought that she was a well-adjusted young woman that didn't need the extra support that the colony could give her. Obviously, her dad had done a great job raising a daughter that wasn't of his blood. She was curious about her ancestry, and her race, but not an overwhelming need to be among them and accepted by them. He hoped that didn't change. Her race could use an ambassador like Kiara.

Kiara sat quietly for a moment, silently digesting the conversation so far. Suddenly, something else that Jax said came back to her. "Why did you say that she doesn't have my abilities? You've only seen me do one thing."

"True, I've only seen you do that one thing, but, something you may not realize about that one thing. I've only seen a handful of Guardians pull that off, and due to my empathetic nature, I could feel how strong your abilities were, with that field."

"Oh."

"Had you done that move before—setting a protection field that was separate from you?"

"No, actually, I hadn't. I've done several around me and Elvis. Don't you think that this little guy is the reason my abilities are so strong?"

"Not the strength of your abilities, but perhaps the speed at which they are progressing can be attributed to him. We honestly haven't had much experience with drayeks bonding with Guardians, so some of this we'll be figuring out as we go."

Kiara's com unit signaled, and she looked down to see that they were needed back on the Acadia. They both stood up to leave, Elvis climbing up to her shoulder for the walk back.

"How did you know how to throw your field like you did?" Jax asked her as they walked back to the ship.

Kiara remembered her dreams, but thought that walking down the space station hallway was not the best place to discuss it.

"I guess that's a story for next time," she told him as they reached the docking tunnel. Kiara could see through one of the windows in the tunnel that cargo-loading robotic arms were making some last-minute adjustments to the load, so it appeared they would be ready to leave shortly. They went back through the docking tunnel and entered the ship. Kiara immediately went to her navunit to start programming the route to give to Frankie.

She was entering information in when Elvis, sitting in her lap, jumped up and chirped at whoever was approaching her station. She turned to see Frankie looking at her with a concerned look.

"What is it Frankie?"

"Just wanted to check on you. You okay?"

"Yes, why?"

"Well, we don't know Jax all that well yet, so I'm going to be checking up on you for a while."

Kiara started to frown, but reminded herself that all of her shipmates had promised to look out for her, so she smiled instead. "I'm good, Frankie. We had an interesting conversation. I'm learning about myself, but I'm also learning about him."

Frankie nodded and headed back to his seat, and Kiara saw him nod, very slightly, at Blackburne. She turned back to her navunit and giggled. Looking down at Elvis, she whispered, "Like I wouldn't know that Blackburne told him to come over and ask me if I was okay." Elvis chirped his agreement.

After making sure everyone was on board and the cargo secure, Frankie released the docking clamps and slowly eased them away from the space station. They'd only gone a short distance when the com channels suddenly filled with calls of alarm and ships in distress. Frankie brought up the screen that showed the space station, and they could see Mercenary ships shooting out of the transgate, firing on anything in their path. Blackburne barked out the order for Frankie to turn them around, but Frankie was already maneuvering them. Kiara got the shields up, and she heard Jax behind her shout that he was on the weapons. Blackburne yelled into the ship's com for everyone to brace for battle so the Bendanites would know what was happening. She heard Blackburne trying to communicate with Transgate Control to shut down the transgate, but he was getting no response. Kiara got off a message to her dad that they needed help before they were in the thick of it.

Kiara heard Frankie say that he counted nine enemy ships in the area, but thanks to the shield upgrade that they had received from the Rangers, their shields were holding as the first of the weapons fire hit them. The weapons upgrade that the Acadia had received was also helping, as first one, and then another of the enemy ships exploded. Kiara acknowledged in the back of her mind that Jax was really good with the weapons, even as she monitored their shields and engines. Blackburne, watching the enemy ships, concluded that they were targeting the transgate and space station, and that the other ships in the area were secondary. They seemed to only target the Acadia if it got too close. The transgate and space station, both being small, were taking heavy fire, and Blackburne knew it was only a matter of time before they were damaged beyond repair. He instructed Frankie to get them closer and try to defend the transgate. At least no more enemy ships were coming through.

Kiara watched another Mercenary ship explode, before another flew out of control into the space station. She could tell from the impact that the shields were nearly gone on the space station. She knew the Acadia was having an impact on the battle, but it seemed so hopeless. They were outnumbered and outmaneuvered, and she didn't think they were doing enough. Kiara could see that there were still five Mercenary ships left, and they were inflicting heavy damage. She turned to look at Jax, wondering if she should try to do more. She didn't know whether she could and doubt in her ability weighed heavy on her. Jax looked up, caught her eye, and in that second, she knew that he knew where her thoughts were going. He held her gaze for a second before he simply nodded.

Kiara turned back to her console, and the dream she'd had where Mirona had used a different type of energy to destroy a ship entered her thoughts. She looked down at Elvis, silently willing him to help her. Elvis stood on his hind legs and put his front feet on Kiara's cheeks. She could feel the power within her building, and it felt a little like it had in the dream. Unaware that as her power built, she seemed to glow, her body flushing a dark blue.

Jax looked up briefly from his weapons fire, a fierce grin on his face. He knew she was special!

Kiara closed her eyes, and was briefly surprised that she could still see the battle in her mind. Concentrating, she focused on one of the tight groups of three ships heading for the transgate. She centered her thoughts on the middle ship, and with a push, sent her energy to it. At first, nothing happened, and Kiara feared that they were too far from the ship, or perhaps she hadn't done it right. As she watched, her energy finally hit the ship, but it didn't have the impact she had hoped for. She could see the ship slightly deviate from its course, before it corrected and continued on, its weapons fire wreaking destruction on the upper half of the transgate. Kiara looked back around at Jax, doubt and despair written all over her face. Jax yelled for Blackburne to take over weapons control, and with an affirmative from Blackburne, Jax jumped up and crossed quickly to Kiara.

"I can't do it!" Kiara nearly wailed. The distress calls and screams of those hurt or dying were coming over the com, and it was increasing her anguish. Jax squatted down to her level, his eyes boring into hers. He grabbed her hands, Elvis still on her lap between them. Elvis was making a noise of distress as well.

In a calm and reassuring voice, Jax simply said, "You can."

Kiara could feel the calm and confidence coming from him, and it transferred slowly to her. Elvis, too, quieted down, and Kiara, her eyes still locked on Jax, willed the power to build again. Elvis placed his paws on top of Jax and Kiara's clenched hands, and Kiara could feel it help focus her. With her eyes still open, she could see the battle, and found the three ships she had targeted before. This time, she told herself, she would stop them. They were coming in hot to the space station, and Kiara knew that people would die if it didn't work this time. Her eyes turning a deep violet, her skin glowing, this time when she sent her power, she screamed her determination. Blackburne and Frankie snapped their heads around to look at Kiara, and in that instance her energy reached the Mercenary ship. Everyone looked back at the screen as the middle ship started to wobble, and Kiara despaired that she had failed again. But, as everyone watched, instead of righting itself, the wobble increased until the ship exploded.

The explosion was so violent; it took out the two ships next to it.

"Yes!" Jax shouted.

"How many are left?" Frankie yelled, as he maneuvered the ship around to go after a lone Mercenary ship heading for the transgate. Blackburne targeted the ship and destroyed it, and Jax scanned for any that were left. The last enemy ship came into range, heading for the transgate as well. A few well-placed shots from Blackburne and it too was destroyed.

The battle was over, but the destruction was massive. Kiara could tell just from looking at it, that the transgate was heavily damaged and out of commission. The space station had taken heavy fire, but was still holding its position, and the shouts over the com units had changed from screams for help, to logistics to help the wounded and evacuate those in need.

Blackburne turned to Kiara and calmly asked her for a damage report, and as Kiara checked the ship for damage or other problems, she could see her hands shaking. She tried to steady them, but it just got worse. Soon, her whole body was shaking, and she could feel tears starting to stream down her face. What was happening to her? The battle was over, and now she was shaking so bad she could barely use her console.

In a shaky voice, she told Blackburne that the Acadia had no major damage or issues. Blackburne looked at her with a question in his eyes, clearly worried from the shakiness of her voice. Before she could answer, Jax had crossed over to her and squatted down to her level again.

"This will pass," he said quietly.

"The shakiness?"

"Yes, it is the aftermath of the battle and using your powers. The adrenaline alone is enough to make anyone shaky, but using your powers in such a manner will also have an effect."

"Okay," Kiara replied, the quiver in her voice still very apparent.

"Here." Jax handed her a small tube of energy gel.

Kiara took it, not quite sure her stomach could handle anything right now, but willing to try. With a quick swipe at her cheeks, she downed the energy gel and willed it to stay in her stomach.

"Take some slow deep breaths, it will help calm you down and ease your nausea."

Kiara smiled weakly. She was starting to feel better, and at least the tears had stopped. She could deal with shakiness, but crying in front of everyone was too much.

Jax, seeing that Kiara was recovering, stood up and crossed over to Blackburne and Frankie to see if they needed his help. Kiara looked down at Elvis. He was looking up at her with adoration in his gaze.

"We did it, didn't we?"

Elvis gave her an answering chirp.

Taking a deep breath, Kiara turned back to her console, ready to help.

"Blackburne, the transgate is completely out of commission," Kiara told him. "We've got help coming from the nearest planets, but the space station is holding for now. They're telling me that most of the docking clamps are damaged, so we are being advised not to dock with them."

"Do they need our help transporting wounded?"

"Negative. We are being advised to clear the area. A medical transport ship is approaching from the nearest planet, so we're not needed."

Blackburne nodded. "We'll need another route out of here since the transgate is damaged. Let's deliver our cargo, and get the hell out of here."

Kiara sent a quick message to her dad that they were okay, and the status of the transgate. He responded back that Rangers were on the way, but it would be days before they would get there due to the transgate being damaged. He also questioned why they would hit that transgate, but Kiara didn't have an answer.

"We're getting reports from the transgate and space station that was hit this morning. Major damage to both. The transgate has been shut down," the Ranger reported to the Senior Logistics Officer.

The tall, dark woman standing near the bank of windows at the GTA headquarters smiled. As the Senior Logistics Officer of the GTA, she had access to transport, materials, money and information for everything and everyone that dealt with the GTA. She turned back to the Ranger standing behind her. "Good."

"We did have one issue, though." At the frown he received, he hurriedly continued, "the female Trandorian— she managed to take out three of the Mercenary ships during the battle."

"I thought you were keeping an eye on her!"

"Yes ma'am, but we were taken off of her detail, and there was no inconspicuous way to accompany them on this trip. Besides, I had no idea she had that kind of power yet. We've only gotten reports of small things so far, so this was completely unexpected."

"Didn't you say that there were Galdorians hunting her?"

"Yes ma'am, but they haven't been successful yet. She has someone from Soltus teaching and protecting her. It's going to make it almost impossible for a Galdorian attack to work."

"Is her father suspicious?"

"Of us? No."

"Perhaps we need to help the Galdorians meet their objective."

"What?"

"With her father helping the Rangers, it stands to reason that she will eventually get pulled into the conflict, even more than she has." The SLO paced in front of the windows. "We can't have her jeopardizing our operations."

"She's only one person; surely she can't have that much effect on what's happening."

"We know there are others like her, and if she manages to get them involved as well, we may have an issue. If her powers are advancing as fast as your reports are indicating, she may be a force on her own." At the conflicted look on the Ranger's face, she became enraged.

"Do you have a problem, Ranger?"

"No, ma'am," he said as he backed up a step.

"Then get back out there, and make sure the Galdorians take care of business, even if you have to do it for them."

Kiara was exhausted. Since leaving the crippled transgate, they'd been on high alert in case there were any other attacks. Although it had been quiet so far, no one seemed to want to chance it. She'd sent Frankie the course to drop off the cargo and get to the next transgate. Blackburne wanted to get back to the space station they had left earlier today, but it was going to take days and several transgates to get there. She did another scan of the area, and still found nothing. The energy gel Jax had given her had long since worn off, but she didn't want to appear to be the weak link and ask to leave. In the end, Blackburne ordered her and Jax to leave the bridge and get refueled and rested. They would take the next shift.

As they approached the kitchen, Curly and Larry were approaching from the other end. Elvis immediately began to jump up and down on Kiara's shoulder, making high-pitched chirping noises. Kiara laughed, and was grateful to have that brief moment of happiness. They all reached the kitchen doorway at the same time, and Larry gestured for Jax and Kiara to precede them into the room. Elvis jumped to Curly's shoulder, his little paws combing her face while he chirped at her. At Kiara's concerned look, Curly quickly reassured her.

"He is good right here."

"Thanks, Curly. Are you guys okay?" Kiara asked.

"Yes, we are good." Curly reached out and grasped Kiara's left hand. "You are tired and need to eat." She squeezed her hand. "You kept us safe."

Kiara blushed. "At least I didn't have to keep our ship from falling apart this time."

After grabbing something to eat, Kiara went to her cabin and threw herself into her bunk. She fell asleep almost immediately, and just as quickly started to dream about Mirona.

Kiara found herself in a cityscape, and her mind recognized it from the pictures she had seen of Trandor before the war. She tried to see and feel everything she could, since none of this existed any longer. She could feel Mirona's sadness at her thought of it all being gone, so Kiara deliberately pushed that thought from her mind, and concentrated on what she was seeing.

Mirona was walking along a busy street with different types of motorized vehicles whizzing by, and everywhere she looked, she could see other Trandorians. It was glorious! She could see buildings that rose into the sky, and the hustle and bustle of everyone and everything moving to their destination. This place was busier than any of the busiest space stations she had visited. Mirona's amusement filtered into Kiara's thoughts.

Where are we going today? Kiara sent the thought to Mirona.

To my home. You can see my family, see where you come from.

I'm grateful to have this time with you.

Have you been practicing with your powers? I can feel how tired and drained you are.

We were involved in a battle today. I remembered how you used your power to destroy an enemy ship, so I tried to do that. So many people would have died if the enemy had succeeded with their attack, so I had to try.

Did it work?

It took me two tries, but I finally destroyed the ship.

You are so young and inexperienced—you will get better.

I hope so. I have someone with me who is protecting me and helping to teach me.

Another from Trandor?

Mirona's excitement was coming in loud and clear in Kiara's head.

No, not from Trandor, he is from Soltus. He has helped others from Trandor develop their gift. He helped me in the battle.

Ahhh, Soltus. Yes, they are good allies for us. Here is my home.

Kiara could see a multifamily housing building, with beautiful colors, flowing lines, and wonderful arches. The buildings were made of native stone and glass, with beautiful stone and glass balconies. The stone used for the buildings ranged in colors from muted reds, browns and yellows to wonderful blues and greens. As they moved closer to the building, Kiara could see the colors changing, depending on her angle to the spot she was looking at. The view was so wondrous, she felt as if there wasn't enough time to absorb it all. They entered the building and took the lift to one of the upper floors. Mirona entered her home, and was immediately swarmed by a group of people that ranged from elderly to infants.

This is your family?

Yes, I am blessed.

You said I come from you. Are you my mother? Grandmother?

This I do not know. I do not know how much time has passed. War has not yet started. I am sorry.

Don't be sorry. I'm grateful for this.

A couple of the older women broke off from the group, and with Mirona, they went out onto a balcony area that overlooked part of the city. Other multifamily homes, gardens, and parks could be seen. Clearly, the city planners had wanted a good feel for their city. Buildings were spaced far apart, and almost everyone had a view of a park or garden. Kiara was so focused on absorbing everything about the city, that when she felt the jolt in her hand, through Mirona's hand, she almost lost the connection with Mirona. They struggled for a moment to hold the connection. They both relaxed as they felt Kiara would stay, at least for a little longer. Mirona looked at the two older women standing with her on the balcony, holding her hands.

Mother, grandmother.

This is your mother and grandmother? They look so much like you.

Shhh. Listen and feel.

It began as a hum, and built to a roar in Kiara's head. The power that the three generations of women produced, standing on the balcony and holding hands, was amazing. Kiara could feel it, and almost taste it. The power had a feel that was familiar, and she realized it was because she was related to these women. She reveled in the feeling, storing the memories for when she would need to use her power again. Suddenly, Mirona's mother snapped her eyes open, her gaze boring into Mirona. Kiara felt as if the gaze could see into her into her as well.

"You have someone with you? She is one of us?"

"Yes, mother. She is from us. She is here to learn."

"Welcome, little one." Mirona's mother sent a different type of power into Mirona, and Kiara could have sworn that it was like receiving a warm hug, from the inside. The feeling was incredible!

The connection with Mirona was snapped again, this time by her com unit signaling. Kiara sat up, rubbing her hands together. They were still tingling from the connection with the other women. She checked her com unit and saw that Blackburne had given her and Jax an hour before they were to relieve the others. She tapped into the main computer, checked their course and the latest scan of the area. She didn't see any problems reported, so she got up and changed her clothes, and wondered if Jax was up as well. She wanted to talk with him about the dreams she was having and see what he thought about them. She sent a quick message to Jax while she tidied up, and was pleasantly surprised when he answered her right away. Her heart jumped when her com unit signaled the message from him, and she scolded herself not to fall for the guy that was supposed to be protecting her. That would surely lead to disaster. He probably thought about her like a little sister or just a client, and would most likely be annoyed or embarrassed if he thought she had feelings for him. Sure, he was very handsome, with compelling dark looks, and the physique to make any girl swoon. He was confident and obviously smart and capable, and she struggled to think of something negative about him. Nothing came to mind. She sighed. If he were as empathetic as he claimed, he was going to figure this out in no time at all. She couldn't avoid him, he was supposed to be protecting her and teaching her. Her thoughts whirling, she read his message that he wanted to meet in the flex-space before assuming their shift. She sighed again.

Kiara entered the flex-space and found Jax running a workout program. Kiara finally pulled her eyes away from the muscles bulging under his workout clothes, and realized it was one of her favorite programs that she routinely worked out to. He looked to be nearly done, so Kiara supposed he hadn't slept as long as she had. She noisily cleared her throat, and when he turned and looked at her and smiled, she shyly waved back at him, and then groaned.

Really, waving at him? What was she, two years old?

"Do you want a few more minutes to finish your workout?" she quickly asked him.

"No, I was nearly done anyway." Jax picked up a towel and mopped at his face. "Did you get any rest? You still look a little tired." He was studying her face carefully.

"I did get some rest, but it will probably take me a little longer to get back to normal." For the first time that she could remember, she wished that she had spent a little more time on her appearance.

Jax walked over to the wall console and shut down the program, so Kiara thought that now was as good a time as any to bring up the dreams she was having and see what Jax thought of them.

"Remember when you asked me how I knew I could throw my protection field?"

"Yes, you said it was a story for another time."

"Well, I started having these dreams a little while back," Kiara said as she struggled for the right words. "It's like a dream, but not like a dream." Kiara wandered over to the wall by the door, and pushing a button, extended a bench to sit on. While she sat, she tried to gather her thoughts into something that made sense. She didn't want Jax to think she was crazy or hallucinating.

"Dreams of your ancestors?"

"Yes!" Kiara exclaimed on a happy sigh. He already knew about this kind of thing!

"Others I have helped have also told me of these kinds of dreams. The dreams are something that your race has to help younger generations of Guardians. Is this where you learned to throw your protection field?"

"Yes. I have been going back in time to visit one of my ancestors. She says I am from her, but we don't know exactly when. I was with her when she was protecting a ship from an attack. She threw energy at it and destroyed it. She is—was—very powerful." Kiara laughed a little bit. "It only took her one shot to destroy the enemy ship."

"This is very good news. It will help with your training."

"Do you think it can help me discover who my parents were, and maybe how I ended up in that destroyed ship?"

"Perhaps." Jax sat on the bench next to her, his look serious as he studied her face. "Be careful in this endeavor. Many times it is nothing but heartache at the end of the search. Sometimes, we find nothing, sometimes, we find answers that disappoint."

"I know." She shifted uncomfortably on the seat. "I've always known I was adopted, and I have all the love I could ever need from my dad." She looked down for a moment before looking back up at Jax. "But since all this has started, I can't shake the need to find out more."

"I understand. We will find out what we can," Jax said as he stood. "I'll go get cleaned up and meet you on the bridge," he told her as he headed out of the room.

Kiara sat for a moment on the bench, thinking about her past, about Mirona, about finding more information on where she came from. She was determined that this need for information about her past would not destroy her relationship with her dad. She wouldn't let it. At that moment, her com unit signaled an incoming message. She looked down and saw it was a message from John. He wanted to know when she would be back at the space station; he wanted to take her to dinner. Kiara smiled. John wanted to take her on a date! She frowned as she looked toward the door where Jax had just left. Was it weird that she might like two guys at the same time? Did that happen to others? She looked down at Elvis, sleeping in her lap. He was still trying to get caught up on his sleep too. Sensing her gaze, he sleepily opened one eye and looked at her. When she didn't say anything, he closed it again. No answers there, Kiara thought. Getting up from the bench she sighed, but she still had a smile on her face. She would run it by her dad; he would know what to do.

Chapter Eight

Kiara, bent over at the waist and breathing hard, fought to keep her lunch in her stomach. She reminded herself that she had asked for this. She'd wanted to get better with her powers. She'd wanted to learn how to protect herself. She'd just had no idea that Jax was going to work her this hard. Jax was standing to the side, a sword in his hand, not breathing hard at all. Of course, he wasn't the one throwing up protection fields at the drop of a hat. She'd discovered early in her training that she wasn't nearly fast enough with her protection fields, and that small things, like swords or lasers, could go right through if she didn't focus hard enough. She looked at Elvis, sitting on the bench by the door and chirping at her. Jax had wanted her to try without the little drayek, and it was practically killing her.

"Maybe we should take a break for a few minutes?" Jax asked her.

"Good idea," Kiara replied between big gulping breaths.

Jax laughed. "Not what you thought, huh?"

Kiara finally straightened up, thinking that perhaps she wouldn't lose her lunch after all. "Definitely not what I thought. But it's good."

Kiara hobbled her way over to the bench to sit by Elvis. Jax had told her that all her race was athletic, and that she should use that to her advantage. Instead of standing and waiting to repel an attack, he had her running, jumping, spinning, and flipping while simultaneously protecting herself. Once she had mastered that, he was going to have her practice throwing some energy around for an offensive move, but he wouldn't go that far until she had the protection part down pat. She was really going to be sore tomorrow she thought.

Tomorrow. They should be back at the space station by then. Her dad was there waiting for her. She could tell by his last conversation with her that he was worried. They hadn't run into any more trouble on this trip, but she knew that wouldn't make her dad relax until he saw her in person. She'd also made a date with John for tomorrow evening. Blackburne had told them that they would have at least a day of downtime when they arrived. She looked forward to getting there, she was running low on her supplements, and her chocolate supply was nearly depleted. They'd stopped yesterday at a space station to refuel and gather some supplies, but it didn't have her supplements or the chocolate that she liked. She was glad she always kept extra of both on hand, but this time it was cutting it a little too close for comfort.

Jax came over to stand by Kiara and Elvis, and the little drayek surprised them both by rumbling at Jax. Elvis tried to maneuver himself between Jax and Kiara, rumbling and looking suspiciously at Jax. Kiara looked at Elvis in amazement.

"He's trying to protect you," Jax said after a second. "He knows your vulnerable right now, you're tired, and he's sensing that."

Kiara reached over and soothed Elvis, murmuring to him that everything was okay. He eventually crawled into her lap, but still kept an eye on Jax.

"Maybe it's because you've been attacking me, and he doesn't understand that it's for training."

"That's probably it."

Kiara knew she'd better attempt to fix it, or the little drayek would be constantly trying to keep Jax away from her. She wasn't sure how she was going to communicate 'training' to Elvis, but she had to try. Taking a deep breath, she closed her eyes and practiced the deep breathing techniques that Jax had also been teaching her. Focusing her thoughts, she sent calming thoughts to Elvis. She could feel him relax in her lap. She pictured her and Jax training, and he tensed up again. She kept picturing it, but each time she ran through it, she pictured herself better. She sent Elvis good thoughts about Jax. He seemed resistant to her thoughts at first, and she didn't think he was getting it. Suddenly, he gave a loud chirp in her lap, and she could feel the resistance from him completely fade. Opening her eyes, she looked at Jax.

"I think he gets it now."

"That would be good," Jax said with a smile. "You are getting better, but you are also much better with his help. I had hoped we could keep you from being dependent on him, but it appears that you have bonded in a way that it will be detrimental to separate you. At least in the beginning."

Jax sat on the bench next to her, and Elvis immediately jumped into his lap.

"Well, that's a good sign," Jax said as he stroked the little guys front feet. "Why don't we quit for today? I'd like you to practice the breathing and meditation techniques that I've been teaching you."

"Okay, I can do that."

"One more thing, Kiara. I have worked with other Guardians that were able to communicate with their ancestors once they mastered their meditation. They were able to communicate without being asleep."

"Really?"

"Yes. I did not want you to be surprised if it happened to you." Jax coaxed Elvis back to Kiara's lap. "I think it will take quite a bit more practice, but you have been surprising everyone from the beginning with the speed that you are progressing, so I wanted you to be prepared."

"Thanks. Am I doing okay?" She hated to ask for his praise, but found herself doing it anyway.

"Of course." He studied her face, seeing the self-doubt. Reaching out, he took hold of her hand, watching her pupils expand as they both felt the jolt that passed between them. He'd trained many Guardians over the years, and the rule that Stryker had always drummed into him was not to get personally involved. He'd felt attraction to several he had trained, and always managed to keep his emotional distance. Kiara was definitely going to test his resolve. She was special, not just because of her abilities, but her personality, her dedication to help those in need, her big heart. And of course, he thought as he looked down at their hands clasped together, they had the chemistry as well. He cleared his throat, let go of her hand and looked out into the room.

"You are an exceptional student."

"Um, thanks." Kiara tried to sound upbeat. It had seemed as if they were going to share a moment there, before he broke whatever connection she thought they had. Her thoughts turned to John and his request for a dinner date. She supposed it was probably for the best. She wasn't experienced with dating, so trying to date two guys at once was just asking for trouble.

Kiara looked out the small window in her cabin, and saw that Frankie was expertly bringing them into the space dock. This trip had ended up being significantly longer than they had planned, and quite a bit more stressful. She opened her cabinet where she kept some of her supplies, and noticed again that her supply of supplements was extremely low. She sighed. So was her supply of chocolate. True, she had eaten most of it herself, telling herself that it was helping her stress, but she had also shared some of it with Curly.

With docking complete and the space dock open for people to walk around, Kiara exited the Acadia and went to look for her dad. He'd told her that he would be at the space station when she arrived, and she was excited to see him again. While they were docking, she'd sent him a message, and he replied back that he was in a lounge area outside of the store where she picked up her supplements. He knew that she would need to replenish her supplies. Kiara approached the store, and Elvis found her dad before she did. He actually jumped from her shoulder, and with a couple of flaps of his little wings, made it the twenty feet to where her dad was sitting. Elvis landed on her dad's shoulder, and Kiara laughed as she saw her dad jolt in surprise when the little drayek landed on him. He recovered quickly, and as Kiara approached, she could hear her dad talking to Elvis, who seemed to be answering with a series of chirps and low huffing noises. Her dad jumped up at her approach and enveloped her in a big hug. Kiara hugged him tightly, more comforted than she would admit to having him here.

"Hi, Dad," Kiara's muffled voice came from the front of Kyle's shirt. He finally let go of her.

"You're okay?" He studied her face. "You look really tired."

"I'm okay, but I am a little tired. We had a rough trip back, with training, and taking shifts to keep a lookout and scanning for trouble. I feel like I can't catch up on my sleep."

"Do you have some downtime here?"

"Yeah, Blackburne says we have at least a couple of days. That could change if he gets us another job, though."

Her dad gestured for her to precede him into the store, and Kiara walked in first, still talking.

"Jax has been training me, it's like nothing I could have imagined, but it's good. And he helped me focus when I helped out with those Mercenary ships."

Behind her, Kyle smiled, enjoying her chatter. A com unit conversation could never take the place of this. She finally wound down, and turned around to him, her small shopping basket filled with chocolate.

"Did your mission go okay? You never said what it was, not that I expect that, but did it go okay?" Kiara had finally wound down enough to ask her dad about his mission.

"Yes," Kyle answered her, his gaze locked on the amount of chocolate in her basket. It finally penetrated Kiara's brain that he was staring at the large mound of chocolate she'd collected, and she blushed as she defended herself.

"I did say it was a rough trip, didn't I?"

He shook his head. "It's okay, honey." Reaching out, he touched her face. "I forget how much you like chocolate, and seeing your basket reminds me of it. You didn't forget your supplements did you?"

"I found them. They didn't have very many, so I sent a request for them to order more right away."

"Speaking of requests," Kyle said as they headed out of the store after Kiara had paid with her com unit. "John was asking me about you the other day. Did he contact you?"

Kiara blushed again. "Yes, he asked me out on a date. We're going to dinner tonight."

"That's good, right?" Kyle studied her face, sensing that there was more to it.

"Yes, it's good."

"But?"

"I like John; at least I think I do. I haven't spent that much time with him."

Kyle waited patiently, he knew his daughter, and there was definitely more she wanted to say. They continued their walk through the space station as they made their way back to the Acadia.

"Well, I think I like Jax, too."

"Ohhhhh." Kyle drew the word out. "Not sure what to do?"

"I knew you'd understand. You know I haven't dated that much, what am I supposed to do? I don't want to upset anyone."

"Has Jax done anything to make you think he returns your feelings?"

"Not really. I mean nothing overt. I thought we shared a moment the other day, but maybe I just imagined it." She sighed.

"Then you don't have anything to worry about. Go on your date with John, enjoy yourself, and if Jax starts to come around, we'll talk."

"If Jax starts to come around?"

"Honey, you are a beautiful, caring, compassionate, lovely young woman. A man would have to be dead not to notice you or want to be with you. He may be avoiding his feelings because of his role in your life right now."

"I did think of that," at his look, she hastened to add, "about avoiding me because he's supposed to be training me." They both smiled.

Kiara finished getting ready for her date, taking extra time with her hair, and putting on her favorite dark-blue tunic. She was a little nervous, and hoped her nerves didn't prevent her from having fun. She exited the Acadia and headed for the restaurant to meet John. He'd found another restaurant for them to try, and had encouraged her to bring Elvis along. She decided to leave Elvis with Curly instead. She had wanted this to be a real date. Jax had actually tried to talk her out of going, saying he was worried about her safety, especially since she was going to leave Elvis behind. She'd tried telling him that she knew John, he'd help to keep her safe, but Jax hadn't been convinced. In the end, she'd gone anyway, telling Jax that she wasn't going to live her life by hiding. He'd wanted to come with her, but she'd quickly squashed that idea. What kind of date would that be?

John met her in front of the restaurant, and immediately moved in for a hug. Kiara felt a little awkward, but hugged him back.

"I'm glad you're okay," John told her when he let her go.

"Why wouldn't I be?"

"I heard about the Mercenary attack you were involved in. Did the ship come out of it okay?"

"Oh, the attack. I didn't know you knew about that."

"Well, to be honest, I've been trying to keep track of you." He looked a little embarrassed, but at her look, quickly added, "Not in a stalker sort of way! I'm interested in you, and wanted to make sure you stayed safe." He was actually blushing by this time.

"Thanks, John, that's sweet." Now she was blushing.

"Where's Elvis?"

"I left him with Curly. He likes her, and he's good about staying with her."

"Okay, let's go eat."

John got them a table near a bank of windows, and they had a great view of the ships going in and out of the transgate. Without asking, John ordered a Coke for her, and she was happy that he remembered she liked the earth drink. They both ordered a dish that was from one of the neighboring planets, and John held up his drink for a toast. Kiara, remembering what her dad taught her about toasting, immediately held up her drink to clink it against John's.

"To new relationships," John said, and they both drank.

Kiara looked at her drink with a frown after she set it down.

"What's wrong? Did they bring the wrong drink out?"

"I'm not sure, it doesn't taste the way they usually do."

"Hmmm. I'll ask for another when the waiter comes back."

Kiara looked at the drink, a feeling of unease coming over her. She looked back up at John. She was starting to feel funny.

"Kiara?"

"I don't feel so good." Her vision started to blur, and Kiara panicked. She tried to stand, but her legs weren't working. "John, help me." She tried to reach for her com unit, but her hand was moving so slow, it didn't seem to want to get there. She looked back up at John. Why wasn't he helping her? She tried to focus a protection field around her, but before anything could happen, the world went dark.

Jax, sitting in the kitchen on board the Acadia, was debating with himself on whether or not he should go find Kiara and make sure she was okay. Sure, she was on a date with John, the Ranger, a guy that Kyle probably trusted, but he rarely trusted anyone. Was his overprotectiveness because he was responsible for her safety and training or because of the romantic feelings for her that he had been fighting? He was just about to stand up and head out to find her when Curly appeared in the doorway. Elvis was on her shoulder, and the little drayek was emitting a moaning noise that Jax had never heard before. Before Jax could ask what was wrong, Curly started shouting at him.

"Something is wrong with Kiara!"

"With Kiara?" At first, Jax thought the language barrier had made her say the wrong name. He could tell, just by looking at Elvis, that something was wrong with the little drayek.

"He is bonded to her—something is wrong with Kiara!" She came into the kitchen, and Jax could almost smell the fear coming from her. Curly bared her teeth and snarled at Jax. "You must find her, now!"

Jax didn't question it. He jumped up, grabbed the still moaning drayek from Curly, and brushed by her, shooting out the door. He yelled instructions at her as he ran down the hallway.

"Get Blackburne and Frankie! Tell them to stop all ships from leaving the space station! Tell them to find her dad!"

Skipping steps, Jax jumped off the ship, heading into the space station. He refused to let the panic surface; instead, he brought all his training into focus. As he ran, he checked his com unit to see if Kiara had tried to contact him. When there wasn't a message, he tried to find her unit by the locater built into it. Nothing came up, and he knew it was bad. Someone had disabled her com unit. He entered the space station, trying to determine where to look for her. The space station was huge, and she could be anywhere.

His com unit signaled, and Blackburne's voice came across.

"No ships are allowed to leave, and none have left since Kiara left the ship, so she's got to be on the space station. Kyle's heading up to the restaurant that John said he was taking her to. Frankie and I are heading in to help look for her. We're pressuring the space station to let us see security camera footage."

"Good." Jax took a deep breath, his eyes going to the drayek on his arm. Elvis looked back at him, his color now turning slightly gray, his eyes sad, and his ears drooping. "Elvis!" The little drayek perked up slightly. "Help me find her!"

It seemed to be what the little drayek was waiting for. He turned on Jax's arm, his nose in the air. Jax didn't think he was trying to smell, he thought he was trying to sense her. Suddenly, his whole body stilled, and he jumped from Jax's arm. Flapping his wings until he landed on the floor, he turned to look at Jax and chirped at him.

"Right behind you!" Jax yelled as Elvis took off down the hallway. The little guy sure could move fast. Jax programmed his com unit on the fly to connect with Blackburne and Kyle so they could follow him. He yelled into the com unit that Elvis seemed to know where she was, and immediately got a response back that everyone was following his com unit. Elvis turned down a narrow hallway, stopping at a door that warned it was for authorized personnel only. Jax never even paused. He was in full-combat mode, and hit the door with the baton he always carried, his body hitting the door shortly after it. The baton carried an electric charge that disabled the door locks, and

179

as his body hit the door, it flew open. His eyes adjusted quickly to the darkened room, and he could see he was in one of the large maintenance hangars of the space station. Large enough to fit a small ship, it had a large open area, surrounded by smaller rooms, ladders and catwalks leading to upper levels, and pieces of machinery everywhere. He took all of this in on the run, as Elvis was still moving quickly, heading for the back of the hangar. He couldn't see any lights, and couldn't hear any voices.

Elvis reached the back of the hangar, and jumped onto a ladder that led into one of the upper areas. At any other time, Jax would have been impressed by the athletic ability of the little guy as he used his legs, wings, and tail to propel himself up the ladder at an incredible rate. Jax was barely keeping up with him. They reached the top and Elvis stopped for a fraction of a second before making a sharp left turn and heading farther back into the upper level, jumping wires, pipes, and pieces of metal. He reached the back of the upper deck, and stopped in front of another door. Jax could see a small, faint sliver of light coming from beneath the door. Elvis turned to look at him, and Jax could see his eyes glowing, and his teeth were bared. Jax took that to mean that Kiara was in there, and she wasn't alone.

Slowing his breathing, he moved closer to the door and tried to listen and determine how many might be in there. He could hear at least two voices, and closing his eyes, he could sense four heartbeats. Expanding on his empathy, he could tell that one of the heartbeats belonged to Kiara, but it was weak. Opening his eyes, he backed up a step and readied his baton. He looked down at Elvis, who still had his teeth bared, and nodded at him, hoping the little guy understood that they weren't going to wait for anyone to back them up. He was going in to get Kiara, and heaven help those who had her.

Jax charged the door, hitting it with the baton, immediately following that with his body as he had the previous door. The door bounced in, and his eyes took in the scene in a fraction of a second. Kiara was tied to a chair, and two men were arguing about whether or not they should kill her before leaving the space station. The third man was sitting to the side watching the other two argue. As the door busted in, everyone jumped, and the man sitting to the side reached for his weapon. Instead of aiming it at Jax, he was swinging it toward Kiara. Jax had launched himself in the air, his baton taking out one person, his booted foot taking out the other. He felt panic as he realized that he wasn't going to be fast enough to take out the third guy that was going to shoot Kiara. It all seemed to happen in slow motion, as battles sometimes do. He was launching himself toward the third guy, when a steak of blue went by him, an unholy growling noise coming from it. The third man never knew what hit him. He was so focused on eliminating Kiara that he never saw Elvis coming at him. The little drayek hit him and ripped out his throat, killing him instantly, his weapon never even fired.

Jax whipped around at the noise coming from behind him, and saw Blackburne and Frankie running into the room. Kyle was right behind them. The guy that Jax hit with the baton started to move and rollover, and Kyle kicked him hard, silencing him. Jax turned back around and rushed to Kiara. Her breathing was shallow, but steady, and Elvis had already chewed through the bindings holding her to the chair. She slumped forward, and Jax put his hands to her face. Closing his eyes, he tried to sense if she were hurt, or drugged. Kyle joined him, his worry evident. When Jax opened his eyes, he looked at Kyle.

"I think she's been drugged."

Kyle nodded, and reaching down, picked her up and started to carry her out of the room. He looked over at the dead man still holding the weapon, his throat completely ripped opened. "Your work?" He asked Jax.

"No, that one was Elvis."

Kyle looked at Jax in surprise, then at Elvis. The little drayek was clinging to Kiara, quietly chirping at her and stroking her hair.

"He'll never let her out of his site now."

"That makes two of us," Jax said grimly.

They reached the ladder, and much to Kyle's relief, Frankie had found not only the lights for the hangar, but a working hoverlift. Loading everyone on it, Frankie maneuvered them to the other end of the hangar.

"We can get to the Acadia through that door there," Frankie said, pointing at a door that led to the space dock.

Everyone hustled through, and Jax could hear Blackburne on his com unit telling Curly to get the med-bay ready for them. Hearing Blackburne contact security for the space station to let them know about the men in the hangar, Jax sent a message to Stryker as well. He wanted some of Stryker's men to get there first so they could question the kidnappers. He knew that the security team on the space station would be caught up in the procedures and regulations for harming a protected race, and there would be forms to fill out, and red tape to wade through. If Stryker's men could get there first, they could question the men the way they needed to, in order to get answers. It was obvious to him that those men worked for someone, and their orders were to kill Kiara at all costs.

They reached the med-bay, and after placing Kiara on the bed, Blackburne performed a quick diagnostic with the equipment. He quickly administered a counteragent to the drug that Kiara had been given.

"This should work pretty quickly," Blackburne told everyone in the room without turning around.

Kiara came awake with a start, screaming for them to leave her alone. Elvis was still clinging to her, and she wrapped one arm around him and threw up a protective field with the other. Jax had been expecting it and had taken a step back, but the field caught everyone else by surprise. Luckily, since Kiara was weak and disoriented, her field only pushed everyone back a step or two.

"Kiara, you're safe," Kyle said into the sudden quiet.

"Dad?" Kiara asked as she struggled to sit upright.

"Yes, Baby, I'm here." He moved into her line of sight, his heart breaking at how vulnerable she looked, and how this reminded him of the first time he'd ever seen her.

Seeing her dad, she dropped her field. He immediately went to her and held her. Looking over his shoulder, she could see Blackburne, Frankie and Jax all crowded into the med-bay, and Curly's face peering at her from the doorway.

"Dad, what happened? How did I get here? Am I okay?" She looked down, and seeing the blood on Elvis, which was now on her, she panicked again. "Elvis! What happened to Elvis!" She grabbed the little drayek, trying to feel for broken bones and looking for open wounds.

"Honey, he's fine, it's not his blood."

Kiara stilled her hands at her dad's words. "Whose blood is it?" She asked quietly.

"One of the men that was holding you," Kyle said quietly.

"Kiara, who drugged you?" Jax asked, but didn't hold out much hope that she would remember.

"John."

The silence was deafening. Her dad took a deep breath. He knew John, trusted John. But with the absolute certainty in which Kiara had said his name and the look on her face now, Kyle knew that John was guilty. Kyle looked over at Blackburne and gave him a quick nod. Blackburne backed out of the room, reaching for his com unit.

"Did he say anything to you? Like who he was working for, or what they wanted with you?" Jax asked into the quiet.

Kiara shook her head. "He must have worked something out with the staff at the restaurant—he ordered a Coke for me, and they brought it right out. When I started to feel funny, he didn't help me."

"That doesn't necessarily mean he had anything to do with it, Kiara." Kyle was reluctant to believe that any Ranger would betray someone like that.

"I know, Dad." Kiara looked at her dad and Jax. "I woke up a couple of times. He was arguing with somebody about where to kill me." She swallowed, hard. "He kept telling them to wait until they left the space station, and they wanted to do it right there." She finally asked the question that had entered her mind when her dad told her whose blood was on Elvis.

"Is John dead?"

"I don't think so," her dad told her. "He wasn't in the room when we found you."

Blackburne quietly came back into the room, and gestured for Kyle to leave with him. Kyle shook his head.

"Better just tell everyone what you discovered. I'll be telling them later anyway."

Blackburne looked grim. "John left the station right after we found Kiara. They lifted the freeze on departures, believing that we had everyone. He's disabled his locater, so we don't have any idea where he is."

Kyle muttered an expletive.

"That's not all," Blackburne continued. "When they arrived at the room where we found Kiara, only the dead guy was there."

Before Kyle could mutter another expletive, Jax stepped up.

"I asked Stryker if he could have one of our contacts here grab them up to question them. Let me find out if he did, or if they are gone as well."

"Good thinking," Kyle said as Jax worked his com unit. He turned back to Kiara. "Are you feeling better?"

"A little. I still feel kind of light-headed."

"Here, why don't you let me clean up this little guy," Kyle said, reaching for Elvis.

Elvis, however, wouldn't let go of Kiara. She finally coaxed him to go with her dad, and Kyle took him over to the little sink and gently washed him off. Kiara smiled, because even though Elvis went with her dad, he kept looking around him so that he could still see Kiara.

"Kiara."

Kiara looked up to see Curly pushing her way into the room, holding some extra clothes.

"Oh, thank-you Curly!" Kiara reached out to take the clothes, but Curly had already turned around and was pushing everyone out of the med-bay, including her dad. Curly put the clothes down, and took over the bathing of Elvis. As soon as the door closed behind her dad and Jax, Kiara swung her legs off the bed, intending to clean herself up and change her clothes.

"Wait, I will help," Curly told her.

"That's probably a good idea," Kiara said with a sigh. "My head still feels a little funny. If I landed on the floor, the guys out there would probably bust the door down to see what happened."

Curly chuckled at that. She moved a now clean Elvis to the bed, and turning, helped Kiara to the sink. As Kiara washed up, Curly told her how Elvis had helped to rescue her.

"Suddenly, he jumps!" Curly gestured with her hands in-between holding Kiara up at the sink. "His look—," Curly moved her hand up and down in front of her face.

"His face?" Kiara tried to help Curly with the words. Curly shook her head no, and moved her hand from her face to encompass her whole body. "Um, his color?"

"Yes, yes!" Curly said excitedly. "His color was bad. He looks to me, and I think, something is wrong with Kiara."

In clean clothes now, Kiara sat down in the chair next to the bed while Curly cleaned up the bed.

"I ask Elvis, is it Kiara?" Curly helped Kiara back into the bed. "He pulls here," Curly gestured to the hair on her face, "and his color gets very bad. I know we must get Jax."

"Thank-you, Curly." Kiara reached out and hugged the large Bendanite. "I think you saved my life."

Curly hugged her back. "We are friends." It was that simple for her.

Curly opened the door and pushed her way past the four men huddled outside the door. She turned as she passed Jax, grabbed him and hugged him. His feet actually came off the floor. When she finally put him down and started to walk away, Jax just stood there staring after her. He turned back to the med-bay full of people staring at him.

"Well, that was a new one for me," he finally said.

"Tell Kiara what we know," Kyle said into the quiet.

Kiara looked from her dad to Blackburne to Jax. Frankie was now standing next to Kiara, his hand on her shoulder, his other hand stroking the tufts of hair on Elvis' head. Kiara was feeling more protected and cared for than she ever had. Jax, now looking down at his com unit told everyone what he knew.

"Stryker's men grabbed the two men that were still alive before station security got there. We're going to let security think the men left—it will make it easier to question them." He looked up at Kiara. "One of the men was killed while they tried to move them to a more secure location. The other is badly injured. They put up quite a struggle while they were transporting them, and one of them was able to grab a weapon, which is why he is now dead. The other was injured during that struggle. He is not saying much now, other than they were paid to kill her. He did verify that John is the one who brought Kiara to them."

"We need to figure out if it's the Galdorians, or someone else that wanted this," Kyle grimly told Jax.

"Who else would want to hurt me? I'm just a navigator on a cargo ship. I'm nobody." Kiara watched her dad and Blackburne exchange looks. She saw Jax alert on that look as well.

"If you know something, you should tell us," Jax said forcefully. "I'm charged with protecting her, and if I don't know where the threat is coming from, I cannot do my job!"

Kyle stood up, his stance aggressive as he faced Jax. "Where were you when John was drugging her?!"

Kiara looked in alarm at her dad and Jax. What the heck was this?

"Where was I?" Jax shouted back. "He was one of your 'trusted' friends! Where were you?!"

Kiara looked at Blackburne, who looked mildly amused. Men! Her dad and Jax were still shouting at each other, and Kiara thought they were going to come to blows at any moment. She'd had enough, weren't they supposed to be figuring out what to do about keeping her safe, not fighting with each other? She looked down at Elvis, and grinned wickedly at him. He mimicked her grin with something that looked more like a snarl. Gathering a small amount of power, she sent a bubble of energy toward her dad and Jax, and when it reached them, she expanded it between them with a forceful 'pop'. The force knocked both men back a couple of steps, and cut off their shouting instantly. Her dad hit the side of the bed and almost fell on it, and Jax fell back into Blackburne, which wiped the amusement from Blackburne's face. Everyone turned to look at Kiara. At the intense looks, she started to shrink back into her chair. Telling herself to be strong, she sat up straight again.

"Maybe we should work together on this instead of fighting with each other?"

It surprised Kiara when all the men looked sheepish for a second. She looked at her dad. "What else do you know?"

When Jax opened his mouth to start in again, Kiara sent him a warning look that had his mouth snapping shut.

"Just some rumors going around that your help in a couple of battles have caught the attention of some at the GTA and the Rangers," Kyle said.

"That's a good thing, isn't it?" Kiara asked. She looked at Blackburne before looking at her dad. "Why is that bad?"

"Blackburne and I have been trading theories back and forth about possible corruption in the GTA," Kyle told the group. "They would have access to the transgates, to the Rangers, and with the right people, unlimited access to ships and weaponry. If you posed a threat to that plan, they would want you gone."

"Then we need to question that guy that Stryker's men have." Kiara looked at everyone. They were all nodding their agreement, but nobody was moving. "I mean, now, all of us."

"What?!" All four men shouted at once.

"Let's all go," Kiara said calmly.

"Absolutely not!"

"No!"

Jax and her dad voiced their objections, Blackburne just tried to frown his objection at her. Frankie, however, turned out to be her ally in this.

"You know," Frankie said, "maybe we should take her. If they were told to kill her, they are probably thinking it was for a good reason. We could use it to our advantage, scare him into talking."

"Yes!" Kiara said.

"We just got you back here safe and sound, and now you want us to put you back into danger?" Jax growled at her.

"Look, I'm feeling better, as you can tell, and besides, I'll have all of you to help keep me safe."

"This could work," Blackburne said. Kyle still looked doubtful, but in the end, Kiara and Frankie convinced them.

Everyone gathered outside the ship and Kiara started to laugh.

"Why are you laughing? This is a serious matter," Her dad admonished her.

"Look, Dad," she pointed to the group standing around her. "The whole space station is going to know something is going on."

Kyle looked around, and he, too, started to laugh. The whole crew, including the three Bendanites, were standing around Kiara, and everyone had a mean look on their face. Blackburne and Frankie were armed, the Bendanites were all growling and showing their teeth, and

Jax was in a combat-ready stance, his baton out and ready to be used.

"Okay, I see what you mean," Kyle told Kiara. "Perhaps we should limit the number of people that go on this little adventure?"

"Good idea," Kiara told him.

It wasn't easy to convince some of them not to go. Everyone wanted to go and protect Kiara, and most of them wanted a turn at beating the guy to a pulp. Kyle managed to convince Frankie and the Bendanites to stay behind and keep an eye on the Acadia. He was worried that the ship and its crew would also become targets. It helped Frankie to know that he wasn't just being dismissed. Kiara went up to him to thank him, but his words made her laugh.

"I'm better off staying here anyway, Kiara. I'm a lover, not a fighter. I'd probably lose my lunch at the first sign of trouble or blood."

Jax followed the directions he received, arriving at a locked door in a less populated area of the space station. The locks were disengaged almost as soon as they reached the door, so Kiara supposed that whoever was on the other side was keeping an eye out for them. The first person she saw as they entered was a Volterran, which surprised her. Typically, Volterrans didn't get involved in conflicts or violence of any kind. The reptilian-like race was intelligent and multitasking, and she wondered at the Volterran's role in all of this. Jax exchanged greetings with him, and they all entered. Jax had told them on the way that no names were going to be exchanged, so Kiara knew she wouldn't get any more information about him. They followed a narrow, dimly lit hallway, and at the end of the hallway, the Volterran opened another door, and gestured for them to enter. Her dad entered first, followed by Blackburne, then

Kiara, with Jax entering last before getting a few last-minute instructions from the Volterran.

As Kiara entered, she was surprised to see another, smaller Volterran in the room, standing next to a man strapped to a chair. She instantly realized that the Volterran in this room was female. She opened her mouth to ask a question, and was instantly cut off by the sound coming from Elvis, who was on her shoulder. A strange, growling noise was coming from him; his teeth were bared and the little claws on his front feet were sticking out. He looked ready to attack at any moment. Kiara realized that he recognized the man in the chair, and she quickly reached up and grabbed him before he did something. The blood that he had on him when she woke up flashed through her mind, and she shuddered.

"Elvis, we need him, for now."

The man in the chair shook his head to clear it, and opened one swollen eye. He peered at everyone in the room, and a gurgling snicker came from him.

"What's this, reinforcements?" He snickered again, and immediately began coughing up blood.

Kiara could see his blood was red, so she knew he wasn't a Galdorian. She saw that besides the damage done to his face, one leg appeared to be broken at the ankle, and his left shoulder was most likely dislocated. She stepped forward so she was in his line of sight. Seeing Kiara, he spit at her, his disgust at seeing her alive evident on his face. Jax stepped forward, his baton ready to strike the man, but Kiara help up her hand and stopped him.

Jax looked at her and smiled. The spit from the man was hovering in a protection field in front of Kiara. She was definitely advancing quickly.

The man, clearly surprised, was staring at Kiara, his apprehension now apparent.

"We need to know who sent you," Kiara said quietly.

The man, still staring at his spit floating in front of him, shook his head.

Kiara took a deep breath, building her power. Her skin turned a dark blue, her eyes started to glow. The man began to whimper, his terror at the unknown beginning to crack his resolve. Kiara guessed that men like this were used to dealing with beatings and physical pain, and she hoped that scaring him with something that looked like magic might have a better result. She watched his pupils dilate, and bloody spit began to run down his chin. She released a small amount of power, tilting the man and his chair backward. Before he could hit the floor, she pulsed some energy behind and had him sitting up straight again.

"We need to know who sent you." This time, as Kiara asked him, her voice shook with the power she was holding.

The man was starting to shake violently, and she watched as he lost control of his bladder. Still, he shook his head no, but Kiara could sense he was breaking. Almost there.

Concentrating hard, as she didn't want to permanently maim him or kill him, she held up her hand, and heard his breath catch. She opened up an energy bubble inside his mouth, about the size of a grape. Panicking, he began to struggle against the restraints. She increased the size of the bubble slightly. His movements became more frantic. She bent over, her face close to his. He stopped struggling, his one open eye locked onto hers.

"I'm still learning how to do this, so I'm going to apologize now if I explode your head."

He began whimpering again. She saw from the look in his eye that she only needed to do it one more time and he would probably tell them whatever they wanted to know. She increased the bubble again, and she saw it physically open his mouth wider.

"We need to know who sent you."

This time, he nodded, and when she released the bubble in his mouth, he exhaled with relief, with more bloody spit flowing down his chin.

Jax stepped forward. "Tell us. Now."

"I don't have a name," he blubbered out.

Kiara stepped forward, panicking him.

"Truly, I don't have a name, they never told me."

"Who are they?" Jax asked.

"My buddies and I usually fly the Mercenary ships. They replaced most of us with CyRAINs, so we were looking for any work we could get. One of my contacts said I could get a big paycheck for getting rid of someone."

Wow, Kiara thought. Once he opened up, he really opened up.

"Who put you in contact with John? Was it someone from Galdor?" Jax demanded.

"Galdor? No. I was told it was some high-ranking official at the GTA."

Kyle stepped forward this time. "Who was it?"

The man looked around the group. When he didn't answer right away, Kiara stepped forward again and raised one hand. He immediately started blubbering again about conspiracies, being kept in the dark, and something bigger than just Kiara. He finally gave them the only name he knew, his contact that started this series of events. When he stopped talking, and it became apparent that he'd told them everything he knew, Kiara left the room. The adrenaline and intensity of the last few minutes was beginning to take its toll. She was starting to shake, and she was pretty sure that whatever was left in her stomach was going to end up on the floor. She was glad she didn't have to do this every day. Give her the bridge of a ship and a navunit any day.

Elvis, sitting on her shoulder, was combing the loose hair back from her face while Kiara tried to breathe through the nausea. She heard footsteps behind her and turned to see Jax coming toward her. He didn't say anything, just wrapped his arms around her, letting his strength and warmth seep into her.

When the shaking finally stopped, she stepped back and looked up into his dark face.

"Thank-you."

He nodded.

"I'm not cut out for this kind of thing."

"You fooled everyone in there, especially the man we needed answers from."

"But not you."

"Not me."

Kiara smiled, for the first time in what felt like years. Jax, seeing the smile, knew she was going to be okay.

Chapter Nine

Back on the Acadia, the group got together on the bridge to discuss what they'd discovered so far. Kiara didn't think they had much. John had gotten away, and it appeared that someone in the GTA had sanctioned her murder. They still needed to consider the matter of the Galdorians that wanted her dead. They had a name of someone to pursue, but from what they could glean from their captive, the person they were looking for wasn't on this space station, or even in this sector. Different strategies were discussed—should they try to go after John on their own? Should they pull in the Rangers or the GTA? Then there was the pesky matter of working. None of them could afford to go very long without a job, except Jax. He was already working for free on the Acadia, and from her conversations with him, she learned that he got his money from those who helped the Trandorians.

"I don't know who we can trust," Kyle told the group.

"Agreed," Blackburne said.

Frankie was pacing around the bridge, his frustration evident in his movements. "We can't just sit around and wait for them to strike again, either."

Discussions continued, with no real consensus on what to do. Jax had contacted Stryker about trying to find the Mercenary contact, but that was as far as anything had progressed. Blackburne suddenly looked down at his com unit, and asked the group to quiet down. Moving to the far side of the bridge, he answered the call. Kiara couldn't tell who he was talking with, but from the sound of it, Blackburne was being asked to take on a job. When he came back to the group, his face looked grim.

"Well, part of our decision has been made for us." Blackburne looked at Kyle. "We're being asked to make another cargo run for the Rangers."

Kyle stood, his agitation apparent. "Did they mention anything about John?"

"As a matter of fact, they did," Blackburne responded. "They know that he's been accused of being involved in a kidnapping and attempted murder plot. The call was from the DG Ranger himself, and he apologized for assigning us a Ranger that was a possible traitor."

Kyle stopped pacing. "We just don't know if he can be trusted. If a high-ranking official in the GTA is corrupt, there could be corruption in the Rangers as well."

"I agree Kyle, but I'm afraid we don't really have a choice," Blackburne said, looking just as agitated as Kyle. "We need to keep working. If we're going to discover who is behind this, I don't think we should tip our hand just yet that we know some of what's going on."

Kyle nodded at Blackburne's statement and turned to Jax. "Not exactly what you thought you were signing up for?"

Jax, with a fierce grin, replied, "My experience has been that this kind of power—," he gestured toward Kiara, "brings out more than the Galdorians."

Kiara actually groaned.

"I think we need to take this job, but we'll go in suspecting to run into more than our fair share of trouble. Kyle, you won't be able to come with us, it'll draw too much attention."

"Agreed." Kyle looked at Jax. "Keep her safe." At the nod from Jax, he continued, "Maybe I'll go do some hunting of my own."

"I would like to go with you—John will need to pay dearly for his treachery. However, I will need to stay with

Kiara," Jax said as he brought up his com unit. "I will do the next-best thing." He entered some data into his com unit before looking up at Kyle. "I believe Stryker may enjoy a hunting trip as well."

Kyle nodded his thanks to Jax, and went to where Kiara was still sitting with Elvis. He looked at the little drayek, his hand reaching out to touch him. "He helps you, and he protects you."

"I know."

"Ask Jax to tell you what happened when he went into the room where they were holding you," Kyle said as he scratched the top of the little drayek's head. "I didn't know they were capable of that kind of violence, so I'm glad he's on our side. Reminds me of an Earth dog called a German Shepherd. Great with kids in the family, but protective as hell."

"I will." Kiara stood and grabbed her dad in a fierce hug. "Please be careful."

"You be careful, too. I love you, little one."

With her dad and Stryker out hunting John and the Mercenary contact, the Acadia crew readied for their next cargo run. Kiara programmed their route through the transgate and sent it to Frankie.

"Kiara, are you up for this? You haven't had a moment to catch your breath since we rescued you," Blackburne said from behind her.

Kiara turned to him. "I'm okay. I got some food when we got back on the ship, so I'm starting to feel more normal." She shrugged slightly, still uncomfortable with being the center of attention. "Jax also gave me something to help even out the drug that knocked me out and the drug that woke me up. Between the two drugs, I was feeling jittery, but sleepy."

"Better now, though? We're going to need everyone at their best."

"I'm good."

Blackburne nodded and went back to his station. As they approached the first transgate, Kiara completed her scan, gave the all clear to Frankie, and monitored their status as they entered the transgate. They were headed to a bigger space station a couple of sectors away to pick up supplies, before dropping them off at an area that was currently cut off from supply routes. They were to meet their Ranger escorts at the space station.

Traffic was light, and they made it to the space station with no complications. While they waited to load up, Blackburne ordered Kiara to get some rest. She was happy to follow those orders since she was so exhausted. As she headed down the corridor to her cabin, Jax was approaching her from the other direction.

"Taking a break?"

"Yes," Kiara answered. She could also feel the exhaustion coming from Elvis. The little guy was curled up tight in her arms. When she looked down at him, his eyes were already closed. She sighed. He was sleeping already.

Jax smiled. "You two need it. We'll keep an eye on things while you catch up on your rest. I believe we have a few hours here?"

"Yes, that's what Blackburne told me. See you in a few," Kiara said on a yawn.

Kiara fell asleep as soon as her head hit the pillow, and fortunately, didn't have any dreams to interrupt the sleep she so desperately needed. When she woke, she could feel the slight vibration of the ship that told her the engines were doing more than idling, and wondered why no one had contacted her to come up on the bridge. Sitting up in the bunk, she still felt a little groggy, and checking her com unit, discovered that she'd been asleep for nearly four hours. She looked down at Elvis, stretching and blinking sleepily up at her. Kiara quickly cleaned up and changed her clothes, and sent a quick message to Blackburne that she was on her way up to the bridge. She checked their location, and saw that they were on their way to the next transgate, and would be there in a couple of hours. She was just about to head out, but hesitated. She still felt listless and tired. Thinking perhaps she had missed taking her supplements, she turned back around and grabbed some, along with some chocolate, and headed to the bridge.

Blackburne turned and looked at Kiara as she entered the bridge. His frown turned more severe as he watched her walk to her station. Something wasn't right. He looked over at Frankie, but Frankie was looking down at his console and didn't see her come in. Still frowning, his gaze went back to Kiara. Her skin color was lighter than usual, her gait slightly uneven. His eyes moved to Elvis. The little drayek was the same light color as Kiara, and the little guy looked drained as well. Did this have something to do with Kiara using her powers? Was she still tired? He watched her sit down a little unsteadily, so he made his way over to her.

"Kiara, are you feeling okay?" Blackburne asked her.

Kiara looked up at him, her face a pale blue, her eyes a little glazed. "I think maybe I'm still tired. I slept really well, but I feel as if I can't wake up all the way."

"Let's go to the med-bay and check you out. Maybe you're having a reaction to the all the medications you've been given."

"I just took some of my supplements, and I think I'm starting to feel better. Maybe we can go later if I'm still feeling tired?"

Blackburne considered ordering her to the med-bay, but decided there was no harm in waiting. He'd help keep an eye on her. He thought about sending a quick message to Jax, but decided he might be overreacting. Jax was still trying to catch up on his sleep, and he didn't want to bother him unnecessarily. He walked over to Frankie, and in a quiet voice got him up to speed on his worry about Kiara so they could both keep an eye on her. Frankie agreed that she still looked tired, but neither seemed to know what to do about it.

Kiara, unaware that Blackburne and Frankie were talking about her, was checking the latest scans of the area, and realized that she was starting to feel a little bit better. Perhaps using her powers as much as she did earlier had drained her, especially after being drugged and nearly killed. She smiled down at Elvis, earning a quiet chirp from him. He was starting to look a little perkier as well. She turned to look at Blackburne.

"Where's Jax?"

"It's his turn to take some downtime," Blackburne said while he studied her face. Her color was starting to come back, and her eyes were starting to clear. "How's our scan looking?"

"Everything's clear."

Kiara sent a message to her dad, letting him know that she was all right, and asking how his hunting was going. She received a quick reply that he was okay, but they hadn't found anything yet.

A few hours later, as they approached the transgate, Kiara checked her scans, and contacted Transgate Control. Receiving the normal response, and getting a clear scan, she sent the navigation information to Frankie. Her earlier recovery seemed to be fading again, and thinking that perhaps she needed more supplements, she told Blackburne she was going to her cabin for a minute.

Halfway down the corridor, she started to feel a little shaky. By the time she reached her cabin, she felt as if she could barely stand. She quickly took her supplement, and sat down on the bunk. Her cabin was empty; Curly was probably in the cargo area with the other two Bendanites. She waited a few minutes to see whether the supplement would work like last time and perk her up. Looking down at Elvis, she saw that he was curled into a ball in her lap, his eyes closed. Becoming alarmed, she tried to stand, but her body didn't want to obey her. Her skin looked almost transparent now, and she panicked that whatever was wrong with her was affecting Elvis. That little bit of adrenaline saved her life. It gave her just enough of a jump that she was able to hit her com unit and send a distress message to Jax. She slumped over in her bunk, one hand holding Elvis, the other on her com unit.

Jax had just finished eating and was heading to the bridge when his com unit went off with the emergency message from Kiara. He sprinted down the hallway to her cabin, his confusion over what could have happened while they were on the ship evident on his face. He reached Kiara's cabin, but the door was locked. He began pounding on the door, yelling Kiara's name, but he didn't get a response. The locater in her com unit said she was in there, but she wasn't answering. He grabbed his com unit and told Blackburne to override the lock on the door. He could tell from Frankie's response in the background that they were about to enter the transgate. He yelled to hold their position, and roared for Blackburne to override the lock on Kiara's door. His panic was escalating with every moment that he couldn't get into the room. What could have happened? He knew that no one had gotten on the ship unnoticed. Did they have another traitor on board?

Finally, he heard the locks disengage, at the same moment that he could hear Blackburne running down the short corridor toward him. He slammed the door open and saw Kiara slumped on her bunk, still holding Elvis. They were both so pale; he feared they might be dead. Jumping forward he grabbed them and turned back to the doorway, his intent to get them to the med-bay. With her in his arms, he could feel her heartbeat, but it was slow, and very faint. Was this a delayed reaction from the drug that John had given her? Blackburne reached the room and Jax yelled for him to make way so he could get her to the med-bay. They sprinted down the hallway to the med-bay. Blackburne put her in the diagnostic scan and they anxiously waited for it to tell them what was wrong. Suddenly, the ship seemed to shudder and shake and they could hear explosions.

"What the hell?" Blackburne bellowed.

Frankie's voice came over the ships' com. "We're under attack. I could use a little help up here."

Blackburne and Jax exchanged looks. The timing of the attack, right when something was wrong with Kiara, was more than a coincidence.

"I've got this," Jax said to Blackburne. "Go help Frankie. As soon as I stabilize her, I'll come up and help."

Blackburne didn't hesitate; he spun on his heel and shot from the room. The ship was still shaking and shuddering, and Jax was trying to will the scan to finish. It finally finished, telling him that Kiara had poison in her system. He looked through the small med-bay for the antidote, but it wasn't there. The poison was obviously something not well-known, and since the med-bay was small on this ship, it didn't stock everything. He asked the computer for alternatives, and found something that would stabilize her, but they still needed the antidote. He administered what he could, and watched her breathing and heart rate come up slightly and level off. Knowing it was all he could do for now, he strapped her into the bed so all the shaking wouldn't knock her on the floor, and headed to the bridge, connecting his com unit to the med-bay so he could continue to monitor her.

He walked in on chaos and panic. Frankie was trying to maneuver them around while Blackburne was firing at the ships, but Jax could tell at a glance that they were outnumbered and outgunned. Blackburne was sending out a mayday, but they weren't getting any kind of response back. He jumped into Kiara's seat and helped fire the weapons, but the ship was taking too many hits. He could see the shields were nearly gone, and the enemy fire had already disabled one of the Acadia's engines. He kept firing, hoping beyond hope that help would arrive, or his promise to keep Kiara safe was going to be broken.

Back in the med-bay, Kiara was floating in a hazy, white cloud, and she felt as if something was keeping her eyes and mouth shut. She could hear someone saying her name, but couldn't make out who it was. Maybe she should just go back to sleep? She needed sleep, didn't she? A resounding 'No!' entered her head, causing her head to hurt, and the beautiful white cloud started to disintegrate. Her eyelids felt so heavy, she just wanted to keep her eyes closed and go back to the beautiful, soft, white cloud. She heard her name again, and this time, she recognized Mirona, her ancestor, as the one calling her.

> *Kiara!*
> *Mirona?*
> *Kiara, you must wake up!*
> *But I need to sleep. I'm so tired.*
> *You are in danger! You must wake up!*

Danger? No. It's so beautiful and peaceful here.

Kiara! You have been poisoned! You will die if you don't wake up!

No.

Elvis will die!

Elvis?

Yes! Elvis will die! You must wake up!

No!

Yes! He will die if you don't wake up!

I can't! Please help me Mirona!

Kiara, you can do this on your own. Use your power. Find the poison in your body.

How? Please help me!

Focus Kiara! Focus! Find the poison!

"Blackburne! The shields are gone!" Jax yelled.

They watched as the attacking ships circled back, and Jax knew that he had failed in his promise.

The enemy ships fired, but nothing happened. Jax and Blackburne looked at each other, before turning and looking at Frankie.

All three, in unison, yelled, "Kiara!"

Jax didn't know how she was doing it, but he was going to take advantage of it. He continued firing on the enemy, hoping Kiara had bought them enough time. Between himself and Blackburne, they were destroying of few of the enemy ships, but it didn't seem to be enough. Suddenly, weapons fire came from another area behind them, and Kyle's voice came over the ship's com. Kyle had a ship more suited for battle, and his entry into the fray turned the tide. Blackburne was yelling maneuvering instructions for both pilots, keeping Kyle out in front to take most of the weapons fire. Kyle's ship also had better weaponry, and he was taking out ship after ship.

With the last ship destroyed, Frankie took them back toward the space station. Kyle went with them, making sure there were no other enemy ships in the area. As Jax sprinted back to the med-bay to check on Kiara, he could hear Kyle's voice over the intercom asking about Kiara and why she wasn't answering her com unit. Unsure of what he would see when he entered the med-bay, Jax entered and found Kiara was sitting up in the bed. Still looking a little pale, the monitors still hooked up to her showed normal breathing and heart rate. At his entrance into the room, Kiara smiled a shaky smile.

"Are we okay?" Kiara asked, her voice barely above a whisper.

"Yes, Kiara, we're okay, thanks to you," Jax responded with a relieved smile.

Jax ran the scan again, and looked at Kiara with a puzzled look on his face. "I can't find evidence of the poison." He ran the scan again, just to be sure.

Blackburne joined them in the med-bay. "Kiara, are you okay?" He turned to Jax. "What happened to her?"

"I'm okay," Kiara responded.

"She was poisoned." Jax said at the same time.

"Poisoned? When did that happen? Was it from the drug that John gave her?"

Kiara watched them looking at the computer scan and postulating on where the poison came from, and what had happened to it. She looked down at Elvis. He still looked tired, so she closed her eyes and connected with him, wanting to make sure he wasn't still suffering from the effects of the poison. She could only detect exhaustion. She opened her eyes and realized that the room had gone quiet. Turning her head, she saw Jax and Blackburne looking at her.

"I'm okay, really."

A slight jarring signaled that the Acadia had landed in the space station dock.

"Where are we? Did we make it through the transgate?" Kiara asked. She swung her legs off the side of the bed, intending to get up.

"Whoa, whoa," Blackburne came over and put his hand on her shoulder. "Hang tight for just a moment. We need to figure out what happened to the poison. If it comes back, it could take you out again."

Kiara opened her mouth to tell them what happened with the poison, but was interrupted by the loud voice of her dad yelling her name. He must have just boarded the Acadia and was looking for her.

"Maybe you should tell my dad where I am, and that I'm okay? I don't seem to have my com unit, and it sounds like he's going to tear the ship apart."

Kyle was still bellowing, so Jax quickly sent him a message. The bellowing cut off in mid-shout, and a few seconds later, Kyle charged into the room. He saw Kiara sitting on the side of the bed, and rushed over to envelop her in a hug.

"Thank God, thank God." He squeezed her one more time before he let go of her. "Are you okay?"

"I'm okay." At his doubtful look, she said it again. "Really, I'm okay."

"She was poisoned," Jax said quietly.

"Poisoned?!" Kyle was back to shouting again at Jax's statement.

Jax explained how he found her in her room, and the poison they discovered with the scan. Blackburne interjected that she hadn't looked well before that, so the poison must have been in her system for a while. They were all almost shouting again, their confusion over what happened to her making their anxiety that mush worse. When they finally wound down and everyone turned to look at her, she calmly pointed to a spot on the wall. A greenish liquid was splattered on the wall about four feet up from the floor.

"That's the poison," she told them.

Blackburne and Jax both walked over to it while her dad made a disgusted face.

"How did it get there?" Her dad asked.

"I threw it there. I managed to somehow wrap my power around it, bring it out, and throw it over there." She looked around the room at the incredulous looks. Kiara looked down, a sheepish look on her face. "I had a little help from Mirona."

"Your ancestor?" Jax asked.

Kiara nodded.

"Can we test it; figure out how she got it?" Kyle asked.

Blackburne nodded and scraped some off the wall and stuck it into the med-bay scanner. They waited, somewhat impatiently, for the computer to tell them something. While they waited, Jax told them the result of the first scan which had found the poison, and that the ship didn't have the necessary antidote to help Kiara. He was only able to stabilize her when the battle had started. The computer signaled the end of the analysis, and Blackburne and Jax crowded around the screen to read the results. They both stood at the same time and turned to Kiara.

Blackburne delivered the news. "It was in your supplements."

"My supplements? How did it get there?"

"I'll go get them from your cabin, we'll see if we can figure it out," Kyle told her. "I have some extra with me, I'll get those so we can start building your system back up," Kyle said as he headed out.

Kiara turned to Jax and Blackburne. "Who attacked us?"

"Mercenary ships," Blackburne told her.

"Was the ship damaged?"

"Yes, we took some pretty heavy damage," Blackburne said. He turned and headed for the door. "Frankie and I will get started on the repairs. Setup or not, we'll need to get the cargo delivered as soon as possible."

"Are Curly and the others okay?" Kiara asked Jax.

"Yes, the cargo bay is intact. Our damage was mostly to the engines and shield generator."

Kiara sighed. They managed to make it through another attack that was aimed at her, and she felt responsible. Jax, of course, was tuned into her feelings.

"This is not your fault."

"You say that, but if it wasn't for me on this ship, none of it would have happened."

"Actually, you don't know that. With all the trouble at the transgates and the Mercenary ships, possible corruption in the GTA and Rangers, it's possible it has more to do with that than you."

Kiara smiled, realizing that he was trying to make her feel better. Her dad walked back in, gave her the supplements that he had for her, and gave the others to Jax to test. He also had some food for her, and Kiara realized she was famished. While she and Elvis ate, the computer analyzed the supplements from her cabin. It only took a few minutes, but they had their answer. They determined which batch was poisoned, and Kiara remembered where she had bought it at. Jax contacted Stryker to see if they could find surveillance of when the supplements were contaminated, but he didn't have much hope.

"Dad, how did you join up with us so quickly? I thought you were with Stryker, looking for John and that other guy."

"I was, but the more Stryker and I talked about it, the more we thought that this cargo run was a setup. I started heading for your position as fast as I could, with Stryker continuing the hunt on his own."

"I'm glad you got here when you did."

"Me, too."

"There is one thing that bothers me, though," Kyle said to Jax.

"What's that?"

"I heard the mayday from Blackburne, but I don't understand why the space station didn't respond and send help. They have defense systems and fighters stationed here, and were well within range to help."

"I thought of this as well," Jax responded. "Perhaps we should go aboard the space station and investigate it further?"

"Let's get Blackburne and see if we can get some answers," Kyle told Jax. He turned to Kiara. After eating and getting her supplements, her normal blue color was back, and even Elvis looked better. He smiled his relief.

"You look quite a bit better," Kyle told her. "Feeling up to helping with repairs? I'll get Curly to help keep an eye on you."

Kiara rolled her eyes. She hated feeling as if she needed a babysitter, but, after the last couple of incidents, maybe she did need one. She stood up from the bed, hoping her legs would hold steady, or else her dad probably wouldn't leave her side. To her relief, she felt steady when she stood up, and she could tell that Elvis felt better as well, when he hopped up to her shoulder with his usual enthusiasm.

Satisfied that she was okay, Kyle left his daughter with Curly and Frankie working on ship repairs, while he, Blackburne and Jax headed into the space station. Kyle used his Ranger credentials to get them in to see the head of security for the space station. At first, they were stonewalled with every question they asked. It wasn't until Kyle made a call to the DG Ranger that they shook something loose. The head of security showed them an encrypted message, origin unknown, detailing the space station's role in the attack. In return for the space station not responding during the attack, the message promised safety for the space station, and the future safety of the transgate. With word of other attacks spreading, and the fear of loss of life and being cutoff, it was an easy decision for the space station to take the deal. Kyle sent a copy of the message, over the very loud protests of the head of security, to Kiara. Out of all of them, she had the most computer experience, and if anyone could help figure out who sent the message it would be her. If they could use the resources of the GTA or the Rangers, they would definitely be able to figure it out, but this way, no one would know they were looking.

The three headed back to the Acadia, feeling as if they had gotten all the information that they were going to get.

"We need to keep the logistics for the rest of this cargo run just with the crew. We can't risk another ambush," Blackburne told Jax and Kyle.

"Did you check the cargo you picked up this time? Was there anything in it that would potentially bring on this kind of attack?" Kyle wanted to know.

"I thought of that, as well," Blackburne said. "We completed the standard check of the cargo as we loaded, and nothing flagged as potentially harmful, or worth this kind of attack."

"It still circles back to Kiara," Kyle said.

They reached the Acadia, and found the crew hard at work. The damaged panels on the outer hull had been replaced, and the work was now concentrated inside. They found Frankie on the bridge, running through diagnostics on the engines.

"Where's Kiara?" Jax asked him.

"Curly and Elvis are with her—she's recalibrating the shield generator. We got the new components for it right after you left."

The three headed back to where Kiara was working on the shield generator. The shield generator was accessible by a small panel in the hallway near the engines and cargo area. Kiara had her head buried in the panel, with Elvis sitting on her stomach, and Curly standing watch in the hallway. At their approach, Elvis sat up and chirped at them, alerting Kiara that someone was approaching.

"Who is it, Curly?"

"Your father, the captain, and Jax."

Kiara scooted out from the panel, space dust covering her face and hair, giving her a silver glow. She smiled at her dad, glad to see everyone back. "I got the file you sent me, but I didn't get a chance to look at it. What did you send me?" she asked him.

"It's a message from an unknown party, to the space station, outlining the space station's role in the attack on the Acadia. They didn't know who sent it. We were hoping you could take a look and see if you could find anything," Kyle told her as he reached down to help her up.

"The space station was told not to help us?" Kiara looked from her dad to Jax to Blackburne, getting a nod from each of them. "That's really scary. Who has that kind of power?"

"They scared them into doing it. They were told they wouldn't be protected from the next attacks if they didn't do it," Kyle said grimly.

"Still, that seems like they took the coward's way out," Kiara said with a frown.

"I agree," Jax said quietly. "But they were thinking not only of themselves, but all those in the space station."

Kiara nodded. She still didn't like it. "I'm almost done with the shield generator, why don't I look at it when I'm finished?

Blackburne nodded. "I'll go get an update on the rest of the repairs from Frankie." He headed back to the bridge, taking Kyle with him.

Kiara looked at Jax, and suddenly felt self-conscious about the dirt in her hair and on her clothes.

He thought she looked adorable.

Curly turned and lumbered into the cargo area, after first making sure Jax was going to stay with Kiara.

"Can I help you with the shield generator?" Jax asked into the quiet.

"It's really a one-person job," Kiara said, getting back down onto her back and scooting into the access panel. "I'm almost done anyway. The weapons fire took out a few circuits; everything else was in good shape."

"Are you still feeling okay? No residual effects from the poison?"

"Nothing so far," Kiara's muffled voice came from inside the panel.

Jax watched her plug in a diagnostic module, swipe the screen, and key in a few commands. The inside of the panel lit up a few times as the commands executed. She ran a few more commands, and contacted Frankie to connect and bring up the shields. When she received the okay from Frankie, she scooted back out of the access panel and with a quick touch to Elvis, closed the panel back up.

"So, are you going to be my babysitter for a while?"

"Babysitter?" Jax wasn't familiar with that term.

"You know, someone in charge of watching the kids while the parents are away?"

Jax frowned. "Why do you think that?"

"Maybe I'm a little grumpy from all the poisoning." Kiara sighed. "I sound like a whiny kid, so I guess it's only fitting that I have a babysitter."

Jax, getting into the spirit of it, asked her, "Does the babysitter feed the kids?"

Kiara laughed. "Yes, I think both kids are hungry." She grabbed the hand that Jax extended to and gained her feet. "Let me go get some of this space dust off, and I'll meet you in the kitchen, okay?"

Jax nodded and Kiara fairly ran to her cabin, feeling lighter in spirit than she had in quite some time. Elvis, riding on her shoulder, caught her good mood, and chirped all the way to the cabin. Changing her clothes, she put on a dark-purple tunic over her skinsuit, and silently hoped Jax would notice how it matched her eyes. She knew he was trying to keep his distance from her since he was in charge of keeping her safe and training her, but she wanted to explore this a little bit more. She headed for the kitchen, and on the way, remembered the message that her dad had sent to her. She'd look at it while she got something to eat with Jax.

When she arrived at the kitchen, Jax already had some food pulled out, and had set a small bowl with Elvis' favorite fruit in it at one end of the table. Elvis smelled the fruit when they entered the kitchen, and with a loud chirp, jumped from Kiara's shoulder to the table to start eating.

Kiara laughed. "I think he was really hungry!"

Jax gestured for her to sit while he put more food on the table in front of her. She smiled when he placed an unopened container of Coke in front of her. She was grateful that he not only remembered that she liked Coke, but that John had drugged her with Coke, so he had left it to her to open the container. Everyone ate hungrily for a while; the only sound was the slurping noise coming from Elvis eating his fruit. It made Kiara smile, and looking over at Jax, she could tell that the noise wasn't bothering him either.

Finally slowing down, Kiara pulled out her com unit and brought up the message that the space station had received. She studied it for a few seconds before dropping it.

"Did you see something?" Jax asked her.

"Not really. I need to connect to the main computer so I can dig into the message some more."

With a few swipes of her com unit, she connected to the main ship computer, brought the message back up, and began digging into it. It only took her a few seconds to get the information she needed. She dropped the message again, and turned to look at Jax. "It was someone at the GTA."

"You could see that?"

"Yes. Let's get Blackburne and my dad, and then I can explain it to everyone."

They took a quick second to clean up their mess before heading to the bridge. Kiara sent a quick message to her dad and Blackburne to meet them there. As soon as they entered the bridge, Blackburne demanded to know if she had found anything. Kiara watched Jax frown at the demand, but Kiara knew that it was just the captain's way of doing things.

"I can tell the message came from someone in the GTA. That's about all I can tell. It could be the head of the GTA, it could be an assistant."

"Is there any way to get more information?" Her dad wanted to know.

"Actually, yes. I found some coding in the message that corresponds to the origination of the message, but as near as I can tell, it's coding that's internal to the GTA."

"What does that mean?" Jax wanted to know.

"It means that if I can get into the building that the message originated at, I can tell which office it came from."

"Do you know which building?" Blackburne asked.

"No."

Blackburne frowned. Kyle looked thoughtful; Frankie and Jax looked slightly impressed.

"What if we got you into a GTA building, could you get more information on where to go, or do we need to get into the exact building it originated at?" Kyle asked her.

Kiara thought about her dad's question, and pulled up the message in her memory. Her excitement began to build.

"You know, I think I can get the building location from any GTA building. If I can connect to their internal network, I can get the codes for the buildings. Then we can get to the right building, and I can do that again, but this time, get the exact office." She looked excitedly around the room. Jax was now frowning, as was Blackburne, but Frankie looked excited. Her dad still looked thoughtful.

Blackburne, still frowning, brought up the doubt and fears that everyone was thinking. "How the hell are we going to get into the GTA and connect to their network without getting detected? If someone at the GTA is doing this, they're going to be looking for us."

"It'll take some planning, and I'll probably need to call in some favors, maybe Jax will need to call in some as well, but I think we can do it." Kyle looked at everyone, his eyes resting on Kiara. "I don't want to do this anymore than you do Blackburne, but we can't go on this way either. Always expecting an attack, trying to do everything we can to keep Kiara alive." He took a deep breath. "There's an old Earth saying, 'the best defense is a good offense'. We need to take the fight to them. I don't think they'll be expecting that. And if Kiara is getting as good as I think she is, we might just succeed."

Kyle looked around at everyone. Blackburne was now looking thoughtful, Jax was still frowning.

"I don't like this plan," Jax finally said. "I don't know how I can keep Kiara safe."

Kyle could tell that he was still reliving Kiara's near death twice now. Jax took his responsibility for keeping her safe seriously, but Kyle was also suspecting that there were other feelings involved as well. Kyle tried to think of something to say to sway Jax to their plan, but Jax surprised him.

"However, as Kyle has said, we can't go on this way," Jax said, his voice resigned. "Kiara is different from others I have guarded and helped. Her powers have increased significantly in a short time, and she is not willing to go into hiding. Others I have helped have gone into hiding, or simply fell off the GTA and Galdorian radar, due to their way of life. Kiara is in a unique position to cause problems for whoever is masterminding these attacks. Perhaps if we expose that person, it will buy her some safety. I think it would be worth trying."

Kyle looked around the room again, and this time, everyone was nodding. "Okay, then," he said. "Let's plan this out."

Chapter Ten

Kiara sat on the floor of the flex-space, taking a break from her workout. She had discovered, during one of her holographic exercise sessions that Elvis liked to play chase with her. Sometimes she would chase him; sometimes she would let him chase her. Today, she had focused on getting in a good workout before she played chase with him. They were both on the floor, breathing hard, and she was scratching his tummy. He was making a noise that she thought was a cross between a cat's purr and a dog's growl. She knew it meant that he was enjoying the tummy rub. They both needed this. She and Elvis had regained their strength from nearly dying, and were working to get stronger and perfect the use of her powers. The plan to discover who was trying to kill her depended on her using her powers with no mistakes.

Elvis, sensing the change in her mood, sat up and crawled into her lap. Kiara stroked his ears, marveling again at the circumstances that had brought them together. She couldn't imagine life without him now. Still sitting on the floor, Kiara sensed that Jax was coming toward the flex-space. Jax had told her that other abilities might start to surface, and sensing the presence of others was one. She thought it was a good ability to have, it should help warn her if someone was approaching that wanted to harm her.

Jax entered the room and smiled at Kiara. They'd been holed up at this small space station in one of the outer quadrants, working on ship repairs, recuperating, and planning. They had arrived here after dropping off the last cargo shipment, deciding to chance the run while the ship wasn't completely repaired. They hadn't wanted to stay where they were, so close to where they were attacked. Kyle had thought of this space station, as it had a small GTA section in it. Security wasn't very tight due to the GTA presence here being more for ambassadorship than anything else. No high-ranking officials were stationed here, which made it that much more attractive to hit. The space station was small, but it was large enough for the Acadia to land in the holding dock.

Blackburne had told the space station that they needed to dock for repairs, and to help extend their time here without suspicion, he had ordered parts that weren't available on the space station. They'd been here about five days, with Blackburne and Kyle taking turns completing surveillance on the GTA offices, trying to determine the best way in. The repairs on the Acadia had been completed, so Kiara supposed they would go to the GTA offices soon.

Jax squatted down next to Kiara, still smiling, and reached out to fluff the tufts of hair on Elvis' head.

"We're going today, in about an hour," Jax told her.

"I figured." Kiara stood, moving Elvis to her shoulder. "I'll go get ready."

Jax nodded. "I'll wait for you on the bridge. Your dad discovered that in about an hour, the offices clear out while everyone goes to eat. There should only be a receptionist in the front."

Kiara nodded her acknowledgment and went to her cabin to get ready. She was anxious, but glad to finally be taking some action. She'd been hiding in the Acadia so when she and Jax went to the GTA, they wouldn't be recognized. Once she was ready, she headed up to the bridge. She looked around as she entered. Blackburne and Frankie were going over engine diagnostics at one of the computer consoles, and her dad was talking to Jax. At least Kiara thought it was Jax.

"Is that you, Jax?"

He grunted at her and Kiara laughed. He looked like Larry, the Bendanite, except slightly shorter. She was disguised as Curly. They hoped the height wouldn't be an issue for anyone monitoring them. They wouldn't be in the disguise for long.

"You okay in there, Elvis?" Kiara asked the little drayek. Hiding Elvis had been the hardest part of this plan. She hadn't been willing to go in without him, and truth be told, after nearly getting killed without him once, no one else had wanted her to go without him. He chirped at her from underneath the furry disguise, and Kiara smiled. She was probably a little bigger around than Curly really was, but it was the only place to hide the little guy. She adjusted her skinsuit and nodded at Jax. "Let's go."

They headed off the bridge after everyone wished them good luck, ready to put the plan into action. Blackburne let them know that the ship would be ready to leave once they were back on board.

Kiara and Jax had been practicing the lumbering walk that Bendanites were known for. They lumbered off the Acadia, with no one paying them any attention. They lumbered through the space station, pretending to look at shops that Bendanites would like. Kiara was glad her face was obscured by the fur, she knew that she wouldn't be able to keep the anxiety she was feeling from showing. They finally reached the GTA offices, and went in. As her dad predicted, the offices appeared empty, except a receptionist at the front desk. Kiara lumbered up to the desk.

"Can I help you?" The receptionist politely asked without even looking up.

"You can help to find family?" Kiara asked in her best Bendanite impression.

The receptionist finally looked up. "Oh, um, yes, we can help you find your family." She looked around a little uncertainly. "Can you work a computer console?" She looked pointedly at Kiara's large hands.

"Yes, yes, I can do."

"Oh, okay, can you come this way?" The receptionist, still looking uncertain, glanced at Jax. "Do you want to come with us?"

Jax grunted.

"This means no." Kiara told the receptionist. "He will want to stay here."

"Oh, okay." The receptionist looked completely out of her comfort zone, and Kiara thought it might work to their advantage. The receptionist took Kiara to a side room with a computer console. She started up the computer, put it on the appropriate screen, and left the room, closing the door behind her.

Kiara waited a few seconds before peeling back the fur from her fingers, just in case the receptionist came back in. She pulled out her com unit, checked the time again, and connected it to the console. With a few swipes, she overrode the system's security, and found the file she was looking for. She knew if she copied the file, it would set off alarms, so she merely found what she needed and memorized it. She looked at a few more files, just to throw someone off if they tried to backtrack where she went. She went back to the ancestry search screen, looked up a few family names, before leaving the screen on those. She knew that her bulk blocked the security camera behind her, so they wouldn't be able to see what she did. She put her fur fingers back on, stood up to leave, and patted Elvis inside her disguise.

Out in the lobby area, Jax had been pacing and pointing at the receptionist, making grunting noises.

Instead of trying to watch what Kiara was doing, the receptionist had been valiantly trying to figure out what the Bendanite in her lobby area needed. When Kiara came back out to the lobby, the receptionist nearly pounced on her.

"Please, he seems as if he needs something, but I can't tell what he needs!" The receptionist fairly wailed it at her.

Kiara walked quickly over to Jax and grabbed his hand. He immediately stopped moving.

"I have it," Kiara whispered.

Jax grunted at her.

Kiara turned to the receptionist.

"He was looking for me."

The receptionist, still looking slightly confused, nodded at them as they headed for the door.

Kiara and Jax left the lobby and headed back to the Acadia. Neither said anything, but Kiara could feel the tension from Jax. Elvis, too, was getting anxious to get out of the costume, but Kiara knew they had to go back to the Acadia the same way they left it, without hurrying. As they lumbered up into the Acadia, Blackburne and her dad were waiting.

"Well?" They both asked as soon as the ship closed up.

Kiara removed the mask from her face. "I got it. I'll send it to Frankie now." She hurried off and let Jax fill-in her dad and Blackburne. She entered the bridge to find Frankie ready at his station. Nodding at him, she entered the information into the navunit so Frankie could get them on their way. She could feel Elvis squirming and knew he needed to get out of the costume. She hurried to her cabin and found Curly waiting to help her out of the costume. As soon as Elvis was freed, he streaked across the room and threw himself on Kiara's bunk, rubbing and wiggling.

"You are okay?" Curly asked her.

"Yes, I'm good. Do you think I looked like you?" Kiara asked with a smile.

"Yes," Curly said, showing all her teeth in her version of a smile. "You are short."

Kiara could feel the rumble of the engines as Frankie got them started on the next phase of their journey. Curly had moved over to scratch Elvis, when Kiara heard her dad at the doorway clear his throat.

"Dad!" Kiara went over and hugged him.

"Did everything go okay? Did anyone stop you? What did you learn?" Kyle asked her.

"Didn't Jax fill you in?"

"Of course, but I wanted to make sure you were okay for myself." The worry on Kyle's face was very evident.

Kiara looked down for a moment, her own anxieties surfacing. "Dad, the message came from the main GTA building, on Earth Delta Nine," she told him. Her dad nodded. "I don't know how we're going to get in that building, much less get close to the planet."

"We've got a few days to figure something out. Frankie is taking the long way, so we don't draw suspicion."

Kiara suddenly realized that they were leaving, but Kyle wasn't on his ship. "What did you do with your ship, Dad?"

"We've got it hooked up to the Acadia, pulling it with us. It'll slow us down a little, but that's okay."

Kyle looked at his daughter and saw she wasn't paying any attention to him. He waved his hand in front of her face. "Hey, where'd you go?"

"Sorry, Dad. I just had a thought about how to get us close enough to Earth Delta Nine."

"And?" He prodded when she didn't immediately continue.

"Let's go up to the bridge and find Blackburne, and I'll explain it up there."

They reached the bridge to find Frankie whistling a tune and piloting them through the slow space area around the space station. Blackburne was monitoring traffic and scanning for threats. At their entrance, Blackburne briefly looked up, nodded, and looked back down. Kiara immediately knew something was going on. Hustling to her station, she brought up her scans, looking for anything suspicious, but nothing jumped out at first. Her dad stood behind her, looking at her scans because he, too, sensed something was going on.

"What should I be looking for?" Kiara finally asked.

"We've got a tail," Blackburne responded with an old Earth phrase.

Kiara's eyes never left her monitor, and within a few seconds, she and her dad had picked it out.

"It looks like the ship that was trying to attack us not too long ago—the one that wouldn't identify itself," Kiara said quietly.

"Exactly," Blackburne responded.

"What should we do?" Kiara felt fear boil up before she controlled her feelings. She was much stronger than the first time he approached them, and she could protect them now, if needed.

"We'll wait and see for now. Right now we're out of weapons range," Blackburne said without looking up.

Kiara smiled. So that's why Frankie had been whistling and going so slow—he'd been drawing the ship out so they could identify it. At that moment, Jax entered the bridge, his Bendanite costume also removed. After Blackburne filled him on the latest situation, Jax took over the scanning. Kyle motioned for Blackburne to join them at Kiara's station.

"Kiara's got an idea for getting us close to the GTA headquarters," Kyle informed Blackburne.

"I got the idea from something my dad said," Kiara spoke without taking her eyes off the scan. "Right now, we're recognizable, due to our transponder and our shape. Anyone performing a scan can figure out who we are, easily." Blackburne and her dad nodded. "Now that we're towing my dad's ship, it throws the scan off slightly. They can still figure it out; it just takes a little longer."

"I don't think that will buy us enough time."

"Of course not," Kiara answered Blackburne's statement. "But it gave me an idea." She finally looked up from her console. "We're going to need to modify the ship slightly, and I can reprogram the transponder to something else. That way, no one will recognize us."

"Modify my ship?" Blackburne nearly bellowed his question.

"Well, yes, but not in a bad way. And we'll have to have a way to deploy the modifications when we need them."

"Of course," Jax said from the far side of the bridge. "Change it when we need it, so we look legitimate when we don't need it."

"It just might work," Blackburne responded with a thoughtful look on his face.

Kyle looked proud, Frankie was nodding his agreement.

"Frankie, run some comparisons of cargo ships. Find something we can easily mimic." Blackburne, fully embracing the plan now, began issuing orders. "We'll need to find a place to do the modifications; somewhere that we won't be noticed."

"I can help with that," Jax responded, his eyes still glued to the monitor.

"Anything from our tail?" Blackburne asked him.

"Tail?" Jax looked confused.

"Sorry, old Earth term. The ship following us."

"Aahh, the tail. Still keeping his distance."

"We don't want him following us to where we're going," Kyle said.

"Should we draw him in?" Frankie asked.

"I've got a better idea," Kyle said, and grabbed his com unit. "Frankie, keep us in this sector for now." He sent a quick message, and looked back at Kiara's monitor. "It shouldn't take long."

All eyes glued to the screen, they watched three ships suddenly converge on the ship that was following them, surrounding it.

Kyle immediately turned to Blackburne. "Quickly, let's go." He turned to Jax. "Tell Frankie where we're going. They won't be able to hold him, but it should be long enough for us to lose him."

"Who are they?" Blackburne asked Kyle once they were under way.

"A couple of Ranger buddies. I knew they were in this sector, so I asked them to detain the ship for a short time."

"What reason did you give them?"

"No reason," Kyle said with a smile. "They did it as a favor. That way, it keeps the number of people that know what we're doing and where we are going to just our group."

Blackburne nodded his approval as they streaked away from the Galdorian ship.

"Kyle, can you take over scanning? I've got a priority message from Stryker." Jax stood up from the console, his eyes on his com unit.

Blackburne and Kiara watched Jax closely as he read the message from Stryker. His face unreadable, he finally looked up.

"It seems that all our investigations are leading us to the same place. Stryker has found the contact that the kidnapper gave us."

At Jax's statement, even Kyle and Frankie turned their attention to him.

"Did he question him?" Blackburne asked.

"Yes, he questioned him extensively. He confirmed the order came through John, but they suspect that a high-ranking official at the GTA gave the order to John."

"Suspect?" Kyle asked.

"Yes. The contact had no direct interaction with anyone except John, but some of what John insinuated made him think that he was just following orders."

"Can we trust the information?" Blackburne asked. "I know it is leading us to the same place we discovered, but are they sure they have all the information?"

Jax smiled fiercely. "I have watched Stryker interrogate others before, and believe me, if there were more information, we would have it."

The bridge fell into silence as everyone digested the information from Jax.

Kyle finally broke the silence. "I'm glad we have confirmation, because it will help our case after this is over."

Since they didn't want to be recognized anywhere, they stayed away from the transgates to get to their destination. It took days, but they used the time to work on a plan, and figure out the best way to disguise the ship. They finally reached the far corner of the sector, where the sun barely reached. They found a small space station orbiting a dead planet, and even the space station looked dead. No lights, no ships. Kiara thought it looked abandoned.

"Are you sure this is where we're supposed to be?" Frankie asked.

"Yes," Jax answered. "I hope you are the excellent pilot that you said you are. You'll have to bring us in without lights, and without navigation help from the space station. It's not big, but it's big enough for us."

Frankie, with a determined look on his face, nodded, and brought them closer to the space station. Jax stood next to him, giving directions on which side of the space station to approach, and where the docking bay was. Frankie slowly brought them in and landed in the bay, soft as a feather. Once they landed, Jax and Kyle suited up in space suits, and went out to secure the docking bay and pressurize and oxygenate the bay.

Once everything was secured, they gathered in the small office off the docking bay. From here they could scan for incoming ships, and control all the functions of the space station.

"What is this place?" Kiara asked.

"It's an abandoned space dock, but our group has repurposed it for situations like this or other emergencies. For any passing ship, it appears abandoned, and scans will show it uninhabited with no atmosphere. For those in our group, we know how to bring it up when we need it." Jax walked over to a console and brought up scans of the area as he spoke. "I had someone stop by and make sure it was in working order, and they dropped off some supplies. We should have everything we need."

Frankie connected his com unit to the space station console, and brought up the image of a ship they could mimic.

"It's an old Earth freighter," Frankie told the group as they crowded around the console. "If we add panels here, here, and here," Frankie highlighted areas of the Acadia, "and these two areas, we'll look like it close enough to fool scanners."

"What about the transponder signal?" Blackburne wanted to know.

"I've got that," Kiara said. "I found the same type of old Earth freighter that was decommissioned a few years back. Because it was recently decommissioned, it doesn't come up that way right away. Unless someone is really digging through the archives, we'll pass first inspection."

Blackburne gave out the orders, and the crew got to work. The work was physical and tough, and Kiara was glad they had the Bendanites to help. The abandoned space station didn't have all the modern hoverlifts and mechanical devices, so most of what they did, they accomplished through sheer physical strength.

A few hours later, Kiara looked down at her clothes, now smudged with grease, space dirt, and all manner of things. She was tired, hungry, and not entirely sure that everything was going to work out. She was feeling pessimistic and defeated, and thought if she didn't eat something soon, she might just pass out. Elvis, curled up on a pile of rags behind her, looked back at her with a droopy-eyed expression that she knew mirrored her own. They were nearly done with the modifications, and so far, their stay at the abandoned space station had gone unnoticed. They'd had a few close calls, but every time they'd detected a ship coming their way, they'd shut everything down and waited until the ship had passed.

Curly and Larry lumbered over to her, and Kiara took a deep breath, anticipating that they would need her help to move something. Jax had wanted her to use her powers to help move or hold panels, instead of practicing in the flex-space. The practice had been good, but it was tiring work.

"Jax says you are done," Curly told her.

"I'm done? But we've got this last panel to finish up." Kiara looked around for Jax, thinking that Curly might have misunderstood him.

"You are done," Curly insisted, and headed over to the last panel with Larry. Moe soon joined them, and together, the three Bendanites lifted the last panel into position.

Feeling oddly dejected, Kiara headed around to the front of the ship, Elvis trailing behind her. Jax was there, conferring with Blackburne over a portable console. Both men looked up at her approach.

"Kiara, you look terrible," Blackburne commented.

"Gee, thanks."

Blackburne turned and looked at Jax. "Are we having her do too much? We're going to need her at her best for this to succeed."

"I'm right here," Kiara protested. She hated it when people talked about her as if she wasn't standing right in front of them.

"She'll be okay," Jax told Blackburne. He turned to Kiara with a smile, knowing exactly what she was feeling. "I asked the Bendanites to finish up the last of the panels. We need you to get some rest and finish programming those transponder codes."

Kiara nodded. "I'm almost done with them. They have to be right, or the first ship we pass will send an alarm if we don't match the transponder, or the transponder malfunctions." She started to climb into the ship, but turned back to Blackburne. "When are we leaving?"

Blackburne looked down at the console. "We should be ready to leave in about eight hours."

Kiara entered the ship and used her com unit to contact her dad. He was finishing up the welds and wiring for the panels. He looked as dirty and tired as she felt. They filled each in while Kiara got some food for her and Elvis. She disconnected from her dad and headed to her cabin to get cleaned up. She looked at Elvis, already asleep on his blanket and smiled. She jumped into the bunk and fell asleep instantly.

When the dream started and Kiara recognized Mirona's home planet, Kiara was relieved and happy. She hadn't dreamed of Mirona in a while, and had feared that perhaps Mirona thought she wasn't needed anymore. In truth, Kiara hoped the connection never went away. She always learned something, and it helped her to feel like she was a part of something. She loved her dad, and she loved Earth things, but she never felt a real connection to Earth. She'd always been the outsider. In just the few dreams she'd had with Mirona, she'd felt a connection she'd never felt before. This connection gave her a feeling of belonging to something bigger than just her immediate family. Kiara realized now that it had also brought her confidence, and a sense of peace that she'd never had.

Kiara looked out into the open area that Mirona was now walking through. Tall, rock-looking formations that had a bluish hue were surrounded by tall, green grasses and bushes. Mirona was following a path through the grasses and rocks, and Kiara could feel her humming. She could sense the happiness coming from Mirona.

You are happy today.

Yes, it is a good day here.

Kiara could sense something else was the cause of Mirona's happiness.

You are with child!

Yes, my dear little one. I am blessed with a child.

I can feel the presence! It is a little girl!

Yes, this is truly a blessing. I have three little boys, but this will be my first girl. I knew, since you had been coming to me in my dreams, that I would be destined to have a little girl. This is the only way to carry on the line of Guardians.

Only women carry the line of Guardians?

Yes. If a Guardian is not blessed with a girl child, then her line will die out. It does not happen often, but when it does, the family experiences great suffering and sorrow.

Mirona reached a great body of water, the color of the water the deepest blue that Kiara had ever seen.

It is so beautiful here. What is this place?

A place set aside by our government for all to enjoy.

Mirona sat on a small rock at the edge of the water and breathed deeply.

I sense that not all is well with you. You have recovered from the poison?

Yes, I have recovered. We are trying to discover who has been targeting me. We have a mission to catch up to them, and expose them. We hope it will keep me safe.

You are much stronger now with your power. I sense your confidence and control. This is good. It will serve you and protect you.

You have been a great help to me.

My understanding is that all in the future must survive an attack by a Galdorian. Has this happened?

I'm not sure I understand. How would you know that, and why would you think that all of us must be attacked?

To better help you, I have merged my thoughts with those who came before, and those who came after. The Galdorians will hunt the Guardians and try to destroy them before they fully come into their power. You have great power now, but I sense that you have not fought a Galdorian.

I have not fought one, no. We have one that has surfaced near us several times, but there has not been a direct attack. We do not know who poisoned my supplements, perhaps that was their attack?

That is not their way, to poison. They will want to physically attack. Be careful, my dear Kiara. They will try for you soon. Use your power to sense when they are near, and to sense their movements in battle. They have underestimated you, and that will be their undoing. Because of those who support you, they have not been able to get close enough to you, so they do not fully realize your capabilities. Use that to your advantage.

Thank-you Mirona. I value all of your advice, and I value this time together.

Be safe, little one. I want many more of these conversations with you.

Kiara woke with a smile on her face, glad that for once her connection to Mirona didn't get interrupted by her com unit. Remembering something that Mirona said, though, wiped the smile from her face. The Galdorian. He would most likely strike at the first opportunity. And if

Mirona was right, the Galdorians weren't responsible for the poison in her supplements. She wondered who else could be responsible. John, the Ranger that had betrayed her? Or some other unknown group? Feeling her rising anxiety, Elvis hopped into her lap, and reached up to put both front feet on her cheeks. Kiara looked down into those trusting eyes, and felt herself calm slightly. She was stronger than before, wasn't she? And she knew he was coming, so that gave her the advantage, right? And Mirona had talked about all those who supported her, so they would help her as well. Feeling more calm and confident, Kiara cleaned up and went to look for Jax and her dad. She wanted to fill them in on the things Mirona had told her before she completed the transponders.

She found everyone except the Bendanites on the bridge, discussing last-minute strategies, and theories as to who was behind the attacks. Kiara knew that she was only a small piece to the puzzle. Whoever was after her was also behind the attacks on the transgates. The Galdorian was just another piece to her puzzle.

Jax, sensing her presence, turned and motioned her over.

"You look more rested," her dad told her.

"I definitely feel better. Plus, I had a dream with Mirona, my ancestor, again. She had some very interesting things to say."

"Tell us," her dad said.

Jax and Blackburne both turned to give her their full attention. Frankie was still looking at something on his com unit, but Kiara knew he was listening too.

"Mirona said that all like me have to survive an attack by a Galdorian."

"Do you think it was the poisoned supplements?" Blackburne asked.

"Mirona said that is not the way the Galdorians attack. They prefer a physical confrontation. She thinks because all of you have been helping to protect me, the attack has taken longer to come to fruition, but she is sure it is still coming." Kiara turned to Jax. "This falls in line with everything you have told me, except the part that she is sure all female Trandorians with power have to be attacked."

"We have always known that the Galdorians have attacked your kind, but we only suspected that it was some sort of requirement." He smiled slightly. "We have found it hard to prove when they will not admit to it when questioned."

"The ship that has been following us—that's the one the Galdorian is in," Frankie said without looking up.

Kiara smiled. She knew he was listening.

"I think I speak for the group—we all think it's him," Blackburne said.

Jax stood and walked over to Kiara. He put a hand an each of her shoulders.

"You are ready for him. He cannot defeat you."

"Mirona said he has underestimated my strength and abilities, since he has not been able to get close."

"She is right," Jax said

"I just don't want him to hurt any of you."

"We'll be vigilant, and you'll be close to keep us protected as well," Blackburne said matter-of-factly.

Kiara nodded, but saw the fear on her dad's face. She knew he would kill the Galdorian himself if he could. She also knew that if he did, the Galdorians would simply send another. She could see on her dad's face that he had come to the same conclusion.

Kiara turned and went to her station; she needed to finish the transponder codes. She'd already completed most of the programming, so it only took a few more minutes to finish. She took a little more time to double and triple check everything, because having it wrong could spell disaster. Satisfied that it would work, she let Blackburne and Frankie know that she was done. Blackburne checked with Kyle and the Bendanites on the installation of the panels, and finding everything was ready, announced they would leave within the hour.

Frankie and Kiara, with help from Jax, had mapped out the route to Earth Delta Nine, and when they would need to deploy the panels and change transponders. Again, they would be taking the long way so as not to draw attention, and it would mean a stop at a smaller space station to refuel and restock supplies about halfway there. Kiara thought it would be a good place for the Galdorian to attack, so she would be extra vigilant.

Frankie guided them out of the abandoned space dock, and put the ship through a few test deployments of the panels. They had to make a few adjustments, but overall, Kiara thought it was going to work well. She sent Frankie the route before she took over scanning. They wouldn't need to deploy the panels until they left the next space station, so Kiara kept reminding herself to be alert for an attack. It would take them a couple of days just to reach their next destination.

After a few hours, Kyle took over scanning, so Kiara took Elvis to the flex-space to put in some practice time and work out the building anxiety. The room was empty, so Kiara entered and started the program that Jax had created for her. Jax had programmed a Galdorian to attack her in different ways, and it was a program that Kiara really hated, but knew she had to practice. She'd never been good at face-to-face confrontations, and this program put her directly in that position. She managed to keep at it for about thirty minutes before she just couldn't take it any longer. Jax had programmed the Galdorian to spew filth at her in his rants, and Kiara found it too much to listen to for any length of time. Jax had once suggested that she use her disgust to fuel her anger at him, and use it against him, but it was hard.

Stopping the program, she went over to the wall and opened the bench seat for her and Elvis to sit on. Elvis, sitting next to her, was chirping and touching her arm, trying to comfort her. Kiara reached over and scratched the top of his head. "I'm okay, little guy."

Still scratching Elvis' head, Kiara sensed that Jax was approaching, and it made her already elevated pulse jump. She worked to even out her breathing before he entered. Her attraction to him would be nothing but a distraction at this point, so she didn't want to embarrass herself by letting him know. She wasn't sure what he felt; sometimes he seemed like he was attracted to her, and other times he acted more like a big brother. Because she was inexperienced with dating, and with men in general, she didn't trust her instincts in this arena. After all, look at what happened with John. She thought he had liked her, and he'd just wanted to kill her.

"There you are," Jax said as he entered. "Did you have a good session?"

Kiara shrugged. She didn't want to hurt his feelings if she told him how much she hated that program he had created for her.

"Ahhh, you were battling the Galdorian?"
"Yes."
"I know you don't like it, but it is good to practice, and to be prepared for the hate you will encounter."

"I know, I know." Kiara sighed. "It's hard to purposely expose myself to that much hate."

Jax sat on the bench next to her, and finally gave in to the urge to put his arm around her. Kiara sighed again and relaxed into his shoulder.

"You will be fine. Use the emotions you have to channel your power. You are strong enough, he cannot defeat you."

"I hope you're right."

Kiara turned her head and looked up into his face. Those dark eyes of his met hers and she could feel her stomach jump in response. She watched his pupils dilate, and knew that he could feel her response. She waited, her pulse racing, her breathing fast and shallow, but when he didn't do anything, she closed her eyes, willing herself to pull back. Instead, she felt his lips press lightly against hers. The kiss deepened, and Jax pulled her closer, wrapping his arms around her. Kiara put her hands on his shoulders, hanging on for dear life. When Jax finally pulled back, they were breathing hard, and it had nothing to do with Kiara's workout. Kiara watched him blink and mentally pull himself back.

"Please don't say you're sorry," she told him before he could speak.

"Okay, I won't." Jax studied her face. "Because I'm not."

"Good," Kiara responded and smiled.

"But we shouldn't be doing this, not now. You and I both need to be focused on what's ahead."

"I knew you were going to say that." Kiara pulled away, disappointed. "But you're right."

Jax looked at her in surprise. He hadn't expected her to agree with him, not after the way she had responded to his kiss.

"So, now what? We just try to put our feelings on hold?" Kiara asked.

"I don't think we can put them on hold, but we need to make sure they don't interfere with what we are trying to accomplish, and make sure they don't put you in any danger."

"So," Kiara hesitated, and averted her gaze, feeling embarrassed. "You do have feelings for me?"

Jax laughed, and pulled her in for a hug.

Kiara, back in her cabin, was getting ready for bed. After her session in the flex-space, she'd gone up to the bridge and taken a turn at scanning. Monitoring the scans was mentally taxing work, but that's why they took turns. When her turn at scanning was finished, she'd met her dad in the kitchen to eat before heading to her cabin. Looking at her bunk, Kiara realized she was tired, but energized at the same time. She just hoped she would be able to sleep. Her shift began early in the morning, and she didn't want to be tired and sluggish while scanning for trouble. Curly was scrunched into her own bunk across the room, and Kiara smiled at the soft snoring sounds coming from that side of the cabin. Kiara finally crawled into her bunk and made sure Elvis was comfortable. She checked her com unit one last time, turned down the light, and fell asleep almost immediately.

When the dream started, Kiara hoped it was another dream with Mirona, but it didn't have the same feel. She realized almost immediately that she wasn't back with Mirona, but was having a dream of her own time. She was on an unfamiliar space station, and she was standing in the docking bay, outside the Acadia. Elvis was at her feet, and as she turned toward the Acadia, she saw her dad and Blackburne exiting the ship. She smiled at them, and raised her hand in greeting. In what seemed like slow motion, she watched as her dad's smile turned to a look of horror and pain, as weapons fire rang out and shots went through his chest. She turned to see who was firing, and saw as she turned that Blackburne too, was gunned down. She saw a Galdorian, a weapon in his hand, filth spewing from his mouth as he continued to fire. In her dream, she threw a force field at him. However, she was so panicked at seeing her dad and Blackburne gunned down, the field she threw was weak, and merely pushed him back a step or two. She'd thrown up protection around her and Elvis, so the weapons fire wasn't harming her, but she hadn't protected her dad. She turned back to her dad, running to his side, but saw that he was already gone. Blackburne as well, was dead. Things were still happening in slow motion, and as she turned back to the Galdorian, Frankie and Jax came out of the ship. Her back was turned to them, and she didn't realize that they had come out until she saw the Galdorian laugh and fire above her head. She heard the scream of agony as first Frankie, and then Jax was gunned down. She seemed powerless to do anything, almost as if she was frozen in one spot. She could hear the Galdorian laughing and spewing filth, she could hear herself screaming in despair. As she watched, the three Bendanites came running from behind the Acadia, and were gunned down as well. Sobbing now, she turned back to the Galdorian, wanting to destroy him, to annihilate him. He was still laughing, and as she took a deep breath to build her power, Elvis shot out from her protection, his rage apparent at seeing Curly and her dad gunned down. The Galdorian killed the little drayek before he made it halfway there. Kiara screamed in agony, feeling his pain. She could hear the Galdorian as he simply walked away from her.

"I may not be able to kill you, but I will kill everyone you love."

Kiara awoke, sobbing and crying hysterically. Curly was standing over her, trying to calm her down. Elvis was standing on Kiara's stomach, emitting a noise that sounded like sobbing. Curly was intermittently crooning to Kiara, and yelling into her com unit for Jax. Kiara could hear running footsteps and yelling from the hallway, and struggled to calm herself. The horrors of her dream were still so fresh in her mind. She grabbed Elvis and hugged him tight, and when that wasn't enough, she reached over and grabbed Curly's arm to hug that.

Jax shot into the room, his baton at the ready, but before he could do more than register the occupants in the room, Kiara launched herself into his arms. She was still sobbing uncontrollably, but was holding Jax so tight that he thought he might have visible bruising in the morning. He finally disengaged himself, and holding her at arm's length, visibly checked her for injuries. He didn't see any physical injuries, and as his eyes met hers, the horror and pain she was feeling shot into him. He dropped his hands and doubled over. He'd heard of this before, but none of his charges had ever had this much power, so he'd never been on the receiving end of their feelings. All dead, all dead, kept repeating in his head. When he was finally able to straighten, he avoided looking straight at her.

"Kiara, who's dead?"

Kiara, still sobbing quietly, said, "Everyone, all of you."

"You were dreaming?"

"Yes. He killed all of you, and I couldn't stop it."

"Okay, okay. Kiara, it was just a dream. We're all still here," Jax reassured her. He could hear Blackburne in the background getting reassurance from Curly that all was well.

"I know it was a dream, but it felt so real."

"Kiara, I need you to pull your feelings back in, can you do that for me?" Jax asked her. He looked down at Elvis, and he could tell that the little guy was also feeling everything from Kiara.

"What?" Kiara looked at Jax in bewilderment.

"Kiara, you are transmitting your feelings of sorrow and pain to me and Elvis," he stole a quick glance at Curly, but she didn't seem to be affected. "I need you to pull them back in."

Kiara took in the look on his face, which mirrored hers, and the noises coming from Elvis. She wasn't sure how she was doing it, but considering how bad she felt with the dream, she didn't want anyone else feeling that as well. Especially since it was only a dream. She closed her eyes, and tried to figure out how to pull her feelings back in. She asked herself to do it, she pictured it, but at first, nothing seemed to work. Finally, calming her mind, she took a deep breath, and willed those feelings to stay with her. She knew she succeeded when she heard Jax release his breath. She opened her eyes and looked at Jax.

"I'm so sorry! I didn't realize I had done that. I didn't even know I could do that."

"I know. It is okay. We are all okay."

"Has that happened to you before?" Kiara reached down and pulled Elvis into her arms. He was quiet now, but still clung to her when she picked him up. She put her face close to his, and sent feelings of love and calmness to him. She could see his face relax slightly, and knew she had helped him. She silently promised that she would keep him safe; she would not let what happened in the dream happen in real life.

"It has not, but I have heard of it. This is a sign of your increasing powers."

"It doesn't sound like a good thing to have."

"Perhaps we can find a good use for it."

Kiara looked past Jax to see her dad standing in the doorway.

"Are you okay?" Kyle asked her.

"I'm okay, Dad." Kiara moved around Jax and went to her dad. He hugged her tightly.

"What happened?"

"I had a dream that the Galdorian had killed all of you. He knew he couldn't kill me, so he killed all of you. In my dream, there didn't seem to be anything I could do about it. It was horrible."

Kyle hugged his daughter tighter. "We'll be on our toes, so we won't let it happen."

Kiara hugged him back just as tight, making her own vow to herself. She wouldn't let it happen. She would make sure she protected all of them, not just herself.

Chapter Eleven

Kiara, sitting at her navunit, watched Frankie bring them into the space station. She'd been going over her dream, again and again since yesterday, trying to figure out how to counter the Galdorian attack. She'd spent hours in the flex-space, running the scenario from her dream, but also running alternate scenarios. Jax, her dad, Blackburne; they'd all try to reassure her that it was just a dream, but she wasn't taking any chances. She knew—she just knew— that the Galdorian would strike here. She went around and made everyone promise not to simply run into danger if there were an attack. She wasn't going to spend any time determining how he found them, she was just going to assume that he was already here, or would be soon. One thing was for certain; the dream had reinforced the need to be at her best. She would do whatever it took to keep those she cared about safe.

Once they were safely in the docking bay, Blackburne made arrangements for some cargo to be loaded. They were trying to look legitimate, and a cargo ship running around empty definitely looked suspicious.

Kiara, still sitting at her station, closed her eyes and concentrated on trying to find the Galdorian, or at least his presence. After a few minutes, she gave up, finding nothing. She didn't assume he wasn't here, she just knew she hadn't sensed him yet. Getting up slowly, she headed to the kitchen to grab some food, making sure she kept Elvis close. She passed Jax in the small hallway outside the kitchen, and he stopped her to make sure she was okay. She held his hand for second, and told him she was fine, before continuing into the kitchen. Jax watched her go, and knew that she was anything but fine.

Jax had already used his contacts at the space station to start discreetly checking for the Galdorian. So far, he hadn't heard anything. He knew, since he wanted to keep things discreet, that it would take time.

For a few hours, everything continued normally. They refueled the ship, the cargo was loaded. They were waiting for food supplies when Jax got the message from his contact that the Galdorian was on the space station. His contact was trying to track down information on the ship and perhaps a picture of the Galdorian. Jax checked his com unit to see where Kiara was, and saw that she was in her cabin. His contact sent him a message to meet outside the Acadia to discuss his findings, so Jax headed that way. He sent a quick message to everyone on the ship that his contact had placed the Galdorian on the space station. Thinking they had all the bases covered, Jax exited the ship, looking for his contact. He didn't see him at first, and as he looked around, he saw Curly and Moe working a hoverlift off to his left, loading the rest of their supplies. As he turned back around, his senses told him that this was a trap. He started to crouch down, swinging his baton out, looking for the threat. He was too late. His eyes found the Galdorian, instead of his contact, hiding between two ships in the docking bay. The Galdorian was already firing at him. He braced for the impact of the weapons fire, his free hand already reaching for his com unit to send a warning to Kiara and the others.

Jax watched in what seemed like slow motion as the weapons fire reached him. Instead of blasting a hole through him, it hit a force field that was around him. The force of the weapons fire hitting the force field was still strong enough to knock him off his feet. As Jax fell, he saw satisfaction on the Galdorian's face as he swung his weapon at the Bendanites. Jax hit the ground below the ramp, and heard the weapon's discharge at the same time that he heard Kyle and Blackburne's shouts. He yelled for them to take cover, but the Galdorian was already shooting into the entrance of the Acadia. He watched Kyle and Blackburne both get knocked over by the force, but he didn't see any blood, and hoped Kiara had protected them as well. Jax gained his feet, trying to stay hidden behind the railing of the ramp into the Acadia, and took a quick glance over at the Bendanites. They, too, had been knocked over, but he watched as both gained their feet, apparently unharmed. Jax smiled. He didn't know how she was doing it, but Kiara was protecting them all.

The Galdorian, still unaware that his weapon wasn't taking everyone out as planned, had now moved to the bottom of the ramp to the Acadia, his intent to enter the ship and finish what he had started. He took two steps up the ramp and faltered as his gaze caught sight of Jax, alive, below him. He pointed his weapon at Jax, before he caught sight of Curly and Moe, now with Larry behind them, approaching the ramp, their teeth bared, their anger palpable. He swung his weapon toward them, when he heard Blackburne's voice from the top of the ramp, telling him to drop it. The Galdorian was starting to panic, his weapon swinging from person to person, not sure of his next move.

"How...?" The Galdorian was clearly at a loss for words, his anger and frustration very evident.

"I can answer that." Kiara stood at the top of the ramp, Elvis firmly clamped to her shoulder.

At the site of Kiara, the Galdorian began firing his weapon, at her and everyone else, while he shouted vile things at her. Everyone around her ducked, their instincts to get out of the way kicking in. Kiara merely stood there and waited for him to realize how fruitless his actions were.

It didn't take long. He finally threw down his weapon, and pulled out a very mean looking sword. Jax had his baton at the ready, but didn't move to use it. He knew that Kiara had to take care of this.

"I won't let you hurt those I care about," Kiara announced.

"You won't be able to stop me when you are dead!" The Galdorian shouted back at her.

"You can't hurt me, much less kill me."

At those words, the Galdorian ran up the ramp, lunging forward with his sword. Clearly, he knew that some Guardians couldn't defend against smaller, pointed objects. He also produced a smaller dagger in his other hand, and when the sword wasn't able to penetrate her force field, he shot his other hand forward with the dagger. He was able to penetrate her force field slightly, but not enough to reach her. It fueled his confidence, though. Kiara knew he wouldn't stop, and she wanted to get the fight away from her dad and Blackburne. Raising her hand she shot small amounts of energy out, each shot driving the Galdorian back down the ramp. She advanced, keeping him in her sights and Elvis firmly on her shoulder. She was about halfway down the ramp when she sensed another Galdorian, then another. Shots rang out, and she knew they were doing it to distract her. She'd planned for this as well. She kept her protection fields up around the others, and she knew they were safe. She didn't need to turn around and look, she knew that is what the Galdorians were trying to force her to do. She heard Jax and her dad as they found the other two Galdorians, and smiled at the surprised look on the Galdorian's face that she was battling. Taking a deep breath, she tried one more time to talk him out of what she considered a suicide mission.

"You don't have to do this. I've done nothing to you."

"I have the right to kill you! I've trained my entire life to kill a *shetanzie!*"

Kiara remembered the slang word that Jax had taught her, and remembered what it meant. She looked at his face, the rage, the hate that it showed. She looked at his eyes, and saw they were slightly glazed, and thought that he may be on some sort of drug to give him courage and strength. "Please don't do this."

In answer, he lunged at her again with the dagger, and again, only penetrated her force field slightly.

Remembering how she had sent her feelings of pain and horror to Jax the other day, she tried a last-ditch effort to bring him down without hurting him. She locked her gaze with his, and sent him all the love she could muster at that point. She knew it was having an effect when he grabbed his head and began shrieking.

"No! No! No! I hate you! I must kill you!"

Kiara tried to hang on, but the hate and the drugs were too much. He lowered his hands from his head, the hate radiating from his eyes stronger now. She watched as he took the dagger and licked it. Aiming at her heart, he threw it with all his strength.

When Kiara saw him lick the dagger, she sensed that it would somehow be able to overcome her protection field, so when he threw it, she used the training from Jax to shift her weight to the side. She knew she wouldn't be fast enough, so she combined her dodge with a shot of energy at the dagger. As suspected, the dagger went through her protection, and her shot of energy was almost too late. The dagger sliced across her upper arm, going through her skinsuit and slicing her skin. The injury gave her the impetus she needed to attack him.

Jumping in the air, she used the ramp to give her the height needed to flip over the Galdorian. Elvis effortlessly shifted his weight as she went, keeping connected to her, but not interfering. Kiara shot energy field after energy field at the Galdorian, keeping him disoriented and eventually driving him to his knees, as she landed on her feet behind him. So in tune with the battle she was in, she began to see his intentions before they became reality. He had two other daggers, and he was going to pull them, lick them and throw them in rapid succession at her. She knew they would hit their target if she tried to defend against it. Before he could grab the daggers, she again threw energy ball after energy ball at him. She advanced on him while she hit him with the energy balls, her intent to take the daggers from him before he could try to use them. She relieved him of both daggers, throwing them underneath the Acadia. In the short amount of time it took to throw the daggers, the Galdorian regained some of his strength and jumped up, swinging a fist at Kiara's face. She realized, an instant before he did it, that he was now inside her protection field. She shot her head back, but he still landed a glancing blow on her chin. She stumbled back, and he immediately took advantage, staying close to her, swinging wildly at her.

At first, Kiara threw up her arms to protect her face, and his blows landed there, but she was still off balance and stumbling back. She sent a thought to Elvis to have him jump at the Galdorian to distract him for a second. Elvis immediately jumped at him, all claws and snapping teeth. The Galdorian paused in his attack of Kiara, swinging instead at Elvis. The distraction was exactly what Kiara needed to take control of the fight. Regaining her balance, she moved up to the balls of her feet, getting into a fighting stance. Falling back on her martial arts training, she landed two quick blows with her fists that further disoriented him. As the Galdorian struggled to land a blow, Kiara dodged and struck at him, using her fists and feet. Her blows drove him across the docking bay. Elvis was alternately on her shoulder hissing at him, or jumping and diving at him. Between the two of them, the Galdorian was stumbling back, no longer able to throw any punches at Kiara. He stumbled to a stop, and Kiara paused in her attack, ready to see if he would surrender. Barely able to stand, the Galdorian, swaying back and forth, raised his head and sneered at her. Kiara, seeing that sneer, knew he wouldn't surrender. She shifted her weight, spinning and striking out with her leg. Her foot connected with the Galdorian's head, the surprise on his face replaced with terror as the force of the blow sent him over the guardrail they were next to. Kiara, reacting without thinking, sent a protection field to catch him. She wasn't fast enough. She heard an impact and a scream of pain. Running up to the railing, she looked over the side. The Galdorian was below her, impaled on a spike attached to a ship below them. As Kiara watched, the Galdorian took his last breath, his hate-filled eyes still staring up at her.

Kiara, tears running down her face, turned away from the dead Galdorian. She looked around the docking bay for her dad and the others. Jax, Curly, and Moe were bringing one of the disarmed Galdorians up to the Acadia. Curly looked as if she wanted to tear his limbs from his body, and from the look on the Galdorian's face, he knew it as well. Behind her, she could hear Larry growling loudly as he and Frankie brought up the other disarmed Galdorian. It appeared that Larry wanted to make sure their captive knew that his life was hanging by a thread.

"Where are my dad and Blackburne?" Kiara asked Jax as he approached.

"They are completing a sweep of the bay to make sure there are no others in hiding."

Both Galdorians were now on their knees at the bottom of the Acadia ramp. They were alternately sending hateful looks to Kiara, and fearful looks to the Bendanites.

Kyle and Blackburne came back, followed by the space station security team. Before they let the security team have them, Jax walked over to stand in front of both Galdorians.

"It's over now, isn't it? She defeated the one sent to kill her, so there will not be any more attacks, right?" Jax questioned them.

Both Galdorians remained steadfastly quiet. Jax looked at one of the space station security guards, and receiving a nod, turned and looked at Curly. He knew she had the most anger at Kiara's attackers, though Larry and Moe were bigger.

"Curly, rip his arm off," Jax said conversationally.

Curly advanced toward the Galdorians, her teeth bared. She was growling loudly, and the sound made the hair on Kiara's arm stand up. The Galdorians started yelling and screaming, looking at the space station security team for help. Seeing no help there, they turned back to Curly, begging her to leave them alone. Curly ignored them, looking at each of them as if trying to decide which to grab. Kiara walked up to Curly and motioned for her to lean down. Curly leaned over, and Kiara whispered to her which one to grab. Kiara could sense his weakness. Curly nodded, and with a loud roar, grabbed the arm of the one closest to her.

"Wait! Wait!" the Galdorian screamed as Curly tightened her grip on his arm.

Jax raised his hand, and Curly stopped, but didn't let go.

"Speak."

"They knew she was more powerful, so they sent three of us."

"Shut up!" The other Galdorian screamed it at him. "Tell them nothing!"

"Will there be others?" Jax wanted to know.

"No, it is only us three. We are sworn to pursue her until we die."

"How do we know he is telling the truth?" Kyle asked.

Kiara, staring hard at him, responded. "He is telling the truth. They won't send any more, but these two will never stop trying to hunt me."

"What do we do with them now?" Kyle asked. Jax and the three Bendanites looked as if they wanted to kill them, but Kiara had had enough killing. She went to stand in front of the two Galdorians.

"Please, no one else has to die," she pleaded. The Galdorians stared at her with hate, but Kiara was hopeful, as their eyes looked clear, so she hoped they weren't on drugs like the other.

"We have no reason to keep going with this feud, or whatever you want to call it. I've never done anything to you or any other Galdorian. Please, can't you just let it go?"

Neither Galdorian said anything. Jax moved to stand next to Kiara.

"You are wasting your time, Kiara," he told her. "They are raised from an early age to accomplish this one thing. I believe it is like your Earth 'brainwashing' for them. They believe what they have been told. I've never been able to talk even one out of their chosen course of action."

"Well, we can't just kill them in cold-blood!" Kiara shouted. She was frustrated with this situation. So much violence, so much death, and there didn't seem to be anything she could do about it. She looked to her dad; his face mirrored her frustration. Blackburne stepped up.

"Perhaps we can give them to security here, and have them turned over to the GTA?" the captain asked the group. "We have proof of their attack on a protected race. I think it will be enough to have them put away for a very long time."

"Do you really think that will work?" Jax asked as he looked at the Galdorians. "We've seen so much corruption, I'd be worried that someone would 'lose' them in the system, and we'll be right back where we started."

"I'll make a few calls to those I still trust with the Rangers, and we should be able to see this through. It's a risk, but it's a risk we'll have to take unless we just want to kill them." Kyle told the group.

Kyle and Jax looked pointedly at the space station security team. After receiving reassurances from them, it was decided to go with Kyle's plan. The security team stepped forward to restrain the Galdorians, and Kyle stepped off to the side to make arrangements with the Rangers. Kiara was relieved that there would be no more killing, but still suspicious that it would work out that way. Jax was right, anything could still go wrong, so they would have to make sure they kept tabs on these two.

Kiara watched as the security team led the two Galdorians out of the docking bay. If she hadn't been watching them so intently, she would have missed it. One of the security team men, pretending to reposition himself around the prisoners, released the electronic restraints on both Galdorians. Kiara immediately sent protection fields around the crew and her dad. She turned and shouted at Jax. As Jax turned, the Galdorians killed the security guards with their own weapons. Without pausing the Galdorians ran toward Kiara, firing their weapons at her and anyone else they could see. When their weapons had no effect on any of their targets, they started firing at the Acadia and anything else they could make contact with. Small explosions began happening around her, and Kiara knew that this had to be ended, now.

The Galdorians had now split up, and were hiding behind some debris, trying to cause as much destruction as possible. Kiara knew if things got bad enough, the docking bay would lose its seal and they would all be swept out to space. She doubted she could keep everyone safe if that happened. She began throwing energy pulses at one of the Galdorians, but they were too far apart for her to reach both. She advanced to the one she was throwing pulses at, and trusted that Jax would head to the other one. She saw out of the corner of her eye that Jax was running for the other Galdorian, his baton already out. She knew he would have no mercy for the Galdorian when he reached him. She approached the other one. Her energy pulses had knocked the weapon from his hand, but he was trying to pull his daggers out between energy pulses. She wouldn't let it happen. She increased the intensity of the energy pulses, and focused the energy, and watched as she broke one of his hands. He looked up into her face, and knew that his time was up. He opened his shirt, and grabbed what looked like a detonator for an explosive device with his one good hand. He smiled evilly at her.

"Let's see how good you really are," he said, and hit the detonator.

Jax had just taken out the other Galdorian with his baton, and turned to see the explosion envelop Kiara and the man she was after. The shock wave from the explosion knocked him from his feet, sending him into a tangle of metal and debris. He fought his way out of the debris, yelling Kiara's name. He gained his feet and began running to the spot of the explosion, the chaos surrounding him barely penetrating his consciousness. The explosion destroyed parts of the two ships closest to it, and set off alarms and fire suppression systems. He barely registered that the explosion didn't destroy the seal of the docking bay, as they were still breathing and not floating out into space.

Jax could see debris from the surrounding ships in a pile where Kiara should have been. As he got closer, he could see blood and remains among the debris, and his heart nearly stopped. Still yelling Kiara's name, he tried to move the debris, not believing she was dead, but scared out of his mind from all the blood and remains.

"It's purple blood."

Jax paused from his frantic yelling and digging at Kyle's statement. He turned to look at Kyle, who had joined him to move debris. Kyle's nose was bleeding, and his clothes were torn and bloodied.

"What?"

"The blood is purple, so it's not Kiara's," Kyle said as he moved out of the way so Larry, Curly, and Moe could move debris. With their strength, Kyle knew they would have the debris moved out of the way quickly. He grabbed Jax by his arm and moved him back. "Jax, you're in shock."

"I'm okay," Jax shook off Kyle's arm, but he stayed back and let the Bendanites work.

Jax and Kyle were soon joined by Blackburne and Frankie, and all of them looked like they'd been through hell. Jax supposed if Kiara hadn't been protecting them, it would have been much worse.

"Come on, come on," Jax heard Kyle muttering.

They stared at the dwindling pile of debris, as if their will alone could bring her and Elvis out of the pile alive. Suddenly, Curly let out a shout, and pushed a large, metal beam to the side. Kyle and the others rushed forward, and as Kyle looked down, he was reminded of the first time he had seen Kiara, in the hull of that destroyed ship. She was curled in a fetal position, Elvis shielded in the curve of her body, and her eyes clinched tightly shut. He could see her breathing, and he let out the breath that he'd been holding.

"Kiara, honey, it's me," he coaxed quietly. Her protection field was still intact, so none of them could reach her until she dropped it. He turned to Curly. "Is the pile stable? It won't come down on her when she drops her protection will it?"

Curly touched his arm. "It is good."

"Come on Baby, I need you to open your eyes," Kyle coaxed again.

"Dad?"

"Yes, Honey, it's me. You're safe, now. Open your eyes," Kyle coaxed again.

"Is everyone okay?" Kiara mumbled.

"Yes, we're all okay." Kyle kept his eyes on her. "I need you to open your eyes and drop your protection. We need to make sure you're okay."

Kiara finally opened her eyes, and quickly found her dad. She saw the pile of debris she was in, and, looking up, saw the concerned faces of the Acadia crew. She looked back down when she felt Elvis squirm against her, and saw that he looked okay. She dropped her protection field, and immediately her dad and Jax jumped down next to her to help her out. Sitting up slowly, she looked at the blood on Jax and her dad's faces.

"I thought you said everyone was okay?" She moaned a little and closed her eyes, as the pain in her head made itself known.

Kyle looked at Jax and smiled. She was coming back to herself.

"Just minor cuts and bruises. Come on; let's get you back on board the Acadia."

Kiara stood up, and swayed slightly as the room seemed to spin and tilt. Jax immediately picked her up, and with help from the Bendanites, climbed out of the pile of debris and headed for the Acadia. Kiara thought about protesting, but thought better of it. She wouldn't have made it two steps on her own. Besides, it felt wonderful to be carried by Jax. She snuggled into his shoulder and closed her eyes, cradling Elvis to her chest. She made a concentrated effort to connect to Elvis to see how he was doing. They weren't hit by any debris, but her protection field only gave them minimal protection against the shock wave. The little drayek's thoughts were clear, and she couldn't sense any injuries. He may have come out of this better than anyone.

Jax took Kiara to the med-bay, and with help from Blackburne, got her checked out. Her injuries were minor as well, the biggest problem, the concussion she suffered from the shock wave. Blackburne treated her, and with Frankie's help, got the rest of the crew fixed up. No one was talking about what happened yet; they were all still focused on assessing injuries.

Kyle took Kiara back to her cabin, and stayed with her to keep an eye on her. Concussions were still serious, even with advanced medical techniques, and in the first few hours they had to be monitored until the treatment could finish repairing the damage that had been done.

Jax joined Blackburne and Frankie on the bridge. Blackburne had sent the three Bendanites to help with the space station repair, as a sign of goodwill, since he felt partially responsible for the damage. Jax asked about damage to the Acadia when he reached the bridge.

"The Acadia only has superficial damage," Blackburne told him. "The modifications we just completed appear to be intact as well, but we can't test those until we leave."

"What about space station security? Have they contacted you?" Jax questioned.

"Oh yeah," Frankie piped in. "They were blaming us for the explosion and damage, but Blackburne set them straight. They're supposedly checking security footage now. I don't know how those two got away from the security team to begin with."

"Kiara may know. She yelled a warning to me when they got free, so she may have seen what happened," Jax said. He sent a quick message to Kyle to ask her. He didn't want to disturb her while she was recovering. He didn't have long to wait. Kyle sent a quick message back.

"Kiara says it was one of the security team that turned off their restraints. She says it was the short guy with the dark hair." Jax read the message he received from Kyle.

"Good, we'll pass that along to the head of security," Blackburne said. "Once they release us, we should head out. We still have a couple of days till we reach our final destination."

A couple of hours later, they were finally under way. Kiara was at her station, ready to change the transponder code when needed. She still felt weak and a little light-headed if she stood up too fast, but she was ready for this task. They reached the part of space where the space station they just left could no longer monitor them, so they deployed the panels, and Kiara changed the transponders. Everything went off without a hitch, and Kiara was relieved. She didn't think she was up for troubleshooting a problem just yet.

Heading back to her cabin, Kiara replayed the fight with the first Galdorian over and over in her head. What could she have done differently? Could she have been faster with the protection bubble to save him? She stopped in the hallway when Elvis chirped in her ear. She realized that she was standing outside the cabin that Jax occupied. She stood there, uncertainty making her shift from foot to foot. Before she could decide what to do, Jax opened the door. He took one look at her face, and pulled her into the cabin and straight into his arms.

"It's okay," he whispered to her.

She began to cry quietly, the last few hours finally catching up to her. Jax just held her and waited for her to speak.

"I didn't mean to kill him."

Jax was dumbfounded. She was upset that the person trying to kill her had died?

"He was trying to kill you, Kiara."

"I know, I know." Kiara pulled back from Jax slightly. "I know you think it's stupid to worry about it, but I never wanted to kill anyone."

Jax moved her to his bunk and sat her down. Sitting next to her, he grabbed both of her hands.

"Taking a life should never be taken lightly. You were put into the position of defending yourself and protecting the rest of us," Jax told her. She opened her mouth to say something else, but Jax wasn't finished. He squeezed her hands lightly, and continued. "You weren't given a choice. This is what you were born into. I think you have done remarkably well, and I'm proud of you, and honored to know you."

Kiara blushed at the praise. She didn't know how to respond.

"In time, the guilt and self-doubt will fade. What you need to remember through all of this is the state of your heart. You did not wish to harm anyone. You are a good person, and the death of the Galdorian that tried to kill you will not change that."

Kiara looked up into his eyes, and saw the sincerity of his words. Elvis, sitting on her lap between them, chirped loudly. Kiara looked down at him and smiled, realizing that she was starting feel better. Getting up, she started to head toward the door, when something from the earlier fight popped into her head. She turned back around to Jax, a questioning look on her face.

"What is it?" Jax asked.

"Something I remembered from the fight earlier," she replied. "The Galdorian licked the dagger, and it penetrated my protection field. I couldn't stop it. Have you seen that before? Do you know why it did that?"

Jax looked thoughtful. "I haven't seen that before. I suspect it has something to do with Trandor and Galdor sharing the same ancestry. I'll pass it on to Stryker, and perhaps when we are done with this, we could do some testing and figure it out."

"I think that would be a good idea."

"In the meantime, you will need to keep that in mind if we run into any more Galdorians."

"I will." Kiara turned and headed for the door again. "Thank-you, Jax." She looked back at him. "I'm so glad Stryker brought you into my life."

Chapter Twelve

Ranger John headed toward the office of the Senior Logistics Officer (SLO) of the GTA, on the outside looking confident, on the inside, he was nearly in a panic. The plan for disrupting the transgates was working fairly well. More transgates were being destroyed, and they were keeping the rest of the Rangers hopping. He knew she wouldn't be disappointed about that. He was worried about the weird obsession she had developed about Kiara. John nodded at someone that passed him in the hallway, keeping the professional Ranger look on his face. He continued purposefully toward the SLO's office, his stride steady. The SLO's obsession with Kiara had started early on, when reports of her powers had become known. The SLO had insisted that she be kept up to date on Kiara's whereabouts, and how her power was progressing. John had sacrificed his ship and nearly gotten himself killed trying to keep an eye on her. The SLO had even ordered John to help the Galdorians kill Kiara, and when that didn't progress as fast as she wanted, she'd ordered John to kill her. That attempt had failed as well, and he blamed himself. He liked Kiara; he really did, so he'd hired someone else to kill her. He drugged her and delivered her to the hired assassin, but he hadn't wanted to stick around to watch. When she hadn't been killed as planned, the SLO had nearly taken his head off. As it was, he promised he would help the three Galdorians chasing her to kill her. He'd had to give them her location, and he'd even supplied one of the Galdorians with an explosive device. That too had failed.

John slowed his steps as he neared the SLO's office. He'd discovered that the SLO hadn't trusted him to finish the job, so she'd also had someone else working in parallel to kill Kiara. He didn't know who it was, but apparently, they had failed as well. The SLO had been livid. They had somehow poisoned her supplements, and had attacked the ship once Kiara had been incapacitated. That attack had failed, and now he was delivering the news that they'd lost Kiara again. He was pretty sure she was on her way here, but they'd lost track of her a few days ago, and he had no idea where she was. The SLO wasn't going to be happy.

Kiara was, at that moment, assisting Frankie with the docking of their ship on the space dock above Earth Delta Nine. Their disguise of the ship so far was working— they hadn't been questioned at all on their way here. They had decided to dock on the outside of the space dock, rather than risk getting recognized inside the space dock. It complicated things, as now they were attached by docking clamps, and had to use the docking tunnel to enter the space dock. Kiara knew it was the best alternative. Once they were safely docked, the crew met on the bridge to go over the plan one more time.

Kiara was nervous. No disguises this time, just a full-on frontal assault. She looked at Frankie; he was staying on the ship with the Bendanites. They would be too far away for her to protect, once she was down on the planet.

"Please be careful, Frankie. Keep Larry, Curly and Moe safe."

"I'll keep us safe up here; you stay safe and bring everyone back."

Kiara nodded. If their plan worked, they would learn who was behind this, and get it out in the open, which would hopefully protect them. If it didn't work, they risked death, or at the very least, prison time.

Kiara, Elvis, Blackburne, Jax and Kyle left through the docking tunnel, and boarded the shuttle that would take them to the planet. So far, they hadn't been stopped or questioned, but all the checkpoints they'd gone through had been more for keeping track of passengers, rather than checking for dangerous passengers. No weapons were allowed on the shuttle, but none of them, except Jax, ever carried any weapons. Kiara held her breath as Jax went through the scanner, but no alarms went off.

The shuttle trip was short, but crowded. Kiara, standing next to Jax, moved her hand slightly and grabbed his. His face never showing any emotion, he returned her slight squeeze, and continued to hold her hand. Kiara released her breath, and felt herself calm. Elvis, scrunched down on her shoulder, huffed quietly in her ear. She knew he was trying to be inconspicuous, but they still earned a few stares.

They exited the shuttle and immediately boarded the transport to the GTA offices. Once they were on the transport craft, Kiara sent a questioning look to Jax. She was curious how he got his baton through the scanners. She knew he had it, she just couldn't figure out how he got it through the scanners. He looked back at her, and smiled. He wouldn't answer her out in public, so she thought she'd have to ask him when they were finished. She hoped they made it through this so she could ask him.

The trip to the GTA headquarters was short, and they exited the transport with a few other passengers. They huddled together near the front entrance, trying not to look suspicious as they scanned for any last minute changes. Kiara took a long look at the group with her. Everyone here had stood by her, risked their lives for her, and now risked everything again to help her. She would be forever grateful to them, and she would do everything in her power to keep them safe. As one, they turned and headed for the entrance.

Jax popped his baton out, and had it hidden against his arm, palmed in his hand. They entered through the main doors and walked to the interactive information center. With a few swipes of her hand, Kiara found the office that the message she had traced come from. She turned with a shocked look on her face.

"It's the Senior Logistics Officer," she whispered. She knew it raised the stakes to have such a high-ranking official be their target. "She's on the forty-fifth floor."

Taking a deep breath, Kiara approached the first security checkpoint. They were still ten feet away from the checkpoint when alarms went off.

"Kiara McCallister! Get down on the ground!" A loud, automated voice blared over the intercom system at the security checkpoint.

Kiara looked at the others and smiled. "Here we go."

Turning back to the checkpoint, she simply continued to advance. The security guards, looking a little worried, continued to yell at her to stop and get on the ground. When she didn't stop, they engaged additional security measures, which brought down locking barriers behind the security checkpoint, and automated weapons appeared in different areas in the walls. One of the security guards ran at her, still yelling for her to get down. Several feet away from her, he hit her protection field and flew backward. The other guards fired their weapons at her a couple of times, but seeing their weapons have no effect, and knowing they couldn't reach her, they backed off. Kiara supposed they would now depend on the automated security measures to stop her.

As she passed the security guards, the automatic weapons began firing, but Kiara's protection was still keeping everyone safe. They walked through the first checkpoint, everyone clustered behind her. She reached the locked barrier, and closing her eyes for a second, sent a pulse of energy at it. It blew a hole in the barrier big enough for all of them to walk through. They walked out of range of the automatic weapons and toward the lift that would take them to the forty-fifth floor. The checkpoint was now eerily quiet; the only sounds were their footsteps and the noise of falling debris. As they entered the lift, Kiara turned back to the guards that were staring at them, and raised her hand. All the guards ducked, anticipating a shot of energy similar to the one that had blown a hole in the wall. Kiara simply waved at them as the lift doors closed. She would keep her friends and family safe, but she would not kill anyone if she could avoid it.

The lift doors had closed, but the building security measures had already disabled the lift to prevent them from going anywhere. Kiara had anticipated this. With help from Jax, they pried open the control panel, and Kiara connected to it with her com unit. As she was bypassing security, a panel in the top opened and someone attempted to throw in a canister. Kiara didn't know what the canister contained, but she wasn't waiting to find out. Her protection field wouldn't allow it to be dropped in, and with an extra flip of energy, she shot the canister back into the opening on the floor above, and immediately sent the security guard after it. Concentrating again on the panel, she bypassed security, enabled power, and shot the lift upward. She left the top panel open, and as they passed openings where security was trying to shoot or fire more canisters at them, she easily repelled them. Just before they reached the forty-fifth floor, Kiara turned to Jax.

"Someone on this floor has a weapon designed for me. You will need to take him out, or this will all be for naught."

"Where will he be?"

Kiara closed her eyes. "Off to the right. He'll be looking for me, not for you. I can't protect you from his weapon, but I can distract him for a time."

"We'll all distract him," her dad growled.

The lift stopped, the doors opened, and Kiara shot out low, firing energy pulses to the right and to the left. Jax, using Kyle and the walls, actually shot out of the lift over her head, hit the opposite wall with his feet, and shot down the hallway to the right. Kiara could hear her energy pulses hit someone to her left, as she heard a grunt and then a thud. She rolled to the far side of the hallway, and gained her feet, looking to the right to see where the danger would be. She saw him, a small security officer, holding an old-fashioned crossbow, a deadly-looking bolt already loaded. She knew it would penetrate her protection field, but the security officer couldn't get a clean shot at her. Jax was flying down the hallway toward him, and Kiara's dad kept dodging in front of her. Jax was almost on him, and the security guard knew it was now or never. He shot the bolt, just as Jax hit him in the head with his baton. The security guard went down in a boneless heap.

Jax turned his head, shouting for Kiara. He watched as Kiara dodged to the left, but it wasn't going to be fast enough. At the last moment, Kyle threw himself in front of Kiara, the bolt penetrating his shoulder. Kiara grabbed him as he started to fall, her panic at seeing her dad shot with a bolt nearly buckling her knees. Seeing the bolt sticking out of him, Kiara screamed her terror and rage, and Elvis, on her shoulder, howled. Her scream sent a pulse of energy that shattered every window on the floor, and flattened anyone approaching them. Jax braced himself against the wall as her pulse of energy shot down the hallway. Racing back down the hallway, he reached them at the same time as

Blackburne, who had been flattened into the lift at Kiara's scream. Kiara was on the ground holding her dad, not sure what to do. They still needed to head to the SLO office, but she couldn't seem to move. Jax stood over them keeping watch, while Blackburne quickly examined Kyle with his portable med-unit.

Kiara looked at her dad then at Blackburne, willing him to be okay. Blackburne looked up from the portable med-unit, his relief obvious.

"The bolt is just in soft tissue, he'll be okay," he said. "Do you think you can use some of your energy, and push it out?"

Kiara nodded, and not looking at her dad's face, she quickly pushed the bolt out. Her dad groaned, but held still. Blackburne immediately applied some powder to stop the bleeding and sat him up. Kiara grabbed him in a hug, trying to avoid his wound, but wanting to hold him. He'd just saved her life, again.

"Thanks Dad, I love you," she whispered.

"I love you too," he whispered back. Then, in a louder voice, "I'm okay. Let's finish this!"

Kiara finally let go of him, and they all stood up. Several security guards were on the floor around them, a few of them groaning, but none of them getting up anytime soon. They headed down the hallway to the SLO's office, and as they passed the guard that tried to kill Kiara, she reached down, confiscated his crossbow and searched him for any extra bolts. She found two more bolts and handed those to Blackburne. The guard groaned, but before she could do anything, Jax reached down and smacked him with his baton again. Jax nodded at Kiara, and they continued.

Broken glass and downed security guards were everywhere. They reached the SLO's office, and found the door locked. Jax looked at Kiara, trying to judge her state of mind. He needed her to be strong for whatever was behind the door. She looked back at him, her gaze clear and determined. He sensed no weakness, and with a nod, let her blow the door open. They entered and found the SLO, with Ranger John and two other security guards in her office.

The SLO stood behind Ranger John and the guards, her face twisted in hate, but Kiara could see and sense fear behind that hate. Kiara, full of power and determination, flicked the two guards to the floor. John moved to stand in front of Kiara, blocking her path to the SLO.

"Kiara, wait," John said and held up his hand to her, his face full of sympathy.

"Wait? Wait for what, John? Wait for you to kill me?" Kiara faced John fully, her anger at his betrayal nearly making her vibrate. She could hear running footsteps in the hallway, and knew they didn't have much time.

"I didn't have a choice," John pleaded to her. "Please, just leave."

"Everyone has a choice." Kiara looked past John to the SLO. "We already know what you did, John, I don't need you to admit anything. I need her to admit what she's been doing."

"You don't have anything on me," John said defiantly.

Kiara took her gaze from the SLO and looked back at John, now sneering at her. She smiled slightly at him. "We have a confession and you on surveillance, which backed up the confession."

At her words, John went pale, and his eyes began to shift from side to side, as if looking for a way out. He took a small step to the side, inciting the wrath of the SLO.

"Stand your ground, you coward!" The SLO shrieked from behind him. Her shriek had the desired effect, and had John straightening and planting his feet.

Elvis, still on her shoulder, seemed to shrink on Kiara's shoulder at the SLO's shriek. Kiara wanted to laugh. The shrieking hurt her ears as well. Raising her right hand, Kiara enveloped John in an energy bubble, and moved him out of the way. The surprise on his face made her want to laugh, except the SLO was shrieking again. Kiara blocked the doorway with energy and advanced to the SLO. She watched the SLO snap her mouth shut as she stepped closer.

"Why?" Kiara asked the one thing that had been on her mind this whole time.

"Why? Why?" the SLO shrieked at her. "You're a *shetanzie*, that's why! You must be destroyed. We have the right to destroy you!"

"You have the right?" Jax asked quietly.

The SLO snapped her head toward Jax. She sneered at him, her disgust at him almost equal to what she felt for Kiara.

"Yes! It is our right!" The SLO reached up and pulled her tunic down at her left shoulder, exposing a tattoo over her left breast. "We almost annihilated your kind, but you keep popping up, like some sort of fungus. But we'll be triumphant in the end! Your kind isn't strong enough; you don't have the killing instinct. That weakness will be your downfall!"

"So you admit to trying to kill Kiara?" Kyle asked.

"We would have succeeded, if it hadn't been for this fool over here," the SLO waved a hand in the general direction of John. "He liked her, so he didn't want to hurt her himself." The last part was said in a singsong sarcastic tone of voice. "If you had just killed her, instead of drugging her, we'd be on to the next one!"

"Shut up, you bitch!" John was now yelling at the SLO, realizing that she wasn't going to defend him anymore.

"Oh, and then giving that Galdorian a bomb—I could have told you that wasn't going to work!"

"Did you have someone poison her supplements?" Kyle asked. He thought it was the only thing that made sense, but he wanted her to admit it as well.

The SLO turned her furious gaze to Kyle. She looked at him in disgust.

"Of course I did!" The SLO spit at Kyle. "You should have killed her when you found her, all those years ago, instead of waiting for one of us to do it!"

Kiara was surprised that the SLO was confessing to so much, until the SLO turned back to face her. All sanity was gone from her eyes. Kiara didn't sense a threat coming from the SLO, but she still felt uneasy.

"You think you've won, don't you, you little *shetanzie*," the SLO looked straight at Kiara as she screamed her insults and threats. "You may have won this battle, but we will win the war!" The SLO looked past Kiara to the crowd waiting outside her door. In the middle of the doorway was her Director, and she knew he'd heard everything.

"We're everywhere, and we will kill you and all your kind!"

With that last parting shot, she walked around her desk toward the doorway, keeping as much distance between her and Kiara as the room would allow. Kiara took down the energy barrier she'd put up in the doorway, and the Director motioned for security to take the SLO into custody. He walked into the office and nodded at Kyle. Turning, he walked over to stand in front of Kiara.

"Please accept my apology, and the apology from the GTA for the threat on your life."

Kiara raised her eyebrows.

"Your father sent me a message once he discovered who was behind the attacks," the Director told her. "He let me know that you were on your way up here and would be working to get a confession from her." The Director looked from Kiara to the others in the room. "I must admit that this is not what I was expecting, but we are grateful that you have exposed corruption in our organization, and in the Rangers." He looked pointedly at John.

"How do we know we can trust him?" Kiara looked from the Director to her dad.

"I trust him," Kyle answered.

"Yes, but you trusted John, and look how that turned out." Kiara looked at John, determining what she could do to him and not go to prison.

"I trusted John because he was a Ranger, not because he had earned my trust," her dad said, not the least bit offended by Kiara's bluntness. "I know the Director. I've known him since you were a little girl. He has earned my trust through the years, and I trust him with our lives."

Kiara watched the security guards take the still screaming SLO down the littered hallway.

"Would you be so kind as to release John, so we can take him into custody as well?" the Director asked Kiara.

"I'm not finished with him yet."

All eyes landed on Kiara at her statement. Elvis, on her shoulder, emitted a kind of hissing noise, and bared his teeth at John. The Director physically took a step backward when he heard Elvis. He wasn't quite sure what the little creature might do.

"I know you're upset with him, but we need to take him into custody," the Director implored her. The look on Kiara's face told him she wasn't swayed at all, so the Director turned to Kyle.

"I don't think she's finished with him yet," Kyle answered the questioning look from the Director. "And frankly, I will also need a few minutes with him."

"I will need time with him, as well," Jax said.

"As will I," Blackburne said.

Everyone turned to look at John, now pale and shaking in the corner. Kiara thought he didn't look anything like a Ranger now.

"Look," the Director stepped forward, worried that this was going to turn into a lynching. "I know you're all angry with him, but let us handle it. I promise he isn't going anywhere."

For a few tense seconds, no one moved. Kiara didn't want to kill him, but she did want him to suffer. She also didn't want anyone else standing here with her to be in trouble if they did something to him. Turning to look at the Director, she saw both the Director and John slump slightly in relief, thinking the standoff was over. John, standing to her right and slightly behind her, also got a little smirk on his face, no doubt thinking that with his connections, he would find a way out.

"You will make sure he is held accountable?" Kiara asked.

"I will," the Director answered.

She nodded at the Director, and turned back toward John. Straightening up to her full height, she closed her eyes, and took in a deep breath. Her skin took on a darker hue, and Elvis, still on her shoulder, began to make a humming noise.

"Uh oh," she heard her dad mutter, and she could hear shuffling as everyone tried to move away from her.

"What's going on?" she heard the Director ask from somewhere down the hall. She couldn't hear all of her dad's answer, but he was saying something about gathering power.

In the room, John was beginning to sense that he wasn't going to get out of this easily, despite what Kiara had just said to the Director. Kiara, her eyes still closed, was gathering enough power to make her hair float. When she opened her eyes, they fairly glowed at him, and the relief he felt earlier was now gone, replaced with dread. He yelled for someone to come and help him, but everyone else had left the room. Kiara advanced on him, and his screams for help increased in volume.

"Say you're sorry," Kiara growled at him.

"I'm sorry, I'm sorry," he blubbered.

Kiara looked inside herself, and found that the apology wasn't good enough. This man in front of her had caused so much pain and death, but not just to her. She would not trust that the system would take care of him.

Letting out a scream of frustration and anger, she sent a pulse of energy at him. It hit him with such force that it sent him through the wall behind him, and out of the building, forty-five floors up. His scream of pain and terror followed him toward the ground. Closing her eyes, Kiara reached up and touched Elvis on his foot. She thought about her conversation with Jax, and found within herself that she could not let him die, not by her hand.

"We won't let him die, not today," she whispered.

She caught him in an energy bubble a few feet off the ground, stopping his fall. She was grateful that she caught him, unlike the Galdorian that had died when she hadn't been fast enough. She waited a few seconds, let out a slow breath, and dropped him.

Kiara walked out into the destroyed hallway, and at the site of her, the Director jumped forward.

"What happened? Where's John?" the Director asked, trying to look past her into the room.

"You'll find John down by the front entrance," Kiara said, and heard Jax chuckle.

"The front entrance?" The Director looked at her in horror. "You threw him out the window? You killed him?"

Kiara assumed her most haughty expression. "I can assure you that I did not throw him out the window, it was through the wall. And, as of right now, he is not dead. Of course, if you don't retrieve him quickly, someone else might just finish what I could not." Kiara continued to the lift, leaving everyone behind her with their mouths open.

It only took a second for them to spring into motion. Kyle, Jax and Blackburne sprinted after her, the Director going in the direction of the SLO's office. Kiara assumed he wanted to verify her story about throwing John out of the building.

In the lift, everyone was quiet. Kiara could feel the energy draining from her, now that everything was over. She turned and looked at Jax, just as her legs gave out. Jax, of course, knew what was coming, and wrapped his arms around her before she fell. She could hear her dad asking if she were all right, and Elvis chirping in her ear, before everything went blank.

Kiara awoke in her bunk with Elvis snuggled up tight against her. She struggled to sit up. She couldn't remember ever being this tired. She fought to orient herself, forgetting for a second where she was and when she was. With a rush, everything came flooding back, and she realized with relief that she was aboard the Acadia, and not imprisoned somewhere. She grabbed her com unit, and discovered that she'd been out for a good twelve hours. She could feel the rumble of the engines, so she knew they were under way somewhere. She sat where she was for a few moments, gathering her thoughts and remembering the past day. Taking a deep breath, she finally swung her legs out of bed and got up.

Entering the bridge, she saw Blackburne studying his screen and Frankie working at his station. Jax was at her navunit, and she was grateful that he could help out. Frankie saw her first, and quickly jumped up to grab her in a huge bear hug.

"You're up!" He yelled, which caught the attention of everyone else on the bridge.

Blackburne and Jax came over, hugging her and asking if she was okay. She thought it was weird that Blackburne hugged her, but supposed after everything that they'd been through, anything was possible.

"Where's my dad?"

"We left him at Earth Delta Nine," Blackburne told her. "The Rangers needed him, so we unhooked his ship and let him takeoff from there. I think he left you a message on your com unit."

Kiara looked down at her com unit and saw the message. Looking back up at Blackburne, he waved her off.

"Go ahead—we've got things covered here."

Kiara headed back to her cabin, and brought up the message from her dad.

"Hey, Sweet Pea! We got you back to the Acadia, and Curly checked you over and said you just needed rest. Jax had some supplements for you, so I know you are in good hands.

"I'm sorry, I had to go. I think you'll be okay without me for a while, but you can call me when you're up and feeling better. I got an update from the Director. John, indeed, was still alive when they got to him, and they have him in a medically induced coma for the time being, while he heals from multiple broken bones and internal bleeding. The SLO is in a special prison while they determine how far the corruption went. I've heard rumors that she had something to do with the transgate attacks, but I don't have anything official yet.

"Even though we caused a lot of damage and injuries, the Director has successfully lobbied for none of us to face charges, so we are off the hook for the attack. The Director was citing 'mitigating circumstances'.

"That's about it on the updates. Stay safe, little one. I love you!"

Kiara smiled. She sent him a quick message that she was up and feeling better, and she would connect with him later. She'd just sent the message off, when she could feel the pitch of the engines change. Checking her com unit, she discovered that they were docking at a space station. Did Blackburne already have a job lined up for them? She headed to the bridge to see if she could help.

Kiara reached the bridge, just as Frankie got them docked. Blackburne and Jax were both gone.

"What are we doing here, Frankie?"

"Picking up supplies, and I think Blackburne has a job for us." Frankie got up to stand next to her, and reached out and grabbed one of her hands. Elvis chirped at him. "Kiara, you need to go talk to Jax."

"Why, what's going on?" Alarm raced through her.

"Just go talk to him. I think he went back to his cabin."

Kiara nodded and headed into the ship. What did Frankie mean? Suddenly, like a fist to the stomach, Kiara realized what was happening.

"You're leaving," Kiara said from the doorway of Jax's cabin.

Jax straightened up from the bag he was packing. He took in Kiara's sadness, but knew there was nothing he could do about.

"I'm sorry, Kiara, it is time for me to go. You are more than capable of taking care of yourself, and I'm needed elsewhere."

He walked over to her and pulled her close. He could feel her tears, both on his shoulder and in his heart. He had gotten close to her, despite his best intentions, and leaving her felt as if he was ripping her heart out, as well as his own.

Kiara pulled back slightly and looked up into his face. "We've known all along that you could only be with me for a short time." She looked down and swallowed the lump in her throat. "It's just hard."

"I know, for me as well." Jax brought his hands up to cup her face. "I would stay a little longer, but there is someone else that needs my help."

Kiara nodded. "I understand." Reaching up, she placed her hands over the top of his. "Will you keep in touch? Maybe we can get together if our paths cross?"

Jax nodded, and moved forward to kiss her. They shared a long desperate kiss, before Kiara stepped back, tears flowing down her face. Jax wiped her tears, before turning around and grabbing his bags. Kiara walked with him off the Acadia, and waved at him as he boarded another ship that was across the docking bay. Taking a deep breath, she turned back to the Acadia, ready to get back to work.

In another office at the GTA headquarters on Earth Delta Nine, the man staring out the window addressed the young GTA security guard standing behind him. "Has the SLO said anything yet?"

"No sir, she just keeps babbling about her hatred of the Trandorian. They haven't gotten anything else out of her. They suspect she's had some sort of psychotic break."

"They'll eventually give her drugs, and she will end up spilling everything. We can't let that happen."

"No sir."

"Make sure she has an accident she can't recover from."

"Yes sir." The security guard backed up a few steps. "What about the Ranger?"

"He is of no threat. My contacts tell me that he suffered irreparable brain damage. He is alive, but that is all we can say about him. Take care of the SLO."

"Yes sir." The security guard backed out of the office. He could feel the anger coming from the man at the window, and wanted to leave before that anger exploded.

Back in the office, the man at the window used the secure link on his com unit. His barely controlled anger still came through loud and clear. "What is your status?"

"We have CyRAINs ready to go in three quadrants, sir. We're awaiting your command."

The man at the window took a deep breath. Yes, the SLO and Ranger put them slightly behind schedule, but they would be back on track shortly. The delay could actually work in their favor. It could give them extra time to amass more troops.

"Continue to amass as many CyRAINs as you can. We'll wait a few weeks for things to die down before we begin the next phase."

About the Author

Phoenix Halloway is an Electrical Engineer by day and a science fiction fantasy writer by night. Combining her love of science and science fiction with her love of writing, she has published her first book—*Awakening: Guardian from Trandor Series #1*. This first book represents the fulfillment of a life-long dream; to become an author. When she isn't working, she is writing, and construction of the second book in the series is already underway.

www.ingramcontent.com/pod-product-compliance
Lightning Source LLC
Chambersburg PA
CBHW071309200626
46813CB00015B/740